# the BARISTA'S GUIDE to THe PERFECT steam

## VALERIE PEPPER

Cover Design: Sarah Hansen, Okay Creations

Editor: Jennifer Sommersby, SGA Books

Published by Stafford Lane Publishing LLC

# CHAPTER 1
# JODI

$\mathcal{A}$ TRICKLE OF sweat makes its way down the center of my back as steam from the frother billows into my face. I step back, wipe my forehead with my arm, and keep moving. The early-March air that gusts in with every swing of the door isn't anywhere close enough to cool me off.

I shake cinnamon onto Mr. Steele's latte. He keeps telling me to call him Henry, but the man was my high school principal, so no way. I push the drink to him and glance around the shop. The line isn't getting any shorter, which is good. Great, even. But it would be awesome if people could time their need for caffeine in a pattern that made my mornings a little less insane.

I'm grateful; don't get me wrong. Of course I'm grateful. I'd have lost the shop way before now if these customers weren't lining up for their daily dose.

Actually, that's the name of my shop: Daily Dose. I've owned it since I was twenty-two, a whole five years. You know that saying *ignorance is bliss*? Yeah, that was me. Blissfully ignorant, thinking how hard can it be to run a coffee shop?

Ha.

It's hard.

Suck the marrow from your bones hard. But deciding to buy

this place is the only time I've done anything entirely for myself, so I don't mind the work.

I hand Mr. Steele his coffee with a smile.

He takes the cup and lifts it in answer. "You talked to your sister lately? How's she been?"

I force my happy expression to remain. "Oh, she's great. Living it up in Nashville, chasing her dream of being the next big country music star."

He grins as his eyes take on a faraway look. "Next time you talk to her, tell her we still haven't had a singer in the musicals as good as her since she left."

"Of course." He leaves and I shove thoughts of my family down.

"Love of my life, sweetness and sunshine, your behind is so glorious but could you please move." Darius growls that last part at me.

I giggle and shimmy my glorious behind, as Darius so eloquently puts it, out of the way. He's my only full-time employee and he swears I pay him a pittance, but I like to remind him that his goal is to be a published fantasy author by age twenty-five, not a barista, and that usually shuts him up. For about five seconds. The man was born to talk.

"New flare?" I ask.

He flashes me a pleased grin and points to the new pin on his apron, TV hostess style. It's a Pride flag, joining a collection of buttons and pins big enough to make your head spin. "Gotta support my people," he says and winks.

We move around each other, a dance borne from years of barista choreography, and keep the line moving.

"Mrs. Withers!" I beam at the crotchety old lady as she steps up to the counter. "Your usual?"

She smiles at me, and I nearly trip on the floor mat. I keep forgetting that she isn't as grouchy as she used to be. She turned into a fluffy kitten after decades of crankiness when she and Devon, my best friend (and ex-sister-in-law) came up with a plan to sell the house Devon inherited from her grandmother. It isn't right. Frankly, I'm worried her new attitude is going to mess with the Earth's rotation.

"Yes, please. The lavender latte with two shots of vanilla syrup." She insists on repeating her order to me every time she's here, even though I know hers, and everyone else's, by heart.

"Coming right up," I say. A glance at Darius tells me he's halfway through making her coffee already.

"When are you going to start selling my famous lemon squares?" She peers up at me from behind her thick glasses. And I'm only 5'2", so you can imagine what it takes for someone to peer *up* at me.

I smile politely. "You know if I do that, then I'll have to hear about it from Miss Betty, who swears she's the one with the famous lemon squares. And I'm not getting between the two of you." There's been enough animosity between old ladies in this town, thank you very much. I'm not about to be the start of another one.

But I'll be honest: Mrs. Withers' are better. I think it's all those years of being sour.

The old woman sniffs like she knows I'm bullshitting her, then pays and moves to the left to pick up her drink.

Next is Sarina, who owns the burger and beer joint on the other side of the town square, then Jhnae, the best hairstylist on the planet, then Brook, owner of Brook's Books. And more after that. Then it's nine a.m. and the rush is over.

And then.

Sweet mother of all that is holy.

The Joseph Brothers walk in.

Two firemen and a paramedic walk into a coffee shop.

It's as if the movie of my life has gone into slow-mo as three fine-as-hell walls of navy-uniformed muscled goodness walk in, joking and laughing with each other. There's Aaron the para-medic, the blond baby of the bunch who's engaged to Devon and is smiling like he's stupid in love. But he actually *is* in love, so he doesn't make me want to barf. Then there's Will Joseph, the oldest and the darkest and the beefiest, who always looks like he's disappointed with the world and gives off this Very Stern vibe.

But then.

Then there's the middle brother. Price. Melter of panties and primary provider of my alone-time fantasies. His dark blond hair flops deliciously over his forehead and he sports a perfectly-maintained beard that's thick but still manages to look like it'd be soft if he graced you with a kiss.

I have crushed on this man since I was twelve. Is it healthy? Probably not. Do I place the blame for my persistent virginity at his likely pedicured feet? Damn straight I do.

"Ahem." Darius hip-checks me and lowers his voice. "I know the brothers are what our dreams are made of, but try not to let your drool get into the steamed milk."

I glare at him before turning my signature matte-red smile to the trio. "Good morning, guys. To what do we owe the pleasure of all three of you at once?"

Darius snorts, and even as I keep my eyes forward, I can picture the way his dark skin glows when he's laughing at my expense—which is far too often for my liking. Splotches of heat rise on my chest and neck, and I'm a ginger, so it's not subtle.

Will barely looks at me, but Aaron tilts his head and leans in. "You okay? You look a little flushed."

Aaron and I have been, if not friends, then at least acquain-tances for a long time. We weren't in the same grade growing up, but it's a small town and there was only one public school, so close enough. And right now, if it wouldn't mean that Devon would have lost two great loves in her life, I would murder him in his sleep.

"I'm fine," I grit out. The espresso machine chooses this moment to hiss at me, and I flinch.

Aaron narrows his eyes, and all my prayers to the coffee gods that he lets it drop must get answered, because he smirks and lets it go.

"Hellooo, Jodi!" Price bounds to the front and smiles at me.

See, this is the thing. From the way he acts, Price seems to want people to believe he's an overgrown mastiff puppy. And generally, that works for him. It has his whole life, from what I can tell. He was far enough ahead of me in school that I don't think he ever noticed me until I started making him lattes. But I was aware of him pretty much from the time I started noticing boys, and I think there's more to him than he's ever let on, especially these days. I see it in his eyes. His beautiful silver-blue eyes that I'm now staring into. I give him a warm smile. My warmest of smiles. I'm very smiley right now. "Hi, Price. Your usual?"

He nods and winks at me. "You know my weakness."

*I wish I were your weakness.* I don't say that out loud. I would never. Instead, I chirp, "One vanilla oat-milk latte coming right up."

Darius gives me a Look and I give him one right back. His says *Girl.* Mine says *What do you want me to do about it—tell him?* And his replies *Yes, yes I do.* And I laugh. Because right along with death and taxes, there is one absolute certainty in this world: Price Joseph will never look at me as anything other than the coffee girl who makes a killer vanilla oat-milk latte.

# CHAPTER 2
# PRICE

*I* DON'T CARE what anyone says. Vanilla oat-milk lattes are an addiction. They are *my* addiction, and it's all Jodi's fault. She made me one years ago after learning I didn't like regular milk, and I was a goner. I grab the cup from her and smile. "Thanks." Then I take a sip. "So good. *You* are so good."

Jodi smiles back at me, her cheeks flushed, and I lift the drink in a salute. "Best vanilla oat-milk latte ever."

"Thanks, Price," she says softly, her eyes meeting mine for the briefest of seconds.

And like always, there's something in her expression that makes me think she might actually see who I am. Who I could be. My chest tightens.

Will grunts behind me. "You done acting like you're about to fuck it?"

I ignore him. At least he said it low enough that he won't hurt Jodi's feelings. As the little sister of a fallen firefighter, she deserves some respect. But more than that, she deserves it because she works her ass off. She's obviously smart as hell, or she wouldn't have been able to turn this shop around from the pitiful little place it was before she got it. She's a sweet girl, doing good for her age.

Listen to me, sounding like I'm a grandpa. I'm only 34. But sometimes it feels older. Maybe it's the abs.

Last time I was in Atlanta for a shoot, my agent Monica had been all over me about them. *They're not defined enough*, she'd said. I just shrugged. That's what Photoshop was for. My job was to pose for the romance cover. After that, it was up to the designers.

Not that anyone knows about this little side hustle of mine. The shit they'd give me if they did. Plus, all it would do is convince everyone that this is all there is to me: pretty face, pretty decent abs.

I'm more than that. I know I am. Unfortunately, no one seems to be willing to believe that. But it's on me to prove it, and I'm old enough to know I've done a shit job of it. I'm hoping that getting the B&B up and running with Will starts to change things, and then I can turn to what I really want: making Assistant Chief at the station.

Aaron grabs his and Will's drinks and hands one to Will. "Regular drip."

I laugh. "Kind of like you, Will. A regular drip."

Will's expression barely even changes. It goes from regular pissed-off to slightly more pissed-off. "Fuck off, Price."

"See, this is the comedy our B&B guests will pay for," I say, giving him a harder than necessary back slap. "You come up with any names yet?"

He grumbles, and Aaron pipes up as we head for the door. "Still think it should be named after Gigi," referring to his fiancée Devon's grandmother.

"Gigi's Inn? Gigi's B&B? Shirley's Oasis?" I keep throwing them out as we walk the block to the firehouse. "Shirley's Right This Way? Talladega Nights? Speed into Shirley's? Slow Down for Dreams?"

"Shirley's Inn," he barks.

I stop, letting the name marinate for a moment. "Well, damn. Even though you snarled while you said it, I love it. It's simple and to the point. It's perfect."

"I know."

I grin. "You're excited that I like it. I can see it under that grumpy exterior of yours."

His lips quiver faintly. For him, it's a smile. "Fine. You're right."

"Ha!" I pump a fist in victory. "Knew it."

Outside the shop, Aaron and Devon's dogs join us for the one-block walk back to the firehouse. They're hilarious. Daisy's a brindle bulldog and Samson is this scraggly little ugly white mutt, and they're inseparable. If you ask me, Samson's entirely responsible for Devon and Aaron being together.

Aaron says, "Still can't believe you two are running that place. Or that Price had the cash to buy it."

"Just for the down payment. And I'm smart with my money, bro," I say.

"I don't know," Aaron says. "Don't you make less than Mr. Assistant Chief here?"

I shrug and attempt to redirect the attention. "I make Will buy the groceries. Look at him. He obviously eats more than me."

Aaron laughs. "I'm just saying, you go out of town a lot. Maybe you're secretly one of those guys who do the bachelorette parties," he says. "I could see it. You show up in your turnout gear, nothing on underneath except a banana hammock."

Will grumbles a laugh. "That's *exactly* how you had the money. Remind me never to use your gear."

I laugh and keep quiet, because it's a little too close to the truth. I bought the property for a lot of reasons. It's a good investment, for one thing, but I also I didn't want some jerk in Nashville or Atlanta buying it and turning it into who knows what. Devon inherited the house from her grandmother, Gigi. Will, Aaron and I all knew Gigi, but Aaron knew her the best. The old woman had written her will so that Devon had to come home and live in the house, which gave Aaron his chance to get Devon to fall in love with him.

Pretty sure the whole thing could've been a plot for one of the romance novels I model for. I've read all the ones I'm on—at least, all the ones in English, anyway. They're good. I've learned all kinds of things.

I had exactly no plans to be a model of any kind. I fell into it, the exact opposite of firefighting. My dad was a firefighter, and I wanted to do it from the time I was ten. But when I was in my late twenties, I met up with an old buddy of mine for an Atlanta Falcons home game. We were in a park throwing a ball around and it was hot as shit, so I took my shirt off. This gorgeous woman came up to me, almost twice my age, and instead of giving me her number for a night of fun—which is what usually happens when gorgeous women come up to me, not gonna lie—she told me she was a modeling agent and could get me work.

I thought it was the most elaborate pickup line I'd ever heard, and I told her so. She handed me her card and walked away. When I showed up at the address the next morning, still half-believing it was a booty call, I discovered it really was a modeling agency.

So here I am, seven years later, and I'm a secret romance cover model.

I'm not proud of it. There's nothing wrong with it, but since I never told anyone, it's morphed into this huge secret that makes me feel like hell. The money's easy and awfully hard to pass up, but I'm going to quit soon, as part of my Price Improvement Plan. How no one's figured out that I'm on all these covers is beyond me, and I'm certain I'll get found out eventually. And when they do, it'll confirm what they've always thought: that

I'm just "pretty boy Price" with nothing in my head, not good for anything but my face and body.

Buying the house and running the bed-and-breakfast seemed like a good start to being New Price when Devon floated it all those months ago. I've sunk countless hours, sweat, and dollars into renovating it, and we're nearly ready to open. When we do, it'll be a big step toward proving I'm more than what people think I am.

As we're leaving, I catch a glimpse of Jodi talking to a customer. Without thinking, I wave at her, and her eyes slide to me. The smile that blooms across her face is enough to make me wonder if maybe I could ever be worthy of someone like her.

# CHAPTER 3
# JODI

$\mathcal{M}$OST OF MY days are the same. Wake up, apply fire-engine red lipstick, head downstairs, open coffee shop, run coffee shop, fruitlessly lust after my lifelong crush, close coffee shop, go upstairs, relax, dinner, bed. Repeat. Obviously, I have my weekly get-together with Devon and Ceci, my other best friend and wife of Devon's brother Rick, but other than that, I can pretty much be counted on to be inside this building.

Good thing I like it.

I bought it because it was exactly what I'd dreamed of since I was a teenager and I'd come into this very shop to do homework, write bad poetry, the whole thing. It was the one place I could be myself, not Jason's baby sister or Jess's older sister. The owner talked about wanting to sell it, figuring she could get a big check from Starbucks and retire. All I could do at the time was beg her not to. Not that I had anything against Starbucks. But local coffee shops are just better. Period.

By the time I'd finished a marketing degree from Jackson State, graduating through sheer will in the wake of my brother's death, the owner was still here, still running the shop. She'd told me she was waiting to sell it to me.

I'd been floored. Nobody had ever demonstrated that level of confidence in me. For that matter, no one had really ever paid that much attention to me. I'm fairly certain the bank gave me a pity loan because of Jason, and that's probably why it was such crappy terms that first time around, but in no time, I was the proud, naïve owner of this shop at twenty-two.

And now, my twenty-seven-year-old-nose smells something that's off. It's not the same smell as when Darius burns something in the toaster oven (a weekly occurrence), and since the morning rush is over, I head upstairs, following my nose.

My living space needs some major work, but obviously I've had my hands and money full with the shop downstairs. The previous owner didn't live up here, and it was more than a little bit of a disaster when I first moved in, but I've been steadily improving the place little by little. It's one giant open-plan area, with the exposed red brick preening in the morning sun let in by the many windows that need replacing. The saddest excuse for a kitchenette is off to one side, and a bathroom is diagonally opposite. My first project was the bathroom; a girl can only be expected to handle so much, so I brought it up to modern standards with the help of the previous owner's handyman son.

I flip on the light and scan the interior. Almost instantly, the far right wall erupts in a bright flash of light. I blink, then see tiny blue flames licking out around an outlet.

*Shit.*

It's an electrical fire. Can't live a block from a firehouse without learning some things. Moving quickly, I run to the kitchenette and grab a box of baking soda, then toss it onto the flames. It looks like I've stopped it, but I know better than to assume I have it all. I pull my phone out and call the station for help.

Running back downstairs, I shoo the remaining customers out. It's slightly chaotic, but it's remarkable how fast people move when you say the word 'fire.'

In a few minutes, the fire truck has made the block-long trek to appear in front of my shop, and the firefighters run in.

Only then do I realize my entire body is shaking. Darius appears next to me and pulls me into a hug, his bulky frame dwarfing me and keeping me warm in the chill of the early spring morning. "Don't cry."

I blink back the tears and huff out a laugh. "I wasn't going to until you told me not to."

Darius hugs me tighter and I let some tears fall. But I know they won't solve anything—they never do—so I give myself a few minutes and then I'm done.

People mill around, curious now that the building hasn't gone up in flames. Brook is crossing the square from the bookstore to see what's happened, and Mrs. Withers makes her way to me.

"What happened? These nitwits don't know crap." She waves her hands at the crowd on the sidewalk.

I extract myself from Darius's grip and look at the walking fashion disaster that is Mrs. Withers. Most people are still afraid of her thanks to her decades-long feud with Shirley "Gigi" Rayne, but Shirley's long gone and Mrs. Withers has more than redeemed herself. "Pretty sure it's an electrical fire upstairs, but I'll know soon enough."

Chief Suarez walks out of the shop and angles for me at that exact moment, and as I go to meet him, I see Brook corner Mrs. Withers for the intel out of the corner of my eye. Small towns, man. I love it here, but I most certainly am not a fan of being the center of attention.

As I near Chief, I ask, "How bad is it?"

He grimaces. "Let's say you won't be living there for quite a while."

"Electrical?"

"Yep. Only good thing is that it didn't impact the shop. The wiring's different downstairs, updated. Not like the stuff upstairs, which seems to be from the fifties."

My stomach sinks. I don't have any family in town to crash with, and no way would I impose on either of my best friends. Ceci and Rick have four-year-old twins, so their place is chaos, and Devon and Aaron are still so lovey-dovey that they probably have sex every hour in every room in their house. I can't be a witness to that. So, awesome: I have nowhere to live.

Or, maybe not. Maybe I can at least still sleep up there. Maybe Chief is exaggerating. "Can I go in?"

He radios up and after a conversation I don't pay any attention to, he nods. "Price says he'll stay up there."

For once, my body doesn't light up at the mention of Price. Probably has everything to do with the fact that my life has just exploded in front of me.

I head inside and up to my apartment. As I step over the threshold to my living space, I can't help the gasp that escapes. It's a disaster. White powder covers every surface. It's the worst kind of winter wonderland, and tears well up behind my eyes.

"Don't clean it up."

I turn, blinking hard as my brain empties and I fight to keep my jaw from unhinging as Price eats up the distance between us.

Um. *Wow*.

He's holding his helmet in one hand, his face sweaty, and he's wearing his turnout gear, the tan and yellow jacket and pants somehow fitting him like they were tailor made for him. Firefighter Price is hard to beat. Maybe I can clean him up. *Ohmygod, shut up, brain*. I shake my head. "Sorry. What did you say?"

He gives me a wry grin. "People always want to clean, but you should wait until the insurance people have a look."

I nod dumbly, whether from seeing him in full gear in my

apartment, or the legit shock of my apartment being utterly uninhabitable, or the combo, who knows.

Then I look behind him and see my bed. My bed, neatly made, which I now see is only partially covered in the white stuff, and the pristine section is sporting the navy polka dot bra and panty set that I'd discarded this morning in favor of the red set I was currently wearing.

Kill. Me. Now.

Price follows my gaze, and it takes everything in me not to starfish myself onto the bed and shove the evidence into the apron I'm still wearing. The...chambray polka dot apron. I have a thing for polka dots, and right now, I'm regretting it alongside every other life choice I've made. "Oh," Price says, then shrugs. "Don't worry about that. We've seen way worse."

My entire body erupts in flames. They're going to need to use their extinguishers on me. Because not only did Price literally *see* and *acknowledge* the whole thing, he *shrugged.* SHRUGGED.

What am I supposed to do now? How do I exist, knowing he's seen my underwear and shrugged? I am deceased. I have ceased to be. I am no more. Poof. Gone.

I'm moving out of town. That's the only option. I bark out a strangled laugh and it sounds like a hyena trying to cough. Then I blurt, "Those aren't mine."

Price's eyebrows raise. Then, before any more nonsense comes out of my mouth, he speaks. "Tell you what. Everything seems to be done up here, so I'm going to head downstairs. Why don't you pack whatever you need for the next couple of days and meet us outside when you're ready."

I swallow and nod. Then I watch him retreat, a perfect specimen of the firefighter fantasy, and I want to die of embarrassment. "*'Those aren't mine'*? Really, Jodi?" I mutter.

Sighing the sigh of every woman who's ever pined for a ridiculously hot man and then said man has seen her polka dot underwear set and shrugged, I pull a duffel bag from beneath my bed and grab what I need from the bedroom area. I'm painfully aware of my penchant for polka dots and cute under-wear sets as I pack them. Next, I head for the bathroom, which is totally untouched by the disaster. A fleeting thought of sleeping in the tub crosses my mind, but I stop it almost as quickly as it starts. I have standards. My lack of money ensures they're perilously low at this moment, but still.

I schlep my way downstairs and wince at the sight of the abandoned coffee shop. I have to be able to open it tomorrow, because I'm pretty much doomed if I can't. So that's the first thing I ask Chief when I step back outside.

He nods, and I sag with relief. That's at least one problem solved.

Chief glances at where the guys are packing up the truck for its one-block drive, then focuses on me. "You need a place to stay."

I nod. "I do. Figured I'd just see if —"

"You should stay at Will and Price's place."

The duffel hits the sidewalk with a thud. "The bed-and-breakfast?" No. That's insane. I can't do that. It's not even open. Don't they *live* there? Oh, no.

But he's already calling Will over, and as he approaches, Chief says, "I found your first guest."

Will, grumpy as always, barely spares me a glance before saying, "We're not really ready for guests."

I nearly slump in relief.

"Um, hold on a minute, broseph." Price appears and claps Will on the shoulder. "We need to pull the trigger or we'll never do it."

"We don't have food for guests. Or toiletries. Or anything a guest of a bed-and-breakfast would demand," Will counters.

"I'm sure Jodi doesn't care about all that, do you?" Chief looks at me and I swear on all the espresso machines in the world the man has a twinkle in his eyes. And the last time I saw that twinkle was when he was trying to push Devon and Aaron together.

Wait. Does he…? No. He couldn't. But maybe? Does this poor, misguided soul actually think he's going to play matchmaker with me and one of the Joseph brothers? The thought is so *beyond* that I nearly start cry-laughing right then and there.

"Jodi?" Chief looks at me expectantly. "What do you say?"

I blink. "Um."

"C'mon, Jodi, it'll be great," Price says, exuding confidence. "I've got just the room for you, and you have your own girlie stuff, right? Shampoo and whatever?"

Will grunts, and in Will-speak I think it means he's agreed to this as well.

Visions of money swirling down a drain run through my head. "I can't afford…"

"We'll work something out," Price says.

All the dirty thoughts I've ever had about Price flood my brain, and I break out in red splotches again.

"Say yes," Chief urges.

This is the worst idea ever in the history of worst ideas. Really bad. If there was a Guinness Book of Worst Ideas, this one would win. I exhale.

"Okay."

Chief smiles broadly and Will grunts. And god help me, Hot Firefighter Price morphs into Little Kid Price, his eyes bright, his whole body lit up with anticipation, and it's the most adorable thing I have ever seen.

I am so screwed.

# CHAPTER 4
# PRICE

*I* HUSTLE HOME to the B&B—Shirley's Inn,
apparently—after the electrical fire at Jodi's. I was
supposed to be off-shift by now, so the timing is perfect. Will
and I worked it out with Chief to stagger our shifts so that once
we get it up and running, one of us is always able to be there.
Chief has to hire another firefighter, but he's been looking for a
reason to bring Zach on full-time, so this is it.

First things first: shower. I would have normally showered
at the firehouse, but I was a little excited to get here and
prepare for our first guest. So I head to my room and the
ensuite bathroom. We've spent a lot of money upgrading the
place, and now we have six guest rooms, all with bathrooms,
along with the room that Will and I share. He doesn't want
both of us living on-site, but right now, that's what's happening. The inn is a three-story Victorian-esque house, and it took
no small amount of effort to convince the local historical
society to let us do the remodeling needed to make this place a
viable bed-and-breakfast. They actually thought we would just
open the doors to the house as it was, and somehow be
successful. Clearly no one there has ever run a business. I
mean, neither have I, but I read a ton about it after we bought

the place, and there was no way we could make a B&B work with yellowed peeling wallpaper, an overworked water heater, and an electrical system that can't handle a blowdryer and a coffeemaker at the same time.

After my shower, I head to the room I've decided will be Jodi's. It's on the third floor, painted a crisp light blue, and it's tiny and cute, just like Jodi. I think it used to be Devon's, but I'm not totally sure. I put towels in the bathroom and make the bed with freshly laundered sheets, and put one of Shirley's quilts on top of the comforter. Every room will have a quilt made by a local, whether it's new or not so new. Will had looked so surprised when I suggested it, as though I'd never had a better idea in my life. It almost hurt my feelings, but honestly, it was standard.

I head downstairs and nearly trip over my feet when I see Jodi standing in the front room. "Shit. I mean, hello!"

She turns from inspecting the newly installed bookshelves and smiles. "Hi."

"Hi." I already said that. "So, um, welcome to Shirley's Inn." I sound nervous. Probably because I *am* nervous.

Her smile gets wider. "Is that the name?"

I nod. "Will came up with it. We just decided on it yesterday."

"It's perfect."

Seeing that she's practically shrinking under the weight of a duffel that's almost as big as she is, I step forward. "Here," I say, gesturing for the bag. "Let me take that for you."

"Oh, I—" She holds onto the straps with both hands.

"I insist." I move closer.

"I really—honestly," she says, stepping back.

Only when I'm towering over her, my six-foot-two self literally casting a shadow on top of her, do I realize how creepy it is. I retreat. "Sorry. I just—it looks heavy." I gesture helplessly at the bag.

She blushes, a deep rose on her pale cheeks. "It's okay, Price."

I stare at her. When was the last time I saw her out from behind that counter? Because she's standing in front of me in a mouth-watering cotton gray skirt that hugs every curve from hip to knee, leaving her freckle-covered calves on display.

When did freckles get sexy?

"So," she says, drawing out the word, "do you want to, like, check me out? I mean, *in?*" she stammers.

"Yes!" I say it too enthusiastically and lurch into action, because if I don't get my act together, I am going to mess up our very first guest's experience. Who is Jodi, of all people. Smart, hardworking, has her shit together Jodi. Jodi, who looks at me like she believes I can be more than I am.

"Right this way." I lead her to the small reception desk, open the laptop, then stare blankly at the screen. Did I finally get that software up and running? And food—do we have any?

Okay, maybe Will was right. Maybe we weren't ready for guests.

I slam the laptop shut, making Jodi startle, and smile brightly at her. "How about I give you the grand tour?"

She blinks rapidly, like she's trying to determine just how much of an idiot I really am, before giving me a tentative smile. "Sure. Let's do that."

I want to take the duffel from her so badly it physically pains me. She's listing sideways under its weight. But she said she has it, and reading those romance novels has taught me that women are way more independent and stronger than I ever realized, so I grit my teeth and walk her around the bottom floor.

"It looks amazing, Price," Jodi says. "Last time I was in here, it was still Devon's and it was…nothing like this."

I grin. Something I can talk about. "We've put a lot of work into it. Pulled up the carpets and brought the floors back to their original parquet finery, took off most of the wallpaper except some in the dining room, and we painted over that to get this really cool texture thing on the walls. Got Sam from the antique shop to see what he could match to the house, too, so basically if it looks old, it probably is. And all the guest rooms have been remodeled and have private bathrooms. We gutted the kitchen and put in all-new industrial-grade appliances, re-painted everything…we've been busy."

She smiles appreciatively. "I can tell. You should be proud of yourself."

My chest warms at the praise, and for a moment, all I can do is beam dumbly at her. I come back to my senses when she arches her eyebrow and her smile morphs into a *let's get on with it* expression.

"Right. Well, um, let me show you to your room." I sweep past her and head for the stairs, taking them two at a time.

I get to the third floor and wait. And wait. And I'm a complete and utter asshole for not insisting on taking her bag because it takes a full minute for her to make it up to the third floor.

She finally hits the landing and launches a smile at me, breathing a little heavily. "Wow, guess all that training you do means you can just whoosh on up here."

*Yep. I'm an asshole.* My hands itch, begging for that stupid duffel, and I try to laugh. "Something like that. So, this will be your room," I say, leading her down the hall. "It faces east so it gets a lot of sun in the morning and it's really nice. I thought you'd like that. Though I guess you get up early to work and I don't even know if you'll see the sun rise, but if you do, um." I gesture at the window as we walk in to the room. Clearly I need to work on my making-a-guest-comfortable skills.

She follows me in, trailing a faint scent of vanilla and coffee as I struggle—and fail—to keep my focus anywhere but on her. She drops the duffel, thank god, and I swear she grows two inches.

"This is cute," she says, turning in a circle to inspect it. "Does each room have a theme? Or a color scheme? Oh my gosh, is this one of Gigi's quilts?" She grabs the quilt eagerly and clutches it to her chest. It's mainly peach and white, and in the light, it kind of matches her hair.

Which is a little frazzled, come to think of it, and that's not like her at all. She's always so put together.

"It is," I answer. "Do you recognize it?"

She nods. "It was in the living room before." She holds it out to inspect it. "So is this the Shirley room? Or the peach room? Or something different?"

I rub my neck. "Honestly, I haven't thought about it." That's a lie. I've spent hours thinking about it. But in the face of Jodi, who's this amazingly successful businesswoman, I'm too embarrassed to say anything. She'll think I'm stupid, and my behavior the past ten minutes has done nothing to counteract that idea. "What do you suggest?"

Her eyes light up. "You want my opinion?"

"Of *course* I want your opinion. You run a business. You're better at this than me."

Her expression softens, and she lets her arms fall. "Wow." She fiddles with a loose string on the quilt.

My brow tightens. "You know that, right? How impressive it is that you own and run a small business?" I probably sound like a self-help jerk. Or worse, like an over-privileged white guy.

She shrugs. "I guess."

I can't handle this. I round the bed so that we're face to face. "None of that, Jodi. Every day you go toe to toe with chain coffee shops and win. It's amazing. *You're* amazing. Believe that."

Her mouth opens and she clamps it shut, then nods. "Okay. Wow, um, thanks. I just—no one has ever actually acknowledged that. Like, ever."

I put my hands on her shoulders. They're so tiny. Hell, *she* is tiny. Well, stature-wise. Without one of her usual aprons on and a counter to hide behind, there are actually a lot of curves on her that I've never noticed…and I need to stop noticing. She is a guest. Guest guest guest. Guessity-guest. "Well, for what it's worth—which isn't much, I know—I think you're kick-ass." I squeeze her shoulders and step back. "So. Tell me your idea."

Her cheeks and neck are almost fire-engine red as she clears her throat. "Right. Okay. Um, well." She takes a breath. "Sorry."

I frown. "Why are you apologizing?"

She shrugs, her eyes everywhere but on me. "Can I see the other rooms? I want to make sure my idea works."

I gesture for her to take a look and she bolts out of the room. I amble along, staying in the hall as she goes in and out of the ones on the third floor, then the second. By the time she returns to the third floor, her eyes are back to their usual brightness, and she's smiling broadly. "Well?" I ask, leaning against the banister.

"Birds," she gushes.

"Birds?"

"Shirley was *obsessed* with birds. Well, maybe obsessed is too strong. But she loved them. Also, the quilts in every room— whose idea was that?"

The fucking quilts again. "Mine."

Surprise flits across her face—of course it does—but she suppresses it quickly. "That's amazing. I love it. It's perfect. So: birds."

I nod. "Okay. Birds. Tell me more."

She flushes again, then launches into reasons why each room needs to be bird-themed, along with the types of bird that best match each room. I zone out for a second, thinking how amazing Jodi is to have come up with this in mere minutes when I've spent ages trying to do it, and Jodi stops.

"It's a terrible idea, isn't it?"

"No," I say. "Not even close. It's perfect, and I should get something to write this down on."

"Oh! Right. Cool."

I straighten and start to walk, right as she does this stutter-step thing in front of me, and it looks like she's about to fall. She grabs onto my arm and hip, pressing against me in the process.

She's soft.

Very soft.

And now I'm kind of not.

"Ohmygodl'msosorry," she says, jumping away like she's been burned.

"It's fine," I say, my throat tight as my dick twitches. What the hell? I've done clinch cover shoots with half-naked women and nothing, but a half-second of Jodi's curves against me does it?

She seems to be sweating. "I'm, um, gonna—bye." She turns and runs away for the second time in twenty minutes.

I watch her go, command my body to get ahold of itself, and head downstairs to make a grocery list. My phone pings and I pull it out. It's my agent.

MONICA

Got a line on a new job for you in Atlanta in two weeks.

I sigh. I'd rather focus on the B&B and rising up the ranks at the fire station, but one thing at a time. Besides, I can't leave Monica hanging. So I ask her to send me the details.

# CHAPTER 5
# JODI

I WAKE UP sweaty and slapping the alarm off on my phone, my brain fogged with images of a shirtless, soot-streaked Price stalking toward me in only the bottom half of his turnout gear, his silver-blue eyes raking me up and down as I stand naked in front of him. *Jesus.* I need to get a grip.

My head pounds from lack of sleep. I've never been a night owl. Not in high school, not in college, and certainly not now. But apparently staying under the same roof as Price Joseph, where I know at some point he's taken off his clothes and stood under a shower, turns me into a sleepless wreck.

Speaking of showers.

I hustle through mine, trying and failing to delete the feel of Price's bicep beneath my hand out of my head. If I were at home, I'd have made myself a cup of coffee and sipped at it as I got ready, but clearly I'm not home and no way in hell am I heading downstairs without being dressed, even if it is five a.m. and Price is bound to be asleep.

Actually, come to think of it, I have no idea who all is in this house.

*Because you're a* guest, *Jodi.*

Right.

I tiptoe down the stairs and out the door like I'm some kind of criminal, then get in my car for the five-minute commute.

I step into the shop and inhale. The fine layer of espresso dust is in the air, and it almost covers the bite of electrical fire odor. I head up to my apartment to see if it's really as bad as I remembered. It is. In fact, in the pre-dawn of the morning, it's worse. The wall where the fire started is black, and the few pieces of TJ Maxx-sourced artwork are most assuredly ruined. The white powder remains on everything like a misguided snowstorm. I itch to clean it all up, but remember Price's words and keep my hands to myself.

With a sigh, I use the still-pristine bathroom to put some light make-up on and do a side-braid with my strawberry blond hair, and finally, because I'm nothing if not wedded to my routine, I apply matte fire-engine red lipstick.

I'm well into my second cup of coffee and nearly have the shop ready for its first customer when Darius saunters in and looks me up and down.

"So how was it sleeping in the same house as your crush?" He gives me a knowing grin.

I glare at him and point to my face. "My bags are so big I should be going on vacation."

He cackles. "That good, huh?"

"I'll be mainlining the caffeine today."

We finish getting everything ready and I rotate the sign to Open and greet the first customers. For a while, we're so busy that the only thing I can do is keep the coffee coming, adding and tamping the grounds, then dumping them after pulling a shot, steaming the milk and topping off espresso with it before the brew goes bitter.

At ten, there's enough of a lull that I'm able to slip away and call my mom. Part of me thinks I shouldn't bother, but I remind that part of me that we've already lost one brother in this family to a fire, and Mom should hear the news from me and not some nosy busybody. I dial my grandmother's landline.

"Hello?" Grandma's voice comes into my ear and for a moment, all is right with the world. I smile broadly and say hello back.

"You met anyone to settle down with yet?" she asks.

Well, there goes that warm and fuzzy feeling. "No, Grandma. I need to talk to Mom; is she there?"

Mom sold my childhood home and moved in with Grandma in South Carolina about a year ago. She said it was because Grandma needed her help, but it was only a matter of time before she left.

I squeeze my eyes shut and will the memory away. They all left. And it'd all been because of me.

Grandma screeches for my mom and eventually she picks up the receiver.

"Shouldn't you be at work?"

"Hello to you, too," I say.

"Sorry." She tries again. "What do you need?"

I plunge in, needing to get it out. "There was an electrical fire in my apartment yesterday. I'm fine, and the shop's fine, but my place is a disaster and needs major repairs."

I wait.

"You're okay?" There's a slight tremor in her voice.

"I'm okay." I try to sound as encouraging as possible, ignoring the warmth that spreads through me at the realization that she seems to actually care.

She exhales. "Good."

I keep going before I lose my nerve. "I'm staying at a local bed-and-breakfast and, um…"

"Jodi," Mom interrupts. "Sweetie, I hope you're not calling to ask for money."

"What? No." Not at first, anyway. But yes. I was definitely calling to ask for money. "Why?"

"I just sent your sister a little bit to help her out. She's got a lead on an up and coming producer and needed some help to record a demo." The pride is evident in her voice; I can almost see her standing straighter, smiling more, as she says it.

Things she never does when she talks about me.

Also, I am a complete idiot for thinking that Mom would do something as supportive as lend me money to help with expenses while all this gets settled. She's barely got any money to start with, and naturally, my little sister Jess gets all her attention and funding. As usual.

I swipe at the rogue tear that's dared to show up.

"You haven't heard from your father, have you?" Mom's voice is hesitant, and I go on high alert.

"No. Why?"

"Oh, no reason. Just…I haven't, that's all."

I sigh. "Mom, you've got to let him go. He left." *Like a coward.* I keep that part to myself.

"I think he just needs time. Jason—" she halts—"we were all affected differently."

I don't bother answering. Dad didn't leave immediately, but he might as well have. He retreated to the furnished basement and only came out to go to work and occasionally to eat dinner with us, and even then, he may as well not have bothered.

Six years later and Mom still seems to think all Dad needs is an unlimited amount of time to grieve, and then he'll suddenly return to his senses and call her, and they'll get back together. News flash: it's never gonna happen.

But I said as much, along with a lot of other things I'd never said, and once I did, he left. Followed by Jess, and eventually, Mom.

"I should go. The coffee shop calls," I say, trying to end us on a high note.

"Sure, sweetie. Call if you need anything."

We disconnect and I can't help the cynical laugh that escapes me. I *did* need something. I called. I got exactly nothing for my efforts.

As I round back to the front, it's just in time to see one of my best friends in the world come in with her kids: Ceci and the twins, Luke and Eva.

"Get over here and give me a hug," she demands, while simultaneously shooing the four-year-olds to a table. They do as she says, and because I'm no fool, I do the same. She wraps me in her arms and chides, "Tell me why I had to hear about this from my husband and not you?"

I sigh and pull away. "It's actually impressive that Rick heard about it before you did."

She scowls and flips her impeccable blond hair behind her shoulders. "Is it, though?"

I crack a smile and lead her to the front so that I can get her a drink and the kids some hot chocolate.

She keeps going. "Of course, I got the juicier news from Devon—you're staying at Gigi's?"

I narrow my eyes at her. "Careful what you say next, or I'll charge you full price."

She waggles her eyebrows. "Yes. The *full* Price. Just down the hall, showering after a long, sweaty shift at the firehouse…"

I groan.

She laughs. "You started it."

"Amen, sister," Darius says, sliding her drink toward her. "Double-shot, half pump vanilla latte."

"You are a god among men," Ceci says. "Also, nice face."

Darius preens. Ceci taught him how to contour years ago and he's been obsessed ever since.

I turn to make the hot chocolates and purposely ignore both of them.

"Have mercy," Darius says under his breath.

At this point, *have mercy* always means Will Joseph, eldest and sternest of the Joseph brothers. Darius has already accepted that Will is straight and therefore not interested in him, but it doesn't keep him from looking. And to be sure, Will is definitely nice to look at—they all are—but we've already established which Joseph brother does it for me.

Not that we're talking about Price right now. Because we're not.

Darius turns to pour Will's drink, a regular drip coffee, black. No frills and straightforward, kind of like the man himself.

"Hi, Will," I greet him as he approaches.

He grunts his usual hello, then nods at Ceci as she takes the kids' hot chocolates, steamed to a lower temperature and loaded with whipped cream and a few sprinkles, off the counter. "We need to talk about your stay."

I gulp. "Oh. Um. Sure."

"Here's your coffee, Will," Darius says, sliding the cup across the counter and damn near fluttering his lashes at Will in the process.

Will's eyes flick to Darius, then the cup, and back to Darius. "Thanks."

Darius will be on cloud nine after getting an actual word out of Will. I ring him up and grab my own cup, and lead him to a set of overstuffed chairs in the far corner. I don't sit so much as perch on the edge of my chair, worried about appearing too relaxed in front of Will. The man manages to make his uniform of navy pants and dark blue t-shirt look like the height of business dress.

He clears his throat and looks at me, not a stitch of humor or good nature on him. "Since you're going to be claiming this on insurance, I don't feel bad about charging you our full rate. The insurance will cover it. And whatever they don't, we'll just waive. Of course, you'll need to pay up front, since we don't know how long insurance will take."

The blood drains from my face as he talks. Pay up front? "I..." I stammer.

"Is something wrong?" He arches one eyebrow, and instead of being kind of fun and kooky like on The Rock, it feels as though a villain is rubbing his hands together and plotting my imminent demise.

"No!" I blurt. "Nothing is wrong." Just, you know, I have absolutely no idea how to pay for any of this, but it'll be fine. I'll be fine. Like always.

"What's your email?"

I blink.

"So I can send you the invoice. Paperwork. Insurance companies love their paperwork."

I gulp and my cheeks blaze as I realize that Mistakes Have Been Made, and I have Regrets. Lots of Regrets. "Can I...do you want to write this down?" I stall.

He frowns. "I can remember an email, Jodi."

Of course he can. Mr. Scary can remember everything and then use it to torture you with later.

Well, can't say I didn't warn him.

"It's coffeegrrlnomnomnom@xmail.com," I mumble.

His eyes widen nearly imperceptibly. "I'm afraid I didn't hear that."

*Oh, you heard it, Mr. Scary.* I stand up. "I'll write it down." Because we couldn't possibly make it any more embarrassing at this point, now could we?

He follows me and reads the email when I hand it to him on a napkin. His eyes flick briefly to mine, then he folds the napkin carefully and puts it in his pocket. "Thanks," he says gruffly.

"Yep." I flick my hand in a weak wave.

Awesome.

As he leaves, Chief Suarez comes in. I head back around the corner of the counter to give Darius a break and am already two steps into making Chief's drink by the time he makes it to me. "Hi, Chief. Your usual?" I try to put my standard pep into the words, but it's hard. Not to mention, I am *tired*.

"Of course, Jodi, thank you." He drops a five on the counter and puts two dollars in the tip jar, and waits silently until he has his iced Americano with almond milk and one raw sugar in his hand. After a sip and a roll of his eyes heavenward, he looks back at me and smiles. "This is always the cure for what ails me."

"Glad you like them." I wipe the counter and keep moving, tidying up from the morning rush. "You here to meet up with Bobby?" Bobby Lent is the town's insurance guy, so I called him yesterday. He's easily seventy-five and I'm told will drink anyone under the table and still get a hole in one on the golf course. I think those stats are supposed to be impressive, but seeing as how I'm a total lightweight with alcohol and haven't ever managed a hole in one at the local mini-golf, I'm not really one to talk.

"Sure am," he says. As he speaks, Bobby himself walks in.

"Morning, Chief. Morning, Jodi. Got any iced tea back there?" His watery brown eyes are kind and the smile he gives me is one of quiet calmness.

I return the smile, a genuine one, and feel a little better. "Sure." I make it and hand it to him, and they head upstairs to determine my fate.

When they eventually come down, Chief nods encouragingly at me and I breathe easier.

Lunch consists of Darius running to Taco House and the two of us taking turns snarfing it down in the kitchen. I have plans to eventually offer more than pastries, things like sandwiches and hot breakfast stuff, but at the rate things are going, it'll be another five years…if I even make it that far.

By the time two o'clock rolls around, we're an hour away from closing and I'm moving like an extra on a zombie show. So naturally, that's when Price chooses to come in.

Gah. He's so…*ungh*. That's all I've got. Words are gone today.

He flashes a blinding white smile at me as he approaches, all six-foot-plus, broad-shouldered, floppy-haired, bearded dirty blond goodness of him.

I repeat: *Ungh.*

"How's it going, Jodi?"

Oh, you know, just watching my life implode, but other than that, peachy. "Good. You want your usual?" I can't ever make his drink until he actually orders, because he switches it up every now and again with absolutely no pattern that I can discern.

He nods, and I drop into the zone pulling together the oat-milk latte with one shot of vanilla. I'm in such a state that I do a heart design in the cup before I realize what I've done. He sees it before I can pretend I've messed it up and toss the coffee and start again.

"Wow, is that a heart design?" he says, sounding awestruck. He holds his hands out, and I hesitate before giving it to him. He grins and pulls out his phone. "You're so talented. This is going on Instagram."

I can't help but huff a laugh and roll my eyes.

Satisfied with the photo, he pockets his phone, then takes a sip. He grimaces.

I startle. "What?"

He takes another tentative sip, then shivers. "Um."

Oh god. Oh no. I've messed it up. I have a vague memory of maybe not choosing vanilla? Maybe? "I'll make another one," I say hurriedly.

"It's okay." He reaches his hand out right as I'm grabbing the cup, and the warmth of his skin combined with the sincerity in his silver-blue eyes is too much. It's the cherry on top. And I can't stop the tears from falling any more than I can stop the sun from rising.

"Oh no," he says, his eyes widening.

I cry harder, because of course I do.

"No no no," he says. "Come here, Jodi…" He rounds the

corner and pulls me out from the counter, and I let him walk me to one of the tables.

We sit and I sniffle, until I say, "I'm so sorry. It's just—this is a lot, and the fire, and your brother, and money, and…"

His brow furrows. "What about my brother? Did Will say something?" He leans forward, his hands clasped on the table.

They're beautiful hands. Even calloused, they were so soft on mine.

Aaaand I'm boohooing again. But after a moment, I manage to pull myself together, so I grab some napkins and dab at my eyes, then wipe my nose. "These recycled napkins are terrible," I mutter.

Price's lips quirk up. "What did my brother say?"

I heave a breath and meet his eyes. "It's not his fault."

"I'll be the judge of that." He crosses his arms. "Between the two of us, we've made you cry, and that's unacceptable. I want to fix it."

And in this moment, with Price Joseph's attention focused solely on me, I can't do anything but word-vomit the whole thing. "I have zero savings. Like, none. Zip. I called my mom to see if she could help me out, just a little money to tide me over since I know a lot will be tied up with the apartment, and as usual, she was more concerned with my little sister. I don't think she even cares that there *was* a fire. Which is insane, right?" I should stop now. But I can't. I keep going. "And then Mis—your brother—he comes in and is all 'we'll charge you full rates because of insurance' and 'we'll require payment up front' and 'we'll send you an invoice' and I just, I just—" I hiccup.

Price's stupidly gorgeous eyes have gotten wider and wider as I've blurted my woes. His fingers twitch. "Will is an idiot."

I grab another scratchy tissue and sniffle out a laugh. "He's Mr. Scary."

He leans forward and grins. "Did you just call him…Mr. *Scary?*"

My cheeks blaze. "Um...yes?"

Price throws his head back and laughs, his entire body shaking with it as he claps. The sound of his laughter spreads a gooey warmth all through me, and a tentative smile emerges on my face.

"Oh no," he says, still chuckling. "Oh, I can't wait to tell Aaron. That's the best thing I've heard in...forever." His eyes are freaking *sparkling* now, all crinkly and gorgeous and trained on me appreciatively and...*ungh*.

At least I've stopped crying, so I've got that going for me. Also, note to self: Go leave a review about this mascara because it has kept up like a champ.

"Tell you what," he says. "Let's forget the whole 'paying in advance' thing. That's not how a regular hotel does it so I have no idea what Will was thinking there. And let's go with half off our regular rate. Does that help?"

"Do I have a choice?" I blurt. "Oh, wow. Sorry. I meant, yes. Sure."

His eyes soften. "Jodi."

The way he says my name, all sweet and kind, it's no good. I can feel tears threaten.

He snaps his fingers and leans forward. "Wait. How about this? You help us with marketing and other stuff and you can stay for free. An exchange of services."

My thighs clench at the idea of *exchanging services* because clearly my thighs are stupid, and what would I know about *services*, anyway? I nod. Wait—I nod? No! "I'm not sure," I stammer. "How would that even work?"

He waves my concerns away. "You're a brilliant business-woman. We've established that. My brother and I don't know shit about marketing, for one thing. We need your help. Or at least, *I* need your help and I'll deal with Mr. Scary later. You'll help us come up with a strategy and maybe help me understand our accounting software?" He dips his head and looks up at me, his expression a combination of mischievous and pleading and sexy that's impossible to resist.

"Okay," I say. He actually thinks I'm a brilliant business-woman? What kind of alternate universe have I walked into?

He sits up, grinning broadly. "Perfect! We've got ourselves a deal."

He extends a hand for me to shake and I take it, sealing my fate of potentially hours sitting across from Price Joseph, acting like I haven't crushed on him since I was twelve.

Again: I am so screwed.

# CHAPTER 6
# PRICE

MIDNIGHT CRAVINGS ARE real. Or maybe it just happens to be late at night and I'm hungry. Either way, I need food. So I sneak out of my room—something I never would have done if we didn't have a guest—and move through the darkened house to the kitchen.

As I approach, I notice the light above the stove is on, illuminating the kitchen in a soft glow. Jodi is in there, and her head is completely inside the fridge as she digs around. And it feels like someone has landed a punch on my solar plexus. Only Jodi's legs are visible, pale and lightly covered in freckles and absolutely luscious, topped with a minuscule pair of silky red polka dot shorts rising up so far that I'm gifted with a view of *all* her legs in their glory, right up to where the curve of her butt begins.

I nearly swallow my tongue.

She straightens, and she's wearing a matching button-down top, her arms full of things from the fridge. I'm still staring when she sees me and yelps. "Ah!"

I throw my hands in the air and yelp a little, too. "It's just me!"

"Jesus, Price! You scared the shit out of me!" she says, her eyes wild.

I exhale an embarrassed laugh. "I'm so sorry, Jodi. I'll help." I lurch forward to help as she leans over the kitchen counter, her back to me, to let everything tumble out of her arms. She's grabbed the makings of my perfect sandwich: sliced turkey, pepper jack cheese, yellow mustard, lettuce, tomato. "I, um, came down here for a snack and…yeah."

She laughs softly as she rights the mustard. "It's okay. Maybe don't creep up on your guests going forward?" As she says it, she turns to face me.

And my jaw might actually hit the floor.

Because now that she's not hidden by sandwich stuff, she is…a revelation.

A soft, pale goddess of midnight, lit only by the half-moon and a too-dim stove light.

Her long, strawberry-blond hair tumbles in soft waves halfway down her back, free of the usual constraints she has it in at work. Her breasts, clearly not in a bra, hang deliciously heavy behind the silk top, which itself shows far more of her chest than I've ever been treated to. It's just as creamy and freckled as the rest of her skin. Her face is bare, putting her wide, hazel eyes on display in a way they never are during the day. But it's her lips that have me ready to sink to my knees. Stripped of their vivid red armor, they're pale pink and plump and I want to rub my thumb over the bottom lip to feel if it's as soft as it looks, and god help me, she actually *licks* them while I'm looking at her.

I cough.

"Right. No creeping on guests," I finally manage to say.

Her eyes widen just a fraction and she averts her eyes as a flush blooms across her chest. "And maybe—maybe wear some clothes?"

"Clothes?" And that's when I realize that I'm staring at her while wearing only black mesh shorts. No shirt.

Her eyes flick up to me and right back to where she's busying herself with the sandwich, and I straighten and puff up a bit. It's habit, really, and I'm so used to being ogled that it takes me a minute to stop doing it. I deflate, because for one thing, she's definitely not looking. And for another, even if she was, she definitely is not interested in me.

"Sorry," I mumble. "I'll go—"

"Stay," she blurts, meeting my eyes before quickly looking down. "I mean, it's your house, your kitchen. You're down here because you're hungry, right?"

"Well...yes." I nod dumbly.

"So, do you want a sandwich?" Her gaze locks firmly on mine.

I recognize the look. It's the one she gives me when she's behind the counter at the coffee shop. Like I'm a customer.

Yeah, she *definitely* isn't interested in me. Which is for the best. I know it is.

"Double meat, double cheese," I say, grabbing pickles from the fridge.

We both go quiet, and I watch as she grips the knife in one sturdy, small hand, then cradles the tomato in her other, moving the serrated edge through the ripe skin, creating even slices to lie on the bread. She's efficient in her movements, each of them seemingly calibrated to maximize her efforts. She is a gazelle, graceful and pure and untouchable as she works, and beside her I am an unsteady, drunk goat, bleating helplessly.

And her scent. Jesus Christ. She smells so utterly feminine, a heady mix of vanilla and coffee wafting toward me with every move she makes. All of a sudden, there is a neon sign and a freaking marching band announcing what an impossibly perfect woman she is, and overhead is a plane with a banner confirming I have exactly no chance.

I might have made her blush being down here partially dressed, but I'm so far from worthy of her that it's laughable. I've spent my entire thirty-four years happily prancing my way through life, getting by on my looks, dating and sleeping with more women than anyone has a right to, and taking on the barest of responsibilities beyond a few at the fire station until recently. Jodi, on the other hand, has lost a brother and is running her own business. I may have been through some family shit myself, but next to Jodi, I feel like a child.

Sure, I'm trying to change, and I will, but Jodi deserves someone who has their shit entirely together. With a 401(k) and a five-year plan, minimum. I'd never treat Jodi the way I treated women in my twenties, but still.

I wonder what Mom would think of Jodi? The thought startles me, because I have never once considered what she might think of someone. I may be the brother with the best relationship with Mom, but that's not saying much. She was an alcoholic for many, many years, and even though she's doing a lot better and trying to be involved, there's a lot of ground to make up.

It doesn't take long before I'm merely handing Jodi what she needs and putting everything away. She clears her throat as she plates the sandwiches.

"So, what are all the baking supplies for?"

I take the plate she hands me and walk to the small breakfast table tucked into a corner of the kitchen, trusting that she'll follow. I forgot about the stack of paperwork on it, which maybe I was supposed to put away, and it means Jodi and I will have to sit side by side. Managing not to hang my head in defeat, I pull her chair out and drop into the one next to her. Another whiff of her heady scent hits my nose. I might actually die before this night is over. If I see just how far those polka dot shorts have ridden up now that we're seated, I really *will* expire.

Clearing my throat, I answer. "I've decided to try my hand at pastries. For our guests."

She nods thoughtfully, her eyes luminous in the dim light. We'd never bothered turning on any lights, so the kitchen stove is punching above its weight tonight. "I'd never have pegged you as a baker."

She smiles gently as she speaks, but it does nothing to ease the sting of her words. And she must notice the flicker of pain that crosses my face, because she brushes my forearm, her fingers smooth and cool. I go still, afraid to do anything that'll make her take it away. My skin tingles beneath her touch.

"I'm certain you'll be great at it," she says. "Being a firefighter means you understand how important it is to follow directions exactly, right? It's the same with baking. Not that I'd know—I'm terrible at it."

My lips curl into a teasing smile. "You? Terrible at something? I find that hard to believe."

She blushes again and looks at her plate, pulling her hand off my arm. Instantly I want it back, but then my eyes fall onto her chest. And I am in heaven. Because in the darkened midnight of the kitchen, the deep V of her silk top hides exactly nothing, and I home in on the space between her breasts. That thin strip of skin, half in shadow, is graced by a line of freckles. I suppress a groan, wanting nothing more than to bury my nose against them in supplication while her fingers scrape through my hair.

"There are plenty of things I'm bad at." She worries her lip with her teeth, and I'm riveted, unable to do anything but stare greedily at the way her bare lips give in to the pressure, then plump up as they escape the drag of her teeth.

None of it manages to help me be any less aroused.

With an effort that I've not put forth since my high school football coach was screaming at me to pick up the pace or the whole team would run another two miles, I drag my eyes up to her face and clear my throat. "I find you being bad at anything hard to believe." *Especially at this exact moment. When hard has a whole other meaning.*

She puffs out a laugh. "You're the only one. I can't be trusted to keep anything alive, for one. Countless fish have met their doom under my care, so I'm completely unwilling to go farther. Even plants are in peril—whatever lives in the shop owes its existence to Darius."

I hope my expression tells her I'm convinced, because it's taking everything in me not to think about picking her up and carrying her over my shoulder to my room. And she is so tiny that it would take no effort.

Her lips part and she takes a deep breath, almost as if she knows what's going through my head. "So, um, anyway," she says, her voice bright, "I should probably, um…I should go. Goodnight!"

She stands quickly, scraping the chair on the wooden floor and putting a wall of red polka dot silk in my eyesight. She is going to put me in an early grave. One I didn't even know I was about to fall into until fifteen minutes ago. Or thirty. I've lost all sense of time right along with my sanity.

She whips around me, trailing that irresistible scent of hers, and I force myself to keep my eyes on the table. *Do not watch her leave the kitchen.*

Yeah, right.

I turn and watch her ass jiggle in those too-short shorts as she practically sprints away and pounds up the stairs. And it's only when I hear the faint click of her bedroom door shut that I scoot my plate out of the way, slowly lower my head to the table, and bang it. Repeatedly.

# CHAPTER 7
# JODI

MUSCLES. I DREAM of golden, broad, tattooed muscles. Nighttime, daytime, it doesn't matter. The muscles are always there, taunting me, achingly close, but I can't touch them. Even in my dreams, I never get near enough to lay my hands on them.

It's been a week of absolute torture. Beautiful, muscle-y torture. I've seen Price without a shirt before—thank you, annual Fall Festival Dunk Booth—but never for such a sustained length of time, and definitely never that close.

He was right beside me. Basically in the dark. A freaking inch from me.

And for one achingly long moment, I'd thought he might actually want me. Which is a whole new level of fantasy, I know. But the way he'd caught his breath, his eyes traveling my entire body while his own stood absolutely still…

Anyway. Fantasy. I'm not so naïve as to think I'd be anything close to what he's used to. I'm a short, pale, not exactly thin thing, and he probably helps himself repeatedly to glamazon women, tall and sophisticated and who know how to do more with their mouths than apply flawless lipstick. Not to mention the customers I know he's dated, like Megan and Mary Alice.

Both of whom are tall, thin, and blonde, and are now members of the Mom Group that regularly comes in. And they're genuinely nice people—especially Megan. Mary Alice got perilously close to being a mean girl in high school, and sometimes she gets a little snippy when she's hungry and not yet caffeinated.

What's wild is that Price is still friendly with them, too, giving hugs and chatting with them at the shop like their history is no big deal. Like *hey, we know what each other looks like naked but we're going to pretend we don't.* I wouldn't know how to do that. Granted, I don't have exes I've slept with, but I can't conceive of dating someone and then being their friend afterwards.

I take a look around the shop. The morning rush has died down, and now the regulars are dotted here and there. Mrs. Withers and Miss Betty are at one of the brightly colored tables, their heads inclined toward each other as they gossip or plot, I don't know which. Chief Suarez is stationed at the table closest to the exit, an iced Americano his only comfort as he stares down a mountain of paperwork. He finally managed to submit his report on my electrical fire to the insurance company, thank goodness. Some of the Mom Group, including Megan and Mary Alice, are over in their usual corner with babies and toddlers galore, and while they probably take up too much space for too much time for a lot of my customers' preferences, I adore them. I love that my shop is the place they've decided to gather while they drink coffees and smoothies and eat pastries. To hear them tell it, this is the only time they get to talk to other adults for the duration of a regular workday, so I'll happily clean up the crumbs and mounds of napkins they go through. Besides, they tip well.

Right on time, Ceci and Devon bust through the door. It's a teacher workday for Devon, and the preschool where Ceci's twins attend is open. Basically, the stars have aligned for a daytime gabfest for the first time in weeks.

"I'll be in our usual spot," I tell Darius, stepping out from behind the counter to grab both women in a group hug.

Ceci wiggles out. "I love you, but I love your coffee more. Where is it?" Her blond ponytail whips through the air as she looks for it.

"Try this," Darius says. "Triple shot half-pump vanilla, half-pump caramel, extra foam, extra hot, no milk." He presents the coffee to Ceci as though she is his queen, bowing and looking up with a twinkle in his dark brown eyes.

"Bless you," Ceci says, grabbing the mug with two hands and lifting it to her nose to take a deep inhale. "Smells like sanity." She exhales with a smile.

"And for you, twenty-ounce iced cold brew, black."

Devon takes the drink with an excited wiggle. "Thank you, sweet Darius."

I gesture with my mug of basic-as-it-gets coffee to the trio of overstuffed chairs in the only open corner of the shop. "Shall we?"

Ceci leads the way while Devon cranes her neck to make sure the dogs, Daisy and Samson, are behaving themselves outside. Satisfied, she loops her arm through mine and leans into me as we walk.

"Missed me?" Ceci asks, her ocean-blue eyes sparkling.

"You mean since yesterday morning?" I counter, hip-checking her.

"Of course. I'm surprised you can even go twelve hours without experiencing withdrawals."

I roll my eyes. "That's Devon and Aaron, not me."

"I can't help it if I love my fiancé," Devon sniffs.

Ceci groans as we settle in. "Don't start, Devon—we are here to get the goods on Jodi, and nothing is going to stop me."

Devon bounces on her chair. "Ooh, finally! We're focusing on someone else's love life for a change."

Their heads swivel to me simultaneously, and I shrink back against the velvet cushion. "Um."

"You know, I think I like it better on this side of things," Devon says thoughtfully.

I scowl at her. "I don't have anything to discuss."

Ceci dips her chin and arches her eyebrows. Then she raises her hand to begin a count off, and I know I'm sunk. "Let's recap. You're staying at pretty-boy Price's bed-and-breakfast. The same guy you've crushed on since time began, apparently. You're single. He's...well, he's not in a relationship, we know that. And it's just the two of you in that giant house, no one else is there. So." She scoots to the edge of her chair and stares into my soul. "When are you going to bang him?"

Devon cackles while I blush furiously. "Ceci!"

She shrugs. "Tell me I'm wrong."

I scan the shop, terrified someone might have heard her. Or, better, for anyone to save me. But alas, no one is around and Darius wants the same questions answered.

"Look," I say, lowering my voice. "He is *not* interested in me."

"I don't know," Devon sing-songs. "I was in here yesterday morning and he was giving you a once-over like he was ready to dive in to that sweet, sweet—"

"Oh my god, *stop!*" I plug my ears and squeeze my eyes shut, unable to take any more of their teasing. It is boiling hot in here. Did the fire impact the HVAC?

Have I mentioned they know exactly nothing about my virginity? It's not shameful or anything—though some days I have to try harder to convince myself of that than others— but how precisely does one go about saying *Oh by the way, ladies, your girl here is 27 and still rocking her V-card?* Because it's dang near scandalous at this point. And I've had boyfriends, but both were in college and neither of them really seemed worth the trouble.

Ridiculous, right? I blame the boyfriends. They were sweet.

Maybe too sweet. It's not my fault that Price set this insanely high bar for the "hot goofy puppy dog" that's apparently my weakness and no one else can step over it. Someone will, eventually.

Anyway. Life has gotten in the way of any other boyfriends, so here I am, the 27-year-old virgin with two best friends who think I'm just gonna waltz into Price's bedroom and ask him to do me.

Nope.

Hard pass.

"Hey," Devon says, reaching over and patting my leg, "we're sorry. It's exciting, this idea of you and Price."

I lift my head to the sky and pray for patience. "There *is* no me and Price."

"Okay, but then why is he standing in the doorway with two notebooks and a handful of pens and looking at you like you're his personal goddess and savior?" Ceci asks with a satisfied grin on her face.

I let out a sigh and look at Devon. "Is this how we treated you about Aaron?"

"Oh, definitely. I'm enjoying this immensely." Devon's eyes track to Price and back again. "But seriously. He really is here for you."

I turn. Price breaks into a wide smile, nearly bowling me over with the force of it. Then he waves, almost like he's *shy*, and my heart squeezes. "I promised him some help with marketing the B&B," I say. "That's all this is."

"Gotta start somewhere," Devon singsongs as I stand.

I shoot her a death glare and make my way to Price, trying to ignore the way Price's eyes seem to darken as they travel over my entire body. He really *is* looking at me differently, but the idea of his interest is so far-fetched that I can't fathom it. "Hi."

He grins down at me. "Hi, Jodi."

We stand there, smiling at each other, until I think that

maybe I was supposed to say something. Finally, he speaks. "So, I thought I'd take you up on your offer to help?"

Wow. He really does seem shy. "Definitely. But, ah, can we do it later? I need to…" I gesture at the shop.

"Oh!" He smiles self-consciously, which I have never seen, and ducks his head. "Sorry. Of course. Okay. Later, then? I'm off-shift till tomorrow morning."

"Sure. Three o'clock work?"

"At home?" He stops. "I mean, the B&B?"

I peer closer at him. He really *is* acting weird. "That sounds good. See you there."

He leaves, and I want nothing more than to get back behind the counter, where everything makes sense. Naturally, that isn't happening, because Ceci and Devon are straight-up blocking my way there.

"You two are a menace." I force my way through them and into the safety of my domain. Instantly I breathe easier, my thoughts growing clearer by the second. Whatever that was out there with Price, it was simply him being nervous about asking for help.

"He is *into* you," Ceci declares, pointing her finger at me.

Darius snickers. "Dude really was acting weird."

"Traitor," I hiss. "Not you, too."

He holds his hands up. "Listen, boss, I'm just calling it like I see it."

I grab a cloth and wipe the frother on the espresso machine. Which does not need it, because it gets cleaned after every use. "Shut up. All of you."

*P*rice is already in the kitchen when I get to the B&B, and he's coated in flour.

"Oh no." I can't help the giggle that escapes me as I take everything in. It's a disaster. Every baking pan seems to have been put to use, the counters are covered in sugar and butter and flour, and the vintagey robin's-egg blue stand mixer looks like it's been to war.

"Price, what are you doing?"

He peers at me through flops of dark blond hair. "Baking?"

Trying—and failing—to ignore how unfair it is that he can be a disaster and still be hot, I sniff the air and catch exactly nothing in the way of pastry goodness. "Really?"

"I haven't gotten that far yet." He wipes his hands on the flour-covered apron that's doing a pitiful job of protecting his clothing.

"Guess not. Should I?" I jerk a thumb toward the stairs, indicating I can come back.

His eyes widen. "What? No!" He pulls the apron off and throws it on the counter. "I mean, no. Sorry. I'll deal with all this later. Let's sit." He hustles to the small table where we sat last week, which is blessedly free of anything but the notebooks and pens he had earlier today.

I take a seat, and he drops into the chair across from me, yawning loudly as he arches his back and stretches his arms into the air. He's wearing a thin white shirt, which does nothing to hide the realistic lion head tattoo on the upper right of his chest that I caught too long a glimpse of the other night, and I take my fill of him as he leans, feasting on the strip of golden skin between the shirt and waistband.

Straightening, he looks at me sheepishly. "Baking is a lot harder than I thought it would be. I mean, I *knew* it would be hard, but what I didn't know was how damn bad I'd be at it. It's frustrating. But I'm not giving up." He runs a hand through his hair and I watch the way his forearm flexes before jerking my gaze back to his face.

Sometimes the force of him is almost too much to bear. Like right now, with the afternoon sun streaking into the kitchen, his eyes are an iridescent silver. His face is angular, probably a photographer's dream if he were ever in front of one, boasting deep-set eyes and a straight nose, with high cheekbones that his soft beard doesn't quite hide.

I clench my fist beneath the table, suddenly overcome with the desire to cup his chin and rub my palm over his beard. "Yeah," I croak. "It's why I don't do it."

He quirks a grin. "I'm not giving up. Not yet. You'll have to be my taste-tester—tell me if whatever I make is good."

I swallow. "Happy to."

He smiles broadly, as if I've just given him a gift. "Thanks. I wouldn't trust anyone but you. So, marketing?"

I smile back, relieved to be in territory I can navigate. "Let's talk about your target audience."

# CHAPTER 8
# PRICE

TWO WEEKS IN and I am losing my damn mind. She smells like coffee and vanilla. She shows up in the kitchen all fresh-faced and sweet, and happily samples whatever terrible pastry I've attempted, looking at me in a way that makes me want to be a better man. And her breasts. Good Christ. How I never noticed before is a riddle for the Sphinx because holy shit. She's still wearing those polka dot silk pajamas in the morning, bless her, but ever since our midnight snack session she wears those lacy things that don't do crap to rein her breasts in but instead just frame them like a gift that I'm not allowed to open.

I can't think about what she does on the mornings I'm not there, where it's Will instead of me. If he's seeing her in those pajamas...*Fuck*. Losing. My. Mind.

I want to know what she'd smell like in my bed in the morning. How it would feel to pull her close and snuggle, then rub my hands over her curves, the dip and swell of her waist and hips. The sounds she'd make as I slid down her body and wrapped her thighs around my head.

Something about her seems so innocent, but even so, I've

caught the heat in her eyes when she looks at me. I know I'm not good enough for her—there's no question—but knowing that hasn't managed to turn my head or my body off.

"Price Joseph, as I live and breathe."

The voice brings me back to the present, on a photoshoot set. I push the thoughts of Jodi away as I open my arms for a hug. "Lisa Cain. My favorite photographer on the planet."

Lisa raises her eyebrows, having grown completely immune to my charms over the years. "They've already covered your tattoos and oiled you up. You're a mess. You really think I'm going to hug you?"

"Can't blame a guy for trying." I wink at her playfully.

"You are so full of shit," she laughs.

I laugh with her. "You know where to find me if you ever change your mind," I joke.

She rests her camera on her hip and gives me an appraising look. "I promise, Price, if I wake up one day and discover I'm twenty years younger and like men, you'll be the first guy I call."

I pistol my fingers at her. "Deal."

"Now, get ready." She waves me into the first scene.

I drop onto the yoga mat they've put off to the side and get to work: a series of push-ups, crunches and bicycle kicks to make the muscles pop. *My abs are still good, dammit.* When I'm done, I hop up and head to the spot an assistant has marked for me.

Wordlessly, I stand while Lisa takes a few test shots and an assistant sprays more oil on me. Today's shoot is a series of scenes for contemporary covers, so we'll get shots of me, then of me and another female model. I'm starting off shirtless and will put on more clothes as we go along. Typically it's the other way around, but Lisa wanted to take advantage of the spring sunlight coming through the willow tree, so here we are. Given it's only seventy degrees outside and I'm already burning up, I'm more than grateful we're not shooting a historical cover, which would mean stifling period clothes. I'm usually considered too bulky for those, but not always.

There are easily five other people running around, darting between here and a tent they've set up for me and the other model to relax in between shoots. We're a lot closer to Talladega than I'd prefer, not even over the border in Georgia this time, but it's not like anyone is going to suddenly appear from home and see me.

"Let's do this, Joseph," Lisa says.

I get into position and run through the poses as she directs me. It's fast work; we've done countless shoots together and I know exactly what she wants. After about twenty minutes, she calls for the female model. The woman approaches, her hair long and jet black, and I see her eyes widen appreciatively as she looks me over. There was a time I'd capitalize on that interest, but thoughts of Jodi have ruined any chance of me pursuing a night of fun with the model. And isn't that something? Two weeks of Jodi in my house and I've completely changed my tune.

"Chrissy," she drawls, holding her hand out for a firm shake.

"Price. You done these before?"

She shakes her head, and I clock the nervousness in her pretty blue eyes. Eyes that have nothing on Jodi's.

I give her what I hope is a reassuring smile. "Don't worry— I'm not a creep. We'll have to get close, but my hands only go where Lisa wants them. Cool?"

She nods and breathes out a laugh. "Cool."

Lisa appears. "Seems like Price has handled the introductions. Chrissy, you're in good hands, I promise. You two ready?"

*I*t's late afternoon when I finally get home, and my pulse kicks up when I see Jodi's white Civic parked in the driveway. She isn't downstairs when I step inside, and I need a rinse, so I head to my room. I step under the too-hot water, letting my muscles relax, and try not to think of how Jodi might also be taking a shower. I've learned that she takes one after she gets back from the coffee shop, and I've learned that for just a little while afterwards, she smells like roses and lavender. I also know that sometimes, she puts her hair into a loose braid after she washes it, and little curls escape and frame her face as it dries. At the coffee shop, she is buttoned up and pulled together, her red lips like body armor. But here? She is relaxed and open, bare-lipped, hair down, and a smile that knocks down every last bit of self-preservation I have.

I finish up and step out, then throw on some sweats and a faded black tee. Before I leave my room, I gather up my laundry. Baking, it turns out, is messy business. Or at least it is for me, and I'm down to almost nothing clean.

But I slow as I approach the laundry room, because Jodi is in there, her back to me, her hips swaying as she hums something that must be playing in her earbuds. Even though I'd love to stand and watch her, I don't want to have a repeat of the midnight kitchen. I call her name.

She startles and turns, her hand on her heart. "Price!"

I shrug and point at her ears. "I swear, I was trying not to scare you."

Jodi smiles sheepishly and pulls them out, pocketing them in her hoodie. "I believe you. I hope you don't mind—I was desperate for some fresh laundry."

"Same." I indicate my basket.

Her eyes dart to it and back, and her chest pinks. "Right. Of course. I'm, I'm so sorry, I didn't—"

I step to her and touch her arm, unable to help myself. She's so soft. "It's okay. Tell you what, let's make it a night. I'll go grab us some takeout and we'll hang?" The words are out of my mouth before I really comprehend what I've done. Also, I'm still touching her. I pull away.

"Oh," she says, following my hand as I drop it. She swallows and meets my eyes. "Um, sure. Yeah, that'd be, um, good."

I smile. She's clearly flustered, and in a normal situation, I'd know exactly how to handle it. I'd move in, cup her chin and tip her lips to mine. But this is Jodi we're talking about. Jodi, who not only deserves someone better than me, but who is a guest of the inn. There's probably some hospitality rule against sleeping with guests. And I *know* Will would definitely have something to say about it. So I step around Jodi to put my basket next to hers, and try to keep my eyeballs in my head when I see the rainbow of polka dot silk pajamas and underwear in a tidy pile, waiting their turn in the washer.

I clear my throat and pivot. "Thai?" I choke out, already heading toward the kitchen to get the menu.

"Sounds great!" she chirps, probably eager to pretend I didn't just see her underthings.

But, holy shit, I did. And now I can add *wears silk polka dot panties in every color of the rainbow* to the growing list of things I know about her.

I command myself to behave as I thrust—god, thrust, really? —the menu at her. "I already know what I want." *Do I ever.* "So. Just, let me know. It's on me."

Her eyes widen. "No. I can pay—"

"Jodi." I practically bark her name out, and hold a hand up in apology. I soften my words, unable to care about what I'm about to say. Blame it on the polka dots. "I want to buy you dinner. Please. Will you let me do that?"

She blinks up at me, rendered speechless, and I start to

worry she's going to turn tail and run on me. But then she licks those deliciously bare lips and gives me a shy smile. "Okay," she whispers.

Thank *fuck*. "Okay."

# CHAPTER 9
# JODI

*H*AS ANYONE EVER died of want? Because I might be there. Price in low-slung heathered gray sweats and another thin tee, this one black and tiny enough to showcase the bottom half of what looks like a tribal tattoo on the right bicep, with bare feet.

Jesus. Did he write the manual on how to render a woman mute?

Like, I've run out of words.

All the words. Gone. Poof.

I turned and there he was, and my brain basically short-circuited. Then he says we should make a night of laundry, because that's apparently a thing, and then. Then! He sees my panties, *again*, and offers to buy me dinner.

I have no idea what's going on.

Only that I'm a hot mess, clad in ratty yoga pants and a hoodie, because that's about what I was down to. I kept thinking that I'd get at least one night to myself, where I could do my laundry in peace, but no. One of them has been here every night, though admittedly Will just stalks around like a surly older brother, and I'm not really sure what Price does once the dinner hour is over. After running into Price in the kitchen early on, I'd done my level best to stay in my room when I'm here.

But now, I'm apparently having dinner and doing laundry with Price Joseph.

What even is my life right now?

Price had said something about a movie, which is a whole additional layer of anxiety, but he'd pointed to the old-school dinner trays as he left, so I guess he meant it. I go about setting the trays up in front of the television, then do the same with napkins and silverware and glasses of water.

Thing is, I'm going to need some liquid courage to get through an entire evening next to the hottest man in the universe. So I grab the bottle of red that hasn't been touched in the two weeks I've been here and get it open. I've poured a healthy portion into my glass and taken a few sips before Price returns, holding the paper bag of Thai like it's an award.

He sets the bag on the counter and pulls the food out. "You drink?"

"Does a one-legged duck swim in a circle?"

He quirks a grin. "Fair. I've just never seen you."

I grab my chicken Pad See Ew. "You've never seen me do a lot of things."

His eyebrows raise, and he nods at my container. "That's true. I would have figured you for a chicken pad Thai woman, for one thing."

"It's good, but not my fave." Then I tuck the bottle of wine in the crook of my arm, pluck the chopsticks out of the bag, and swivel on my heel to take everything into the living room. Price follows with his own meal—some sort of lightly sauced, stir-fried chicken and veggie healthy thing with rice on the side, because of course it is—and surveys the set-up.

"Why'd you put us on separate couches?"

I look up, half-way through propping pillows behind my back so that I can eat comfortably on this couch that's clearly made for giants. "Because that spot has the best view of the television?" I indicate the set-up he's standing in front of.

He shakes his head decisively. "No way. We sit on the same couch, and it's the one you're on." He picks up his tray and has himself a mere three feet from me in seconds, and then all I can smell is his body wash, which I'm fairly certain has a name like *Black Chill* or *Phoenix God*. And it smells absolutely divine. Or maybe that's him. I'm still trying to figure it out, because I swear part of my brain just blacks out when he gets this close.

I take him in as he settles in beside me. He's tall, over six feet, with lean muscles and wide shoulders and, as I had the pleasure of learning a couple weeks ago, a set of abs that make me want to sink to my knees and bite them. His body is so ridiculous it almost hurts to look at him. His fucking tiny shirt rises up as he leans to grab the other throw pillow, and I zero in on the skin it reveals above his waistband. I want to lick it. I snap my eyes back to his face as he turns to me and smiles, his eyes a mesmerizing blue and silver tonight.

"What do you want to watch?"

I take a larger-than-necessary gulp of wine. I'm not much of a drinker, but I will be tonight. "Doesn't matter."

He considers me. "I don't believe that for a second. But how about this?" He pulls his phone out of his sweatpants pocket and opens an app, then hands it over.

His phone is encased in one of those old-school box-like cases. Though, given the man is a literal firefighter, I guess it makes sense that his phone needs to be protected. "What is this?"

"It's our problem-solver. We use this at the firehouse all the time. But here's the thing: we *have* to watch the genre it chooses, no matter what." He leans forward and puts his hand next to his mouth, like he's about to share a secret. "You wouldn't believe the number of rom-coms we've watched at the firehouse—or how many guys secretly love them." He sits back up. "So. Click the button that says spin and it'll tell us what movie genre we're watching." His eyes dance. "Push it."

I laugh softly. The puppy side of Price has come out to play. I take another gulp of wine and *push it*, like he wants.

We watch the wheel spin, Wheel of Fortune style, until it finally lands on Murder-Mystery. Price claps and hops in place on the couch. "Perfect. I've got just the movie."

I smile stupidly, caught off-guard by how excited he is, and tuck into my food as he queues up a streaming service and scrolls to one of the newer options.

"Have you seen this?"

Of course I have. "Nope." No way am I doing anything to take that smile off his face, especially now, as it brightens even further.

"It's so *good!*" he says.

An hour later, I've had entirely too much wine and am not even a foot from Price on the couch. He'd cleared the trays and put them away, and when he flopped back down, there he was... closer. And with each little twitch and jump he makes, or every time one of us gets up to handle laundry, he gets nearer and nearer. It's not me. I've been certain to stay in my designated spot, because it's the only thing I can guarantee will keep me from launching myself at him.

But I really, really have to pee. And who knows, maybe it'll be like Christmas when I get back, and Price will be on the couch, naked.

Oh god. Who even *am* I? I shouldn't think like this. Honestly, I can't even fathom him naked. Besides, I wouldn't know what to do with myself *or* with him.

Anyway. "I'll be right back." I jump up like a scared baby deer and practically hop to the bathroom. As I'm washing my hands, I take stock of my reflection. My eyes are bright and my face is flushed, but whether it's from wine or the nearness of Price is anyone's guess. My hair is half out of its braid, so I pull it the rest of the way out and let it hang. I ditched the hoodie a while back—wine makes me hot—so I'm in a peach-colored tank top. It's only now, when I'm standing here, that I realize how the black lace bralette I'm wearing is doing exactly nothing to hold the girls in check. I may be short, but my boobs didn't get the petite memo, and there they are, ready for the world, or at least Price, to see.

I shrug and snicker to myself, too many drinks in to do anything about it.

I sway out of the bathroom, pleasantly buzzed, and flop back onto the couch, tipping over and knocking right into Price's amazing biceps.

"Oops. Sorry," I giggle. I try to sit up, but not only is this couch made for giants, it's also made of marshmallow fluff, and apparently I'm not buzzed, I'm *drunk*, and the more I try to sit up, the funnier it gets, until I'm snort-laughing into Price's lap, and then he's laughing, and we're both laughing, and holy crap *my head is in his lap.*

I grab onto a millisecond of sobriety and launch myself upright, attempting to find some breadcrumb of propriety, but then the fact that my very drunk ass thought the word *propriety* sets me off again.

Price keeps chuckling. "Jodi, what is so funny?"

But even as he asks, he's starting to laugh even harder, and then I catch his eye and my own laughs ratchet up farther. "I'm so sorry," I manage to wheeze out. "It's just..." I giggle.

He smiles at me, shaking with laughter, and when I see the unshed tears glistening in his eyes, I lose it.

"Oh my god you're *crying*," I howl, then throw myself back onto the pillows in another fit of giggles. I cover my face and kick my legs up, then one of them meets something solid.

"Oof," Price says.

"Oh shit," I breathe out, then giggle again. I can get a little silly when I'm drunk, but this is a whole new level. "What was that?"

A warm, calloused hand grips my ankles. Immediately I still, every part of me on high alert.

"Price?" I peek out from behind my hands.

A slow, wicked smile grows on his face as he pulls my feet into his lap. "No more wiggling." His voice is scratchy.

Fully serious now, I try to sit up, but it makes my feet move and he yanks me closer to him in response. Both of his hands are on me now, and warmth pools in my belly as my entire universe centers in on them. I would never have thought of my ankles as an erogenous zone, but right now, they're living their best life. My knees are bent and are inches from resting on his chest, and my neck aches from holding my head up as I stare at him.

His gaze is dark, heated, and I finally understand that it's for *me*. I lick my lips and his hands tighten on my ankles as he watches my mouth. When I suck my lower lip in and bite it, his grip tightens even more. "Jodi," he warns, his voice scraping across me.

I'm light-headed, my skin tingling and my blood fizzing. But I don't know what I'm supposed to do next. Only that he told me not to move. But I do, propping myself onto my elbows.

He snaps, pulling me up and into a cradle position in one swift movement, his arms wrapped around me, the side of my butt firmly wedged against his crotch. My hand has a mind of its own, instantly moving to press against his chest.

He heaves a shaky breath as I focus on his neck, the smooth, delicate skin pulsing with the beat of his heart. But his chest. I'm touching his chest, and it's rock solid, and the tiniest of whimpers escapes me.

"Jodi," he repeats.

I tip my head back and meet his gaze. His pupils are blown, the thin band of irises the color of liquid mercury. He studies me, then brings a hand to cup my cheek. I close my eyes and lean into it, savoring the feel of his work-roughened skin against mine. When I open them, I lick my lips again, and a low growl rumbles out of him as he squeezes his eyes shut.

"You've got to stop that."

"Stop what?" I don't recognize the voice that comes out of me, breathy and remarkably steady.

He sucks in another breath and lets it out slowly, finally opening his eyes and meeting mine again. "Your lips," he grits out. His hand still on my cheek, he moves his thumb to press it against my lower lip, pulling it down, then pushing it back up. Instinctively, my tongue darts out to touch his skin, and I feel something twitch against my hip.

Oh. *Oh.*

He grunts softly, then he releases my lip and threads his fingers through my hair as he cups the back of my head. Word-lessly, he leans lower, lower, until our lips are so close we're breathing each other's air. His face is a blur of tan skin and honey-brown beard at this point, and I know he's waiting for me. If we're going to kiss, then I have to be the one to get us there.

With my hands against his chest, I close the final inch that separates our lips. For a moment, I forget to breathe, focused only on the sensation of his firm lips against mine, the way his beard, just as soft as I'd suspected, lightly brushes the skin around my mouth. Then his arm tightens around me, his fingers digging just a little into the nape of my neck, and I pull him close.

He leans away, and I gasp in some air, only to lose it again as his lips slant over mine, his tongue teasing against the seam of my lips. I open for him willingly, still trying to fully grasp that

I'm kissing Price Joseph, and his mouth is covering mine, and he tastes like Thai food and red wine.

This…is *A Kiss*. I've kissed before, of course, but this. *This* is the kind of kiss I've watched in movie after movie, the ones that make me yearn and ache in every piece of my soul. His tongue dances with mine, gentle but in charge, and his hands continue to tighten, never leaving their posts at my head and back. My entire body is on high alert, warmth and giddiness streaking through me and setting me on fire, but even now, a part of my brain is freaking out. Because it's Price Joseph. I'm kissing *Price Joseph*. What happens next? Does he think more is going to happen? Because he is definitely hard. There is no denying what I feel under me.

"Jodi," he breathes, pulling away and looking at me quizzically. He loosens his hands.

"What?" I ask, panic lancing my voice. Did I mess this up?

"I think I lost you there for a minute." His voice is so soft, and so gentle, and the sweet smile that's gracing his lips makes me want to sob in gratitude.

"I'm, I'm fine," I manage to say. My hands are shaking.

"You're so stiff," he murmurs. Then his lips quirk up mischievously. "I thought I was the only one who was supposed to be stiff right now."

My cheeks burn with embarrassment, and I'll definitely go up in flames if I meet his eyes. "I'm sorry." I am the only woman in this town who can mess up a Price Joseph kiss. It'll be on my tombstone: *Jodi Bristol, died a virgin. Even Price Joseph couldn't help her.*

"Jodi, no," he says, his brow furrowing as he tucks a piece of hair behind my ear. "Will you look at me? Please?"

But I'm too busy scooting off his lap and trying—and failing—to keep my eyes off the impressive tent in his sweatpants. "Nope. No. This was…I'm sorry. I've," I turn in helpless circles, trapped by indecision and mortification. "Thanks for dinner," I blurt.

Then I run. Literally run. Around the couch, through the foyer, and up the two flights of stairs to slam the door and fling myself on my bed. Only to realize that my basket of clothes, neatly folded with all the panties and bras safely hidden from view, is still down in the laundry room, and there is no way in hell I'll be retrieving them tonight.

# CHAPTER 10
# PRICE

*H*oly shit.

She tasted like wine and repentance.

I'm going to need more of that.

A lot more.

*I* SLIDE MY hand down my face, trying to process what just happened. I kissed her. No—*she* kissed *me*. Okay, fine, she kissed me, but I was clearly the instigator.

And now she's hightailed it out of here, and I can't figure out why. Was the kiss bad?

I scoff.

I don't do bad kisses.

And the kiss with Jodi was…shit, it was everything. It felt almost holy, like a puzzle piece locking into place. Like my mouth had been waiting on hers for decades. Her lips were luscious and hot against mine, and the way her mouth opened, welcoming me like I was someone she truly wanted, was enough to make me want to worship her for the rest of eternity. It made no sense, because it was just a kiss, except it wasn't. Kissing her brought me clarity.

She'd felt like everything right and good and perfect. Like home.

So why did she run? The woman literally *ran*. I glance around, as though she's going to reappear if I look hard enough, but I suspect she's not going to come out of her room the rest of the night.

Rising, I adjust myself and set to cleaning up. Will and I trade off tomorrow morning, and the guy will have me by the balls if he comes home to a dirty living room and kitchen.

At the thought of Will, I curse. I've kissed a guest. And not just *a* guest, but our *only* guest.

I can see Will now, growling and muttering how I can't be trusted to do anything right, and the thought of it stings. But it doesn't cut as deep as it normally does, because kissing Jodi?

Best decision of my life.

# CHAPTER 11
# JODI

*I*'M AN EARLY riser. I have to be because of the whole running-a-coffee shop thing, but waking up at four in the morning is a new level of early. I bury my face in the pillow and sigh. What had I done? I'd *kissed* Price. And then, when he called me out on being in my head, I'd fled the scene like a criminal.

Clearly done with sleeping for the night, I roll out of bed, wincing at the hangover headache, and chug the water on my nightstand. I take my time getting ready for work, then realize that laundry is downstairs. Can I go down there and back up without waking Price? Only one way to find out.

But when I ease my door open—and it creaks, of course it creaks—the basket is sitting on the floor in front of me.

Gah. He's *sweet*.

Of course he is. I should have expected nothing less.

I slide the laundry in, after looking down the hall to, what, make sure I'm not being watched? I'm an idiot. I get dressed, try not to think about Price getting an eyeful of my underwear, not to mention an armful of *me* on his lap, throw on my jacket, and get out of there.

It's March, and in Alabama that means temperatures range

anywhere from freezing to the upper eighties. Anything goes, and Mother Nature loves keeping us on our toes. But no matter what, trees and bushes and flowers are in bloom. And I can't help but stop in the darkness and breathe in the smell of the chilly morning, dewy and fresh, and let the birds tell me all about their plans for helping the sun into the sky.

After a minute, slightly calmer than I was before, I hop into my trusty Civic and weave through the darkened neighborhood to the shop. The way it feels outside tells me it's going to be a beautiful, sunshine-filled day, meaning Daily Dose will be packed. So at least I'll be so busy I can't think about The Kiss.

Of course, it's still so early that by the time Darius arrives, I'm an hour and three cups of coffee into opening the shop and have started inventorying lids.

"Um, okay." His brown eyes scan the area behind the counter, then meet mine. He grins. "What'd you do?"

"Nothing." My reply is quick, too quick, because he laughs as he pours himself a coffee.

"Liar. You gonna tell me about it now, or do I have to wait until pretty boy Price comes in here to see what happened? Because I *know* it has to do with him. He's the only one that gets you this riled up. And seeing how you live with him..."

"I kissed him, okay?" I blurt.

"Oh shit." He fumbles the cup in his hand but manages to keep it steady, then looks at me. "You kissed *Price*?"

"You don't have to look so surprised," I mutter, crossing my arms over my stomach.

"That explains...that." He arches a perfectly groomed eyebrow and wiggles his fingers at me.

"What? I look fine." My hair is braided, my eyes are de-puffed and mascaraed, my red lip is in place.

He lifts his cup to his mouth and takes a sip. "Your shirt, honeybun."

I glance down.

*Crap.*

"You know, you could have opened with that when you walked in," I say as he laughs, untying my apron and heading into the room just behind the counter that serves as our storage area. After getting my shirt on right-side-out, I emerge and give Darius the death stare. "I should fire you."

He scoffs. "Girl, please. And don't worry, I already texted your posse to give them the news. You'll see them soon."

I hang my head. "You're mean."

"Love you, too."

At six-thirty, just as the morning rush is kicking into gear, Devon and Ceci walk in together, the pair of them practically vibrating with excitement as they get into line. I scowl at them, then scowl harder at Darius.

"Tell us *everything*," Ceci demands, then hands over her credit card. "I got Devon's."

I scoff. "Devon's is free for five years. Don't act like you don't know." I look around. Chief isn't here, and Helen from the Piggly Wiggly isn't in yet. If she hears it, the whole dang town knows. Darius slides the coffees forward, because the meanie knew they were coming, and gestures to the next person in line. After confirming that the customer isn't anyone who will care, I lean in and lower my voice.

"I kissed him."

"Holy *shit!*" Ceci exclaims.

The entire shop stops and looks at her.

"Really, Ceci?" I hiss.

Devon waves at all the eyeballs turned our way. "Sorry, folks, nothing to see here." She gives me an appraising look. "Except for that impressive blush you've got going on. Wow. How far down your chest does it—"

"Oh my god I will murder you two." I shove the card back at Ceci and glare at the both of them. "Yes. We kissed. It was the hottest thing I've ever experienced and when it was over, I ran.

Literally ran, because he called me stiff and I was embarrassed."
I straighten and bring my voice out of the hiss-whisper thing I'd
had going on. "Okay?"

"Oh, babe." Devon scrunches her face.

"He called you *stiff*?" Ceci says. "I'm going to need way more
context."

"How much more could you need?"

Darius clears his throat and I startle. Because of course, the
Joseph Brothers have walked in. I swear the whole place quiets
for a moment, stunned into silence at the amount of hotness
that has descended upon our collective gazes. I'd like to think
it's the way the sun is slanting into the shop, bright and cheery,
motes flitting about in the beams of light, but it's the brothers.

Price's eyes find mine immediately, and they crinkle in a
smile. I can't flee, despite my every instinct screaming at me to
do exactly that, so I jerk into motion, waving Ceci and Devon
along and turning to the customer behind them.

Naturally, my ex-best friends go to the back of the line to
talk to the brothers. So after taking care of Christy, who always
wants an Americano with two Splenda and light ice, I move on
to a handful of other customers, all of them familiar to me. Then
I turn to Joe, an older man who's always in a suit with the
morning paper tucked under his arm, who only wants the
largest regular coffee we have and "one of those delicious poppyseed lemon muffins." He's an incorrigible flirt, and as he drops a
dollar into the tip jar and throws me a wink, I can't help but
wonder if that's what Price will be like when he's that old: still
flirting shamelessly.

And then I remember the way Price's mouth slanted over
mine, the heat of his body as he gripped me tight, the hardness
of his—

"Good morning, Jodi."

The man himself is smiling down at me, insanely gorgeous
in mesh shorts and a navy fire department t-shirt, and the

warmth that shoots straight to my lady parts makes me angry. Beside me, Darius greets Will and Aaron, while Ceci and Devon stand between the brothers, watching me like they would a movie. The only thing they're missing is popcorn. I hate them.

"Hi," I manage to say.

A flicker of uncertainty crosses his face, but he recovers and brightens his smile. "Can I get my usual? And, um"—his gaze darts to the glass display case and then back—"a dozen muffins? Whatever kind you choose. For the guys." He jerks his head in the direction of the firehouse.

"I thought you were off-shift today." Immediately I want to crawl into a hole. Because I shouldn't know his schedule. But boy, do I ever. I can't blame it on living in the same place as him, or even being the owner of this coffee shop. Nope. That's simply the product of having tracked this man's movements over so many years that his comings and goings are second-nature to me. It sounds stalkery, I know, but it's always been innocent.

Except that now, we've had our tongues in each other's mouths and I've blurted this unintentional knowledge out in front of the very people who will use this moment to torture me for the rest of my life.

Without waiting for a response, I move away from the register and start making Price's oat milk vanilla latte. He shifts out of line to stay with me, which is not fair of him at all.

"I'm not working," he says, his voice low and clearly intended only for me. Which is great, except that our friends—sorry, *former* friends—and family likely have sonic hearing and are still going to hear all the words. "I was hoping to find you in the kitchen this morning."

He was? I drop the frother into the oat milk and press the button. "I had to get here early. Inventory." *Liar liar, pants on fire.* I keep my eyes firmly planted on my work, refusing to see the look of pity I know has to be on his face. But it's clear he's not moving, and he's probably still watching me, and I can guar-antee that Devon and Ceci are watching both of us.

I set the latte on the pastry case without looking at Price, and grab a box for the muffins. And then I fill it, *still* managing to keep my eyes on my work, and set it on top of the case as well. I shift back to the register, and of course Price does, too, and only after I say the total do I force myself to look up.

"Jodi."

I need him to stop saying my name. The way it sounds like pure sex coming out of his mouth is simply not fair. *He* is not fair. I bite the inside of my lip. "Yes?"

He gestures between us, his expression serious, and dammit, he's even sexier like this. "We need to talk. We're *going* to talk. I'll see you after you close up, okay?"

I nod tightly, knowing I'm beaten, and take the cash he's holding out.

His face clears and he's all smiles again. "I'll see you later."

# CHAPTER 12
# JODI

*I* TAKE MY sweet time closing the shop, even though I'm bone-tired. We close at three p.m. every day, and while that's maybe a little early in some people's minds, it's perfectly fine by me and Darius. Still, even Darius is giving me side-eye when he's about to walk out at three.

"You *really* think now's the best time to inventory sugar packets? Actually, there's never a good time to inventory sugar packets. You're avoiding. Go home."

I finish my count to one hundred and shrug. "My home is uninhabitable."

Darius sucks his teeth. "You know good and well I mean go to the inn. Quit being a baby."

I glare at him. "Maybe it's time for you to become a full-time writer."

He laughs, not taking the bait. "You wouldn't dare. Not that I don't need the push."

"How are things on that front, anyway?"

He turns and comes back to the counter. "Eh, querying agents. Got a few who have asked for partial manuscripts and some who have asked to read the whole thing after that."

"Darius, that's *awesome!*" I squeal, dropping the packets and forgetting my count. "Wait. Why don't you seem excited?"

He waves me off. "I was excited six months ago when they asked, but they haven't replied yet. It's a long game. Epically long, at this point. Anyway, go home." He yanks the box out from under me and shoves the uncounted packets back in, ruining my progress.

"Ugh, *fine*. I'll go home."

"I'll wait on you to leave." He crosses his arms and smiles smugly.

I roll my eyes. Of course he's waiting on me, because he knows I'd hang out here for another hour in hopes of avoiding Price. "You're the worst."

"Love you, too," he replies.

OUTSIDE THE SHOP, I wave at Brook as she writes something on the bookstore's board, and nod a hello at Chief, who's sitting on a bench outside the fire station's engine bay. I walk quickly to my car, sensing that Chief would be happy to chat me up about Price if I linger.

Price. Why did I kiss him? What was I thinking? I wasn't. That's the problem. I was not even close to thinking, and I've spent the entire day alternating between beating myself up and reliving the way he tasted. The way it felt to be held by him. The way *he* felt. Like, *him* him.

I sigh. Am I so ridiculous today that I can't think the word 'dick'?

Shaking my head, I start up my Civic. I need to face this.

Face Price. It was a mistake. No—it was pity. The only way Price Joseph would give me the time of day is because he pities me. The man can have anyone he wants, so pity is the only answer that makes any sense.

*But what about his dick?*

I scoff at my naïve self. What *about* his dick? It was a pure biological response. He's a guy, and he was kissing a girl. It had nothing to do with me. Not really.

By the time I get to the inn, I've worked myself into a such a state that I barely know which way is up. I let myself in, still feeling weird that I'm the only guest here, and it smells…not good. Like lemons on fire. I walk to the kitchen, and sure enough, Price is in there. The desiccated remains of lemons are on the counter, along with a bag of powdered sugar, regular sugar, the poor, beleaguered stand mixer, and probably every baking implement the kitchen houses. I've got to give it to him. For better or worse, the man is *not* letting up on the pastry effort. And right now, it's worse. So, so worse.

He looks up, and his face goes from serious and focused Price to puppy Price, all happy and wiggly. "Jodi! Hi!"

I can't help the smile that blooms on my face in response. It's impossible not to smile at him, especially when he's got a bit of flour in his beard. "Hi. Were you trying to make lemon squares?"

His grin turns bashful. "I'd hoped to have these finished by the time you got here, but…" he shrugs.

I laugh. "Price, I don't know…I think your talents might be elsewhere."

A shadow crosses his face and I stiffen. *Crap.* I'm not a fan of sad Price. Or whatever that was. "But who knows? Practice makes perfect," I say, hoping that helps.

He pulls the apron off, and I catch a glimpse of that heavenly strip of golden skin between his shirt and mesh shorts. Mesh shorts that don't really do anything to hide…well. My experience is obviously limited to light make-out sessions with two former boyfriends, but I suspect the heat he's packing isn't standard. I bite my lip, and of course, he sees me. His eyes flare and he clenches his jaw, and I have no idea what to do with that.

"I promised you a talk," he says.

"Um. We don't really have to." I start to back out of the kitchen.

His brow furrows. "Jodi. No."

"You're right, no," I say, my stomach pitching. This was stupid. *I'm* stupid.

"Please?" he asks, reaching me before I can escape, his hand lightly gripping my forearm. The way he does it, I can see the bottom half of the eight-point compass rose on the inside of his upper right bicep. This man and his tattoos. I haven't seen all of them, because I can't allow myself to look at him long enough to learn, but it's clear he's working on a sleeve on his right arm.

As he pulls me back into the kitchen, my entire being centers on the bit of skin he's touching. I look everywhere but at him, and there's the opened cookbook on the island, and the coffee mug sitting on top, *World's Okayest Firefighter* emblazoned across it.

My chest loosens at the sight. He's still Price Joseph, goofball extraordinaire. I shouldn't be so nervous. He'll let me down gently. It's probably what he does with all his exes—and now I know why they're all still friends. I've only *kissed* him and I'm practically heartbroken at the prospect of never speaking to him again. I can't do it. Who could bear to not talk to this wonderful man?

"Sit?" He releases me next to the stool beside the island, and instantly my body protests the loss of him.

Sliding onto the stool, I finally force my eyes to meet his.

And crap. He's looking at me like…like I don't know what. I

used to think I knew the guy in front of me, but these past two weeks have proven I don't know him at all. Or maybe that I only know a part of him. Because the Price looking at me now is calm, *serene* even, and not at all the man I'm used to.

He rakes his hand through his hair, tousling it even as he tries to get it off his forehead, and those silver-blue eyes of his practically bore into my soul. "Jodi."

I lean forward, drawn to him despite myself. "Yes?"

"That kiss…"

"Was a mistake," I blurt. "I know. And I need to find another place to stay."

He shakes his head. "That is not what I was going to say."

"It's not?"

His lips tilt up. "Definitely not. I was going to say that the kiss—Jodi, I don't have words for what that kiss was."

I stare at him. "Oh."

He blows out a breath. "I'm not doing this right." He looks away and huffs a laugh before turning those piercing eyes back to me. "I guess what I'm trying to say is, did you…was it not good?"

"What?" I didn't hear him right.

"You ran. Was the kiss bad? Because I thought—"

"No," I blurt. My cheeks blaze but I make myself meet his gaze.

He exhales. "Thank god."

"But," I start.

"But what?"

"You said…" I swallow.

He reaches for me, and I slide off the stool. If he touches me, I'll lose all ability to think.

"Did I do something wrong?" he asks. "What did I say? I'd had more to drink than usual but I would never—"

I back away, shaking my head. Of course. He kissed me

because he was drunk. It all makes sense now. "We're good," I say.

"Jodi, please."

His anguished expression is almost enough to make me hear him out, but I don't want him to tell me it can't happen again. I get it.

So I run away.

# CHAPTER 13
# PRICE

MIDWAY BETWEEN A three-day shift filled with almost no calls, I'm about ready to go out of my mind. There was a cat stuck in a tree over at the Johnsons', which we made the probies handle, because it was the same cat that gets stuck every time. Then there was the usual visit from the Montessori school a couple blocks away, followed by us going to the local elementary school a couple of blocks in the other direction. I love the school visits, because we have to make sure kids aren't afraid if they ever see a firefighter in uniform, but there has been exactly nothing else happening. Chief has had us check and recheck our supplies and turnout gear more than the usual once per shift, the entire place is cleaner than I've ever seen it, and we've even reviewed some annual training ahead of schedule.

I knock on Chief's door and poke my head around it. "Chief, got a minute?"

He waves me in, leaning back in his seat.

I look around at the disorganized office. It's always looked like this, and honestly, I have no idea how Chief manages to keep everything running. And that's what I'm here to talk to him about.

"How's our guest at the inn?" Chief asks.

I startle, because I'd finally had a few minutes with her *out* of my head. "Jodi?"

A thoughtful smile crosses over his face. "Yes, Jodi. You two are…getting along?"

I shift on my feet. I'd like to do more than just *get along* with her, and am desperate to talk with her. Unfortunately, she seems to be just as intent on avoiding me as I am on speaking with her, because I haven't so much as laid eyes on her since the disaster in the kitchen. Even Darius, who I thought would be my silver bullet, seems to be immune to my pleas. I'd brought him a batch of chocolate-chip cookies that I actually got right, which he took out of my hands and promptly told me he was having way too much fun watching the two of us to interfere.

It might have been funny if he weren't talking about me.

"She's the perfect guest," I say, not wanting to get into it with Chief. "I'm actually here to talk to you about something else."

He gestures for me to sit. "Make it quick. I've got to figure out how to make some magic happen in this payroll system."

I tilt my head. "What do you mean?"

"Nothing for you to worry your pretty head over," he chuckles. "Just the usual stuff I deal with."

I try not to let the comment sting, and press forward. "I'd like to be Assistant Chief."

His jaw hinges open, then shuts. He blinks. "You? Assistant Chief?"

Okay, *that* stings. "Yes."

He leans back in his chair. "Son, you're a driver engineer. I thought you liked that. There's—"

"I know," I interrupt. "There are ranks above me. Lieutenant, Captain, Battalion Chief, and *then* Assistant Chief."

Waving the comment off, he says, "I was going to say I've never seen you be interested. Besides, we're not a fancy group of firefighters, Price. We just get the job done. Titles don't mean much around here. Hell, your own brother is Assistant Chief, and you don't see him doing anything much different than the rest of you all."

I take a beat. "You're right. I've spent a long time coasting. But I've changed. Well—trying to. I'm trying to tell you what my goal is. And that's to become Assistant Chief."

"Even though Will is already the Assistant Chief."

"Yes. You clearly need help," I say, gesturing at the piles of paperwork in the office. I almost tell him the rest: that I think Will wants out, and to stop looking at him for help because *I'm* the Joseph brother who will be here for the duration. But I keep that to myself.

Chief nods. "I'll take it under advisement."

Realizing the discussion is over, I stand. "Thanks, Chief."

It's only after I get out of his office that I let disappointment wash over me. Even Chief, the man who was a second father to the three of us after ours died, doesn't seem to think I'm up for being Assistant.

That night, as I attempt sleep in one of the station bunks that is less *mattress* and more *torture device*, it's not just thoughts of Jodi keeping me awake. But when I do get to sleep, it's a fever dream of a shy, strawberry-blond barista who lets me get close enough to catch her scent, then runs away.

Over and over and over.

When I wake up at five the next morning, covered in sweat and the faint smell of coffee in my nostrils, I'm a disaster.

By the time Will shows up at six for shift change, I'm nearly out of my head. "How is she?" I don't even say hello.

Will's eyes widen just a fraction, enough for me to know he's appalled at my behavior.

*Me, too, Will. Me, too.*

"Our guest?" Will emphasizes the word *guest* and I notice, I promise I do, but I can't be bothered anymore.

I follow Will as he heads to the kitchen, where Aaron is certain to be pulling out the ingredients for his standard beginning-of-shift breakfast. He started it after he and Devon moved in together, and now, if he's cooking during shift change, no one getting off shift leaves until they eat. Aaron complains about having too many people to feed, but I think he secretly loves it. "Yes. Jodi. How is she? Is she good? Does she seem different? Did she say anything? Did she mention me?"

Will slows before we get to the kitchen, and even in my hurry to hear about Jodi, I can appreciate that he's not subjecting me to Aaron and Chief and whoever else is in there. "Price. What the fuck." He glares at me in the hall.

I sigh, shoving my hair off my forehead and glaring right back. "I know. She's gotten to me, man."

Will's look intensifies and I'm pretty sure he gets another inch taller out of pure pissed-offness. He's not just the oldest of the three of us, he's also the biggest. Half the time I think he's secretly trying to win Mr. Universe or some shit, because dude is approaching obscene levels of muscles, and we're not going to talk about his disgusting protein shakes. So as we're standing in the hallway and he's glowering at me, he's also attempting to tower over me.

I swat at his chest. "Your intimidation tactics don't work on me, asshole."

"She is our *guest*, Price. Also, she's as innocent as they come. You can't go after her and, and, *sully* her," he growls.

"You should really shave that mustache," I shoot back. "Between it and this big-man thing you've got going on, you're starting to creep me out."

"I'm not losing my bet with Chief," he grumbles. "And stop trying to change the subject. Do not go after Jodi."

I shake my head. "Too late, man."

His jaw ticks. "What do you mean, 'too late'?"

"I mean, I kissed her. And she freaked out, and I want to make it right. I—"

"See?" He jabs a meaty finger at my chest. "That right there. She probably freaked out because you get your dick wet all over the place and she knows it. She's too good for you, Price. Leave the girl alone."

Twin furies of anger and shame rise in me, heating my neck and boiling my stomach simultaneously, and it's a struggle to keep my voice level. "Fuck you, Will. This is different."

He snorts derisively. "Listen to me: That girl doesn't need the shit show you bring."

My head snaps back like he's punched me. *Shit show?*

He keeps going. "She deserves better. So you kissed her. You do a lot more with a lot of girls. Leave this one alone."

"You really think that little of me?" I say.

His face softens by the barest of millimeters. "Come on, Price. You know what I mean."

"Because I know I'm not good enough for her. Hell, man—*no one* is good enough for her. But Will, you have to know that my reputation is much worse than actual reality."

He looks at me skeptically.

"I'm not saying I've been an angel, but I'm not the guy that everyone thinks I am. I never have been." Women are funny, because half the time they say nothing happened with me when it absolutely did, and the other half of the time they say all kinds of things happened when they definitely did not. If all the rumors were true, I'd have slept with literally hundreds of women. But I've never tried to correct the rumors, first because I was an idiot teenager, and then because I'd been quiet too long to bother, so that's on me.

That's not to say there are more women in town who I've slept with than I should be comfortable with, but the past is the past. "Have you realized it's been a year since I've even so much as taken a woman on a date?"

A year of a hell of a lot of work on myself. Not that anyone, not even my own brothers, have noticed. But I'll keep going. Because I'll prove myself to Jodi, and maybe everyone else will see it after that.

Will considers me. "Maybe so. But you're right. You'll never be good enough for a girl like her."

He lands his gut-punch and turns away.

THANKS TO HAVING hours in the house by myself— still no other current guests, but we do have reservations later in April thanks to the Talladega spring race—I manage to bake two batches of scones.

Well, they're *supposed* to be scones.

And I'm cleaning up when I hear voices.

"Told you he'd be in here baking." Will strides into the kitchen, followed by Chief and Aaron.

I turn the water off and dry my hands, taking my time before turning to face them.

"Don't eat them."

Aaron shoots me a self-preserving glance. "Man, you couldn't pay me. Are they supposed to be blueberry?" He leans over the tray on the island and sniffs.

I fight back the wince. "Yeah."

"Son, why are you bothering with baking?" Chief's voice fills the room like always, big and booming to match the rest of him. His thick hair is getting to be more white than silver, and the man's always been able to take down anyone in the facial hair department. Right now, he and Will are the last men standing in a mustache bet to see which one can manage to keep theirs the longest.

Honestly, they both look like they could be cast in a seventies porn movie.

To be clear, I don't mean that as a good thing.

"Baking's not the problem," Will says, picking up a scone in spite of my scowling at him to drop it. "You overworked the dough. These are too dense."

I gape at him. "Are you a baking show judge now? How the hell—"

"Two of you shouldn't have bought this place to begin with," Chief grumbles. He shoots an apologetic glance at Aaron. "No offense to Devon, of course."

Aaron huffs a laugh. "Of course."

I don't bother reminding them that Will and I were the only ones in town willing and able to buy this place and turn it into a bed-and-breakfast. I also don't bother pointing out that had it not been for me, we'd have had no chance to buy it, period. Remarkable how no one asked how I had that much money lying around. Not even Will.

It's frustrating, how no one bothers to actually look at me and see all the changes I've made. And I'm finally getting tired of it.

Jodi's eyes flash through my head, and I realize that this is all her fault. *She's* the reason that after a year of improvement, I'm suddenly fed up with being thought so little of. It's hard to undo what decades of assumptions and actions have wrought, I get that, but when is everyone going to give me a break?

"Why are you three here?" I ask. Then I look out the window and catch a glimpse of the apparatus, her red and chrome gleaming prettily in the sunlight. "Why is Glenda out?"

"Giving the neighbors something to talk about," Chief says.

I raise an eyebrow at my brothers. "You sweet on Miss Betty next door, Chief?"

He chuckles and blushes, then tucks his thumbs into his belt. "Nah."

I think he is. But that's not the point.

"Here to grab some things I forgot," Will says. "Worked a small kitchen fire a few blocks over, figured we could swing by before heading back. Zach's up front."

I lean to the side and sure enough, there's Zach in the driver's seat, and Chief's SUV is visible just behind Glenda.

Will leaves the room and I'm left facing Chief's appraising look and Aaron's far more amused one. "Spit it out." No sense in dancing around whatever these two are going to say.

Aaron holds his hands in the air. "Nothing, nothing. This is cute, though." He gestures at the baking.

"It won't last," Chief says good-naturedly. "Nothing ever does."

I bristle as they laugh, but I don't bother correcting them. Instead, I level a meaningful look at Chief. "I was serious about our discussion yesterday."

Before Chief can respond, Will reappears with a duffle and raps twice on the doorframe. "Ready."

"Don't get bogged down in all this," Aaron says to me.

"Unless it's for a certain little miss?" Chief says, his expression hopeful.

Will scowls in Chief's direction. "Chief. We've talked about this. You can't refer to a woman as a 'little miss.' It's belittling and you're better than that."

Chief sputters a response as he follows Will out, leaving just me and Aaron. He looks like he's going to say something, then he thinks better of it.

"See you around," he says.

Alone in the kitchen that's suddenly too quiet for me, I take stock. The dishwasher's running and I only have a few of the bigger dishes to wash and put away. I've even got time for a shower and a little manscaping. Not that I think I'm going to get to show it off, but it simply needs to happen. For once, I'll finally be prepared when Jodi gets home. And this time, I'm not letting her run away before she hears me out.

# CHAPTER 14
# PRICE

*I* HEAR THE door of Jodi's Civic slam shut and bolt off the couch to scramble for the entrance. I'm sure that someone, somewhere, has a made a fortune telling people that they shouldn't accost someone right when they walk in the door, but guess what?

Don't care.

"Jodi, hi!" I give her my warmest smile as I fling open the door. "Welcome home. I mean, welcome back. Here. To where you're staying."

"Hi?" Her voice lilts up at the end.

I ignore her baffled look and lift grocery bags out of her hands to deposit them in the kitchen.

"Price—"

"You know, you don't have to go to the store. Just let me and Will know what you want, and we'll take care of it." I smile at her again, really not able to tell if this is working or not, but needing to get rid of these damn groceries so that we can get to the point.

"Please stop."

I freeze, my hand halfway into the paper bag that I've put on the kitchen island, and look at her. Suddenly wary of whatever I might find in the bag—maybe it's not groceries at all?—I obey, and back away. "I made you scones."

Surprised, she follows my glance and sees the blueberry scones on the blue toile platter in the center of the island. The platter that I pulled out because the pattern matches the blue in her hazel eyes perfectly. "You made those?"

"I don't know how they taste, but yeah. I made them for you."

A shy smile creeps onto her face. "Me?"

I suppress a groan as I nod. "Yes, you." She has no idea what she does to me. The way she's so fierce and strong one minute, then shy and innocent the next. If I ever managed to get her into bed, which Jodi would show up? Because if I'm being honest, I want them both.

She must see something on my face, because her eyes dim as she looks away and starts unloading the grocery bag, which is, in fact, filled with food, and it looks like it's the makings for a hell of a delicious dinner. Or dinners. I'm a terrible cook and couldn't begin to sort out how the ingredients piling on the counter will turn into a meal. "You didn't need to do that."

I chuckle as she puts everything in the fridge. "Well, I have an ulterior motive," I say. "I'm secretly on a mission to become the lemon square king of Talladega."

A laugh bursts out of her, and warmth spreads in my chest. I made her laugh. Even better, I made her relax.

Her shoulders drop down to their regular height as she walks around the counter, putting the entire island between us. "That competition is already happening between two very intense old ladies who have nearly come to blows more than once. I'd hate to see you get hurt." Her eyes are almost back to their normal glittery selves as she smiles ruefully at me.

"Try one?" I push the platter toward her. "I promise they're not poisonous. After that, though, I honestly couldn't tell you."

She picks one up and smells it. "You haven't tasted them?"

I shake my head, and she pushes the platter back to me. I pick one up. "On three? One, two, three."

We each take a bite.

I know I've messed up the second it hits my tongue.

Whirling around, I spit the nasty thing into my palm, then grab for the paper towels. "Salt," I gasp.

I swing back to her and hand her the roll, and she takes it, tearing off a sheet and putting it to her mouth.

"Well, they *looked* good," she says, grimacing and wiping her lips. "And that's a start."

I grab the platter and dump the rest of them in the trash can, cursing at my inabilities, then rinse it off and set it to dry. "I guess everyone is right," I mutter.

"Hey." Jodi's voice is soft and low as she draws near. Then she's right next to me, and her heady scent of vanilla and coffee is in my nose, and I close my eyes for just a moment. "Fuck everyone else."

Surprised, I open my eyes and look down at her. She holds my gaze willingly, and in the depths of her hazel eyes I see a new strength, one I never noticed. She brings a hand up, then stops, unsure of herself. Finally, she rests it on top of mine. Her touch is cool, a balm to my shattered confidence.

"All it takes is practice, Price," she says. "And since when do you care what everyone else thinks?"

I choke out a sad laugh. "Since *always*, Jodi."

A look of surprise crosses her face. "But—"

"I don't want you to leave." The words are out of my mouth before I'm able to stop them. It's what I've wanted to say the second she walked in the door. "The inn, I mean. The other day —" I break off, take a breath, and try again. "Will you stay?"

She studies me, then shakes her head. "I can't."

"Yes, you can," I say softly. I pull my hand out from beneath hers, then grab it to cradle against my chest. Her eyes widen and she parts her lips on a sharp inhale, and dimly I'm aware of how

I've moved us and backed her into a corner of the counter. She's so *little*. This close, the top of her head only reaches my shoulders, and she has to tilt her chin up to look up at me. Her pulse is racing, the vein on the side of her pale neck beating furiously with every pump of her heart.

I pull back, giving her space. I may be desperate for her touch, but I don't want to overwhelm her.

"I need to leave," she whines softly. "It's just, I'm having a harder time finding a place than I thought, and Nancy—do you know her? Owns the hotel about two miles from here?—says it's booked."

"Jodi," I say gently.

She takes a deep breath and releases it. "Price."

"I want to be very clear about something."

She holds my gaze.

"I really, really want to touch you. But I need you to tell me it's okay."

She blinks. "Um. Y-yeah?"

I crack a smile. "Is that a yes?"

She bobs her head. "Yes."

I step forward and put my hands on her hips. Tentatively, she wraps her arms around me, and as we lock into place—we fit so perfectly, good *lord* she is going to be my undoing—I move my arms around her waist and feel her soft curves against me. She is heaven. My own personal heaven. And she has no clue.

She whimpers, and the noise is all it takes for my dick to come roaring to life against her stomach. So, okay, maybe she knows *that* part.

"Please don't run away from me," I beg, my voice like gravel.

She licks her lips, a pink tongue on smudged red, and I follow the movement greedily. "I'm sorry," she whispers.

"I don't want you to be sorry." I trail my fingers up her pale arm, lightly tracing the freckles dotted here and there, and her skin erupts with goose bumps. I keep going, moving over the fabric of her shirt, desperate to know if she's wearing something with polka dots under the solid green of the tee. I bring my hand to the side of her neck, and as she swallows, I trace the freckles there, too, confirming the heart-shaped pattern I only noticed that night on the couch. I want to kiss every tiny freckle, then lick them, nibble them, hear how she'll sound when I scrape my teeth over them. "I want you to stay."

Jodi lets out a shuddering sigh, and I move my fingers to the nape of her neck. Her eyes close slowly, and when they open again to meet mine, they're darker. Heat flares in them as she looks at me. *There you are.* "Tell me this isn't one-sided, Jodi."

She clenches her jaw and darts her gaze away from me. I hold my breath, but then she brings her hands up, placing one, then both, on my stomach. One tiny finger finds the skin between my shirt and waistband, and I hiss as she slides the rest of her hand onto my heated skin.

"Thank god," I choke out, unable to keep from squeezing my eyes shut in ecstasy. She's so fucking perfect. All softness and curves, with a shyness that I'm certain is hiding something else entirely. I pull her tighter and she makes a sound in the back of her throat, and it takes everything I have not to throw her onto the counter and put my head between her thighs.

She breathes in and out, softly, as she moves her palm up my stomach and to my chest. I almost shudder at her touch, opening my eyes again and locking onto hers. With my free hand, I pull her hips to mine and lean down to her ear. I nip the lobe. "Do you feel what you do to me?"

She swallows and nods, and I keep my lips at her ear, breathing her in even as I tighten my grip on her. Her nails dig into my chest, making me hiss in pleasure, but then they jerk back.

I nuzzle her neck. "Mark me, Jodi. Do what you want to me."

She inhales sharply and pulls her gaze to mine, her eyes still heated, but wide and nervous. "I can't—"

*Fuck it.*

I crush my mouth to hers. I won't give her another millisecond to overthink this, to get into her head and worry about whatever it is that's got her so spooked.

She squeaks out a protest and surges up at the same time, the press of her soft curves against me and nails digging into my skin giving me the answer I was hoping for. I tighten my grip on the hair at her nape and pull, angling her head for me to ravish her. She opens her mouth and my tongue dives in, thrusting against hers in time with the tiny circles and thrusts she's making with her hips. She tastes like peppermint and coffee, and so help me I'll never taste coffee without thinking of this kiss again.

I pull her up and set her on the counter, then push her legs apart, step between them, and yank her back against me in one smooth motion. Her hands are under my shirt, exploring and squeezing and scratching, then she tightens her thighs around my waist, and I'm pretty sure I've never been this hard in my life. The mewling sounds she's making, the heat of her core pressed against my bare skin, Jesus *Christ* give me willpower.

I lick her neck, the scent of her skin on my tongue as it trails over those ridiculous freckles, while I force my hands to behave themselves. The old me would have had her tossed over my shoulder and been moving to the bedroom already, but that's not me anymore. And that's definitely not me with Jodi. I pull her mouth back to mine, needing those lips like I need fucking air. *Hands on legs and back only. Legs and back only. Legs—*

"Price." She pulls away with a gasp, but I follow, pressing our foreheads together as we each take gulps of air.

Her lips are swollen with my kisses and her hair has come undone, half up and half out of the tight braid it'd been in before my hand got involved. Her creamy skin is flushed, her chest heaving.

"Jodi," I manage to say, my voice hoarse.

"You can't—"

"Can't what?" I ask gently, tucking a strawberry-blond curl behind her ear.

She exhales, her body growing tense again. "This doesn't make sense."

I straighten, noting her hands are still on my skin and she still hasn't stopped hugging my waist with her thighs. A quick glance down confirms the peaked nipples I'm already upset with myself about not touching. "Pretty sure the rest of you doesn't think so," I say.

I reach for her hand and she lets me guide it to my dick over my pants, pressing her palm against it and watching how her plump lips open as she blushes. Holding her hand there, I give her a chaste kiss, then release her hand. She doesn't move it.

"Tell me this isn't one-sided," I demand again, brushing my thumb against her temple.

She swallows hard as her eyes search mine. Finally, she answers. "It's not."

I smile, almost slumping in relief.

"But—" she halts.

"But?" I murmur, canting my hips to press into her, feeling her squeeze my growing erection.

She looks at me, both doe-eyed and greedy, and shakes her head dismissively.

Slowly, I aim for her mouth once again, giving her time to object, but she says nothing as our lips meet. I groan. Her mouth is going to ruin me.

No, strike that. It's the tiny sounds she makes in the back of her throat that go straight to my dick.

I ease up on the kiss, pulling back to drink her in again. "Okay," I breathe. "We both kissed. We liked it. So here's what's going to happen. I'm going to go to my room and leave you alone before I take this any farther. Even though I want to. So much," I groan. I kiss her again. "And you're going to do…whatever it was you were going to do."

She nods, the tiniest of smiles playing on her lips. "Okay."

"And you're not going to overthink this."

Her smile broadens. "Okay."

I give her another peck before extricating myself from her thighs.

Which, now that I think about it, *they* might be what ruin me.

I back out of the kitchen, fully aware of the salute my dick is giving her, and head straight to my room for a cold shower.

# CHAPTER 15
# JODI

*U*M.

What.

I think—no, I *know*—Price Joseph just kissed me.

And not just kissed me.

But like *kissed* kissed me.

Kissed me so hard I felt things I have never felt in my entire life. Swirling, aching, empty things. Like I wanted him to ease that ache and fill that emptiness things.

Holy shit.

Holy *shit*.

I slide off the counter, any thoughts of cooking completely out of my head, and walk upstairs to my room.

In the bedroom, I stand in front of the mirror and touch my lips. They're swollen, and the skin around them is a little red from all the friction. My hair…wow, my hair is a disaster. And I'm all splotchy. What must I have looked like to him?

A smile creeps across my face. Because regardless of what I looked like to him, *he* did it to *me*. His hands in my hair, his calloused fingers tracing my neck and jaw.

I flop onto my back onto the bed.

My hands all over his rock. Solid. Chest.

My nails digging into his skin.

*Mark me, Jodi. Do what you want to me.*

My hand slips into the waistband of my yoga pants and under my panties.

His mouth on my neck, the softness of his beard, the way he whispered in my ear.

I'm soaked and swollen, primed beyond belief, and all it takes is a few moments of my fingers on my slick clit, the memory of Price's cock straining against me as I moved against him, before I'm shuddering with a climax that rocks me head to toe.

I breathe out, not even remotely satisfied.

What would happen if I went down there? Walked into his room? Would he be doing the same thing I just did?

My body heats at the idea. To walk in and see him take himself in his hand—what would that even look like? Never in any of my fantasies have I ever pictured it, and now I'm consumed by the idea. Price, his golden, sun-kissed and ink-stained skin, reaching down to wrap a hand around himself. Would he be gentle? No. Rough. Something tells me a man like Price wants rough.

*Mark me, Jodi.*

I shiver.

What the hell is going on? What am I doing? Does Price actually like me?

I take a bath, try to read books, do some yoga, and start and stop about fifty million shows on Netflix before I finally give up. At midnight, I figure I can trust myself to go downstairs. The silk of the green polka dot pajama fabric is cool against my skin as I creep down the steps.

At the top of the landing, I pause, listening for any sign that Price is anywhere other than his bedroom. Hearing none, I move quietly down.

And when I reach the bottom I lose my mind. Because

instead of going left to the kitchen—because I *am* hungry, dang it—I swing right, unable to resist turning toward the room I know is his.

I'll just look at the door. Not creepy at all.

If I get caught, I'll claim temporary insanity based on a lack of glucose.

I turn the corner and suck in my breath. Two thin strips of light angle in an L down the hallway, luring me like a moth to a flame.

I tiptoe closer, ears straining, heart beating wildly.

*This is a terrible idea. I'm literally spying on my innkeeper. What is* wrong *with me?*

I plaster my back to the wall and draw nearer, common sense disappearing with the potential of seeing, well, anything.

I hear something and freeze. A rustle.

Oh no, what if he's coming out of his room?

I look around for a place to hide.

There's nowhere. It is a hall in a Victorian-esque house, and yet somehow, there is nowhere to go.

So I stand pressed against the wall, trying to suppress a giggle at how absurd this is and how ridiculous I'm acting.

I exhale. Okay, okay. I can do this. *Breathe.*

I creep ahead a little more, because Price clearly isn't coming out of his bedroom, and freeze again.

Because it sounds like he's breathing heavily.

And I know it's wrong, but I absolutely *have* to look.

*"Fuck, Jodi, fuck fuck fuck."*

Holycraphe'ssayingmynameishedoingwhatIthinkhe'sdoing?

Quick as a bunny, I do a one-eighty while moving forward, and then I'm hugging the wall and looking through the crack and—

Oh.

Oh, praise baby Jesus and all the baby goats and sheep in the world.

He's on his back in the bed, the navy covers thrown off him, and he's naked, and yeah, I'm pretty sure he's just gotten himself off, because his arms are thrown wide and his chest is heaving.

Wait. He's *naked.*

My eyes snap to catch a glimpse, but apparently the baby goats aren't giving me everything because he brings an arm down that blocks my view, and he swears again, softly.

I grip the wall and try to process what I'm seeing. He's just gotten himself off, that much is obvious, and he said my name while he came.

I'm not sure I can handle this.

Because this. Is. Amazing.

Even though I should feel guilty about looking at him. And I probably will later, and I'll need to find a way to apologize, but right now? I keep watching.

With another swear, he swings himself into a sitting position, his back to me, and rests his elbows on his legs. Then he stands and heads toward what must be the bathroom.

Wow, his butt is *white.* Ghost-level white. Belly of a fish white.

I snicker, then clap my hand to my mouth.

Price whips around and I jerk backwards, pressing my lips together to keep the laughter inside.

"Jodi?" he calls.

And with that, I haul down the hallway as quickly and quietly as possible, aiming for the kitchen and slapping the light on. I whistle to start making noise, then set about making myself a peanut butter and jelly sandwich while giggling about a very, *very* white butt.

*I* don't expect to find him downstairs at five o'clock the next morning, but there he is. He's dressed in what I've learned is his at-home uniform of black mesh shorts and thin tee, this one blue. His broad shoulders strain against the fabric, and I take a moment to enjoy the way they taper down to his glorious (white) butt. His hair is mussed and his back is to me as he looms over the toaster and mutters.

"It'll work better if you plug it in," I say.

He jumps and turns around. "Okay, not cool," he says, a smile blooming on his face. "You can't scare me *and* insult me at the same time."

I grin at him, fighting the sudden bout of shyness that's thrown itself over me. What if he regrets our kiss yesterday?

He plugs the toaster in, and once he's satisfied that it's working, he turns his attention to me. "How did you sleep?"

The image of him laid out on his bed, navy sheets bunched around his naked body, jumps into my head. I feel my cheeks heat as I say, "Fine. You?"

He narrows his eyes slightly, then seems to decide to let it go. "Could've been better."

"Yeah?"

He nods. "Yeah." He pushes off the counter and stalks toward me. "C'mere."

But instead of doing something normal, like doing as he asks and walking to him, I go still like I'm suddenly in a game of freeze.

He tilts his head as he nears me, studying me with eyes that are nothing but kind and curious. He holds his arms out, clearly intending for me to go into them, but I'm still stuck in place.

*What is wrong with me?*

"Jodi? You okay?"

I blink and shake it off. "Yeah. I'm fine." I launch into motion and move into his arms. And I try to relax, I really do, but something about him makes me so unsteady, so unsure of myself. He's too gorgeous. He's a freaking fireman and clearly has his act together. And I'm just Jodi, the girl who owns a coffee shop and is hanging on for dear life just to make it month to month.

He gives me a gentle hug, then steps back and tips my chin up. I look into his eyes, reminding myself that *he* kissed *me* last night, not the other way around, and that I was absolutely not stiff. I was the farthest thing from it.

Then he leans down, the scent of his should-be-cheesy-but-it-works-beautifully-on-him body wash hitting my senses, and brushes a kiss on the side of my lips. He lingers, and I don't know what I'm supposed to do.

He straightens and smiles at me, and it's almost...bashful. "I've been wanting to do that since last night," he says.

I blink up at him, and it's on the tip of my tongue to say *I've been wanting to do that since seventh grade.*

"If I'm honest—" he starts, then his phone rings.

Who would be calling him at five in the morning? It's not even daylight.

He winces. "Sorry. It might be work. I should..." He swivels away to answer. "Monica?" He pauses and looks at me guiltily, then walks out of the kitchen to continue the conversation. "No, I was awake. What's up?"

*Monica?* I stare after him, my worst fears confirmed. There's no one at the fire station named Monica. So whoever she is, she knows him well enough, and means enough to him, that he answers her call this early in the morning. Maybe an old flame.

But everything he said. In the kitchen...*and* his bedroom.

I shake my head. No. Whatever last night was, it wasn't

anything special. He's probably bored, and I'm just a flavor of the month. Convenient.

Not that I want more. Or maybe I do? I'm not sure. Being this close to him, day after day, has only showed me that everything I thought about him was true. He's kind, and good, and thoughtful, not at all the silly guy he portrays to most everyone.

I guess if I'm honest with myself, the crush I thought I had on him was really only pretend. And now that I'm living in the same house as him, it feels a heck of a lot more real.

Crap.

My head and heart a muddled mess, I grab the bagel meant for Price out of the toaster and head to work.

# CHAPTER 16
# JODI

$\mathcal{P}$RICE SHOWS UP at the shop a couple of hours later. He is relentless, something I didn't know about him before…well, *before*. He's in black jeans that make my mouth water with the way they hug his thighs and butt, and a casual white button down with the sleeves rolled up to show off his forearms. If a person didn't know any better, they wouldn't suspect the tattoos he's sporting just underneath that shirt. The effect of the outfit, combined with the ease with which he carries himself and the way he darts glances at me beneath the flop of his dirty blond hair, is enough to make me whimper.

Darius clucks at me as we work. "Have we ever seen him in here looking like that?" he asks under his breath.

I shake my head. "I'm about to pass out."

Darius laughs. "Perfect. He can give you mouth to mouth."

I glare at him and risk another look at Price. He waits in line and chats with Miss Betty, who looks at him like he could be her fifth husband. And honestly, who could blame her? She lives next door to the inn, and she's a shameless flirt, so I guess they have plenty to talk about. Once the duo approach, Miss Betty orders a hot English Breakfast tea. I can feel Price's eyes tracking my every move, my skin heating under his attention.

After I push the tea to Miss Betty, I'm left with Price and Darius manages the line without me. I take a deep breath and meet his gaze.

"Good morning." My voice comes out scratchy and thick.

He smiles, but there's heat behind it. "Good morning."

Fidgeting, I press onward. "Your usual?"

His lips quirk upward. "I'll take whatever you give me, Jodi."

*Good. Lord.*

My cheeks flame and I clear my throat. But I don't have a response for him, so I make his vanilla oat-milk latte. I move quickly, unable to handle the heat of his attention for fear of combusting. When I slide it to him, he drops a ten-dollar bill on the counter and jerks his head to the side, indicating I should come out.

"Please," he says, his voice soft.

As if I'd say no to him. "Be right back," I tell Darius.

He shimmies his hips and hums in response.

Ignoring the pointed stares from Miss Betty and others in the shop, I allow Price to take my hand and walk me to the set of plush chairs at the back of the store. He settles into one and I do the same in the other.

"You're amazing back there, you know that?" he says.

I blink at him.

"I mean, in addition to making the world's best vanilla oat-milk latte, you're just so good at this." He gestures at the shop. "Making everyone feel so welcome, knowing everyone's order before they even say it, creating a space for the community. It's amazing."

My entire upper body flushes. "Thank you."

His eyes drop to my neck, then rest on my lips before raising back to my own. "You should know how special you are."

I swallow, certain my entire chest is crimson at this point. I break eye contact, unable to withstand the force of it.

"So, listen."

At the change in tone, I meet his gaze once more.

He smiles, the skin crinkling around his eyes. "I have to go out of town for an overnight thing."

My stomach drops. *Monica.*

"It's nothing, just some business I need to handle. But I'll be back tomorrow afternoon, and I'd really like to take you out."

Wait. "What?"

His smile broadens. "On a date. I'd like to take you on a date."

I point my finger at him. "*You* want to go out with *me*?" I point back at myself.

He huffs out a laugh. "Yes, Jodi. Very much. Why is that so hard to believe?"

Because of this Monica chick. Or because Price Joseph doesn't date women who look like me. He dates tall, lithe, blond cheerleader types like Megan and Mary Alice. And none of those descriptions belong to me.

"Jodi, you're killing me here. Please?"

Man, if twelve-year-old Jodi could see me now. I should do it. I should go out with him, even though I know that it's nothing. Besides, Ceci, Devon, and Darius would murder me if I said no. So I smile back at him, my own grin just as big as his, and say, "Yes."

He exhales. "Oh, thank god," he chuckles. "After the way you left this morning, I wasn't sure—"

"I'm pretty certain there's a rule whenever a Joseph brother asks a woman out, she has to say yes," I joke.

His eyes soften. "It's *you* I want to take out, not some random woman."

My stomach bottoms out. *Oh.*

He stands and holds out his hand, so I take it and he helps me to my feet. His skin is warm and calloused, and he's pulling me to him before I realize what he's doing. We're so close that I have to tilt my head way up to see him, and those silver-blue eyes are studying me like a puzzle he wants to put together. He tucks a loose curl behind my ear with his free hand, then cups my cheek.

"Can I kiss you?" he asks.

"Here?" I squeak.

He smiles tenderly at me. "Yeah. Here."

Everything goes quiet. I don't know if it's that the whole shop has literally decided to stop and watch us—a real possibility—or if my body has simply blocked out everything that isn't Price. Either way, he is the only sound in my world right now. His touch, the clean smell of him, the clear desire in his eyes that is, unbelievably, for me. And even though I'm sure at least half the shop is watching, because this kind of thing is practically a sport to them, I nod.

With an approving hum, Price wraps an arm around me, pulling me close and angling my chin as he leans down.

The zing that goes through my body at the touch of his lips should be illegal. The way it feels to be held by him, enveloped almost, as he kisses me. I feel safe. He tightens his grip on my waist while his other hand cradles my head.

No, it's not safe. I feel *cherished*.

He finally pulls back, but keeps his palm on my hip as he hums again. "I could do that all day," he grins.

I blush and look away, the noise of the shop coming back at me full blast. At least half the women in the Mom Group are staring at me, mouths gaping, and now I want to crawl into a hole.

He squeezes my hip and I focus back on him, just in time to see a shadow cross his face. "So, tomorrow then? It's a date?"

I nod and smile. "It's a date."

"Good." He leans down to give me a peck on the cheek, then grabs the latte he'd set on the table beside him. "I'll see you then."

I watch him leave, trying and failing to keep my eyes off his butt as he leaves. When I go behind the counter, Darius is waiting.

"Did you—?"

"I did."

"And he—?"

"He did."

Darius winks at me. "Damn, girl! Color me impressed. And also," he leans in, "the Moms seem pretty scandalized." He straightens. "Or jealous. Either way."

I flick my gaze back to the Moms and babies, and sure enough, they keep darting glances at me.

After a moment, Megan approaches the counter, her blonde hair bouncing and her blue eyes shining. "So," she smiles. "You and Price?"

I feel the heat rise on my chest and cheeks as I nod.

Her smile broadens. "Oh my gosh, that's *amazing*," she gushes. She looks back at the table, then to me. "He really is the best. I mean, I love my Thomas, obviously, but there's just something about Price. He *really* knows how to treat a woman, you know?"

I struggle to keep the smile on my face. Because no, I don't know, and this beautiful creature is all but telling me she most definitely had sex with him. Probably a lot of it. And, yes, I assumed as much, but I didn't need it staring me in the face.

She continues. "He was great. Amazing, actually. And so sweet. But I was ready for the whole thing, marriage and babies, and he wasn't." She brightens. "Anyway, I am *so* excited for you! This is amazing," she repeats.

As she leaves, I fight the urge to run to the back and hide. Am I ready to be known as just another Price conquest?

Then I stop myself. Why should I care what anyone thinks? And who said this was anything big, anyway? This is just how Price is. I know that. I've *seen* that.

Greeting the next customer, I ignore the twinge in my stomach that reminds me I want to be something different.

*I* nearly jump out of my skin when, later that night, there's a knock at my bedroom door at the inn.

"Dinner," comes Will's gruff voice.

Dinner? He's never served dinner before. But considering it saves me from eating the sad meal bar I had lined up, I'm not complaining.

I open the door and startle again with a yelp. "I did *not* expect you to be standing here."

Will towers above me like the Hulk's little brother in the dim light of the hallway. He steps back with an apologetic nod of his head. "Sorry. You want dinner?"

"Yeah. I mean yes, definitely."

He turns without another word and heads downstairs. I shake my head. These guys need to work on their guest skills.

I make my way to the kitchen and nearly stumble across the threshold. It's clear that Will has been cooking, and judging by the smells, it's also clear that the man knows what he's doing.

"Try not to look so surprised," Will says. "Unlike Price, I actually know my way around a kitchen."

I duck my head and toss him a sheepish grin. "Sorry. I've sampled some pretty questionable pastry lately."

He laughs, and I nearly stumble again. Will Joseph laughs? Who knew? "I don't think he's giving up on the pastry anytime soon."

"You're right. He's not."

Will gestures to the counter behind him. "Since it's just the two of us, I didn't bother putting anything on serving platters. Hope that's okay. We're having baked rigatoni pasta with sausage and sautéed mushrooms, tri-colored peppers and onions, with thinly shaved Pecorino cheese. Also some store-bought garlic bread." He stops. "Oh, shit. Are you vegetarian?"

I laugh. "I'm not, but it's something you should be mindful of once you have real guests."

He scowls. "You're a real guest, Jodi. Now grab a plate."

"See? That right there."

Now it's more of a confused scowl. "What right there?"

Unsure of where my boldness is coming from, I step up to the dish of baked pasta and grab a spoon. "*Now grab a plate?* You can't just command your guests. Try 'would you like to serve yourself or shall I' or something."

Meanwhile, holy mackerel, this looks amazing. I put more than what's polite on the plate and then grab a slice of bread. When I turn, Will's looking at me like I'm a different person, so it's my turn to look confused. "What?"

He chuckles. "You're not what I expected, that's all."

My cheeks warm. Does *every* Joseph brother make me blush now?

As he dumps heaping piles of pasta on his plate, he says, "Would you like to eat at the table, or would you prefer to go back to your room?" He shoots me a meaningful look. "See? I can learn."

Guess Will isn't the only one being surprised by someone tonight. Mr. Scary isn't nearly as scary as I thought. I take a seat at the table, which is already set for two, and wait for him to join me.

"Want anything other than water?" he asks.

I shake my head as he sits across from me. Not like Price, who has either sat right next to me or as close to that as possible.

I take a bite of the pasta and suppress a groan. "Wow, Will, this is excellent."

His lips quirk up. "Thanks. Had to learn early growing up."

I nearly drop my fork. "Okay, what's going on?"

He chews and swallows. "What do you mean?"

I gesture at him. "This. You're usually the silent, grunty type who'd sooner scare a preschooler than smile at them. Now you're baking pasta, and not only are you carrying on a conversation, you actually dropped a hint about your childhood." I squint at him. "Do you have a fever?"

He smiles. "No fever. Let's talk about you and my brother."

I manage not to choke on the bite of pasta in my mouth. Have I found myself in another dimension? Maybe he doesn't have a fever, but he's concussed. He's *smiling*. And he just asked...oh, god. I take a steadying drink of the water. "Um, what?"

"You and Price." He takes another massive bite of pasta.

I consider pointing out that he's eating like a caveman, but figure it's pointless and he'll accuse me of avoiding the question. Which I absolutely would like to do. But Mr. Scary is back and he's narrowed those Joseph family eyes at me. "Me and Price."

He nods. "He likes you."

I blink.

"I've never seen him like this," Will continues. "And I think you'd be good for him. So I want to make sure you, you know."

No, I don't know. "Make sure I...what?" I prompt.

He huffs out a breath and stabs another forkful of pasta. "That you like him, too." He shoves the bite in his mouth and mumbles something that sounds like *hate talking about this shit*.

I can't decide if I'm amused or intimidated. So I deflect. "You know, this is the last conversation I ever thought I'd have with you. Aaron seems the better choice for this line of questioning."

Will grumbles.

I keep eating, hoping he'll let it go.

"So? Do you?" His voice is gruff.

Guess he isn't. "Yes," I say softly. I clear my throat. "Yes. I like him. Happy?"

He smiles again, transforming from Mr. Scary right back into...well, whatever he is. "Good."

I wait on him to say something else, to, I don't know, expand on that one word a little. But he doesn't. Just keeps shoving delicious pasta into his maw like a machine.

Side note: the mustache is terrible. I'm a fan of facial hair—clearly—but the mustache on its own? Nope. Hard pass. Not my fave.

Finally, I can't take it anymore. "Is that all you're going to say? *Good?*"

He looks up and shrugs. "Yeah."

"No."

"No?"

"Yeah, *no.*"

He puts his fork down as his eyebrows go up. "Really."

"That's not how it works! There's a give and take here, Will. Don't you know how this goes? Do you not have any friends?"

"I have my brothers and the guys at the station," he says, straightening.

"Maybe this is a guy thing." I wave it away. "Doesn't matter. The point is that you've extracted out of me that I like Price. It's now *your* turn to give me some kind of morsel back."

He scoffs, but his face softens as he wipes his mouth with a napkin. When he speaks, the edge is gone from his voice. "Jodi. He likes you. I said that already."

My chest tightens. "Yeah, but—"

"And I said that I've never seen him like this."

I sigh. "But what does that mean?"

He grins. "It means he likes you. It means you've gotten under a Joseph brother's skin."

"And that's a good thing?"

He scoots his chair back to stand. "Put it this way: the only woman who ever got under Aaron's skin was Devon."

The vise on my chest loosens and I'm suddenly boneless. "Really?"

He nods.

"What about you?"

Will's face shutters as he says, "No one." And just like that, Mr. Scary is back.

I narrow my eyes. There's something there—some*one* there—but no way is he giving it to me. Fair enough. I stand and start to help.

"Stop," he barks.

I freeze, my hands hovering over the plate and empty water glass.

"Sorry," he grumbles. "I'll handle this. You're a guest."

I give him my thanks and head up to my bedroom. I flop onto the bed and pull Gigi's quilt up around me, suddenly chilly. Outside, the sun has set, and the temperature has dipped back into the fifties. A car door shuts. Miss Betty is probably watching television and cross-stitching naughty sayings to sell in her Etsy store. Ceci and Rick are likely eyeball-deep in the dinner/bath/bed routine with the twins. If Aaron is off-shift, then he and Devon are probably cuddled on the couch, Aaron massaging her feet while she grades papers.

All around me, the world keeps moving, but mine has come to a total standstill even as I grin so hard my face hurts. Because Price Joseph likes me. He really likes me.

*I* GRIP THE steering wheel loosely, content to chill in the middle lane while I deliver the news to Monica.

"I'm out."

There's a pause, and finally she says, "Out?"

"I'm done modeling," I clarify. "No more."

"Are you sure about this? I can ease up on the assignments, keep you closer to home, whatever you want. Set the terms."

I shake my head, even though she can't see me. "I'm done with it, Monica. Today was the final straw. I've been groped and propositioned and then told it's all in my head too many times." Literally, I've lost count. The women who do it seem to think there's nothing wrong with grabbing my junk or my ass—as though the fact they're touching me without my consent is irrelevant, because I'm a guy.

News flash: that's not how it works.

"What happened?" Monica asks.

"Does it matter?"

"Fuck yes, it matters," she growls. "I want my clients to feel safe, and you're telling me you don't. So what happened, who was it, and who do I need to go after?"

I sigh and mumble, "The photographer's assistant." Which

never would have happened with Lisa, and is another reason why she's my favorite.

Monica launches into a tirade about on-set behavior and sexual harassment that lasts an impressive ten miles. When she's done, she says, "Tell me you still want to work."

"I really don't, Monica. I'm done." What I don't bother telling her is that even though this is a good gig, it's never felt like something I could be proud of. And my hiding of it has eaten away at me to the point where I now feel physically sick every time she calls with a new job.

We end the call, and my thoughts turn to happier things. Like the date I'm taking Jodi on tonight.

Something about this girl has me ready to dive in. I know the shitty stuff, because I worked the fire where Jason was killed. And I know the rest of her family's taken off. What I don't know is why she stayed, or what her favorite pastry is, or the music she listens to, or her goals and dreams.

Listen to me. I sound like a sap. And for all I know, she only said yes to the date because no one says no to a date with me. Sounds pretentious, but it's true. From age twelve to now at age thirty-four, I've never had anyone turn me down. If I'm lucky, though, she said yes because she sees something more.

I roll into the house with just enough time to get ready, and I think I hear the sounds of Jodi with one, maybe two people in her room. Naturally, I need to know what's going on, so I bound up the stairs and toward Jodi's wide open door.

"Ladies," I boom.

Shrieks and a door slamming in my face is the answer.

The hell?

The door opens an inch and Devon's eye meets mine. "Price," she drawls. "How are you?"

I wrap my hand around the door, pushing gently and meeting resistance. "Good. Can't I come in?"

Her eyebrow arches. "No. You cannot. We're busy turning Jodi into a smoke show for you."

See, what they don't realize is that Jodi is a smoke show no matter what. And if they do too much, she and I might not make it out of this house. "What if I bring you snacks?"

"Nope. Nice try, though."

There's a shuffle and Devon is replaced by Ceci, who opens the door a bit more. I glance over her head, but Jodi is completely out of sight. The hunger to see her takes me by surprise, especially since I just saw her yesterday morning.

"You're not wearing that, are you?" Ceci asks, looking me up and down.

I pout. "Ceci, give me some credit. It's a date. I just got home and wanted to say hello to my date before I got ready for the date." I pause. "I'm saying 'date' too much, aren't I?"

Ceci smirks. "You're adorable when you're flustered."

"So I can't say hi to Jodi?"

"Sure you can," Ceci answers. "You just did. Right, Jodi?"

"Um, yes?" Jodi's voice is muffled. "*Ow!* Quit hitting me!" she hisses.

My lips quirk up. "Hi, Jodi," I call.

"Hi, Price!" comes the response.

"Okay, bye," Ceci says, starting to close the door.

I yank my hand back, in serious fear of losing my fingers. "Wait! You really don't want snacks? I have some." I sound desperate. I should stop.

Ceci eyes me, then grins mischievously. "No. Let's make sure our girl is hungry."

I nearly swallow my tongue. "Come again?"

"Oh, let's hope so," she says, waggling her eyes and shutting the door in my face.

As I turn to head downstairs, I can't decide if I like Ceci and Devon, or if they terrify me.

*A*N HOUR LATER, watching Jodi's skirt swish around her legs as she descends the stairs, I decide I love her friends. She's done up like a siren from the fifties or sixties. Her lips are her usual red, but her strawberry blond hair is curled up and back from her face, highlighting the curve of her neck and showing off almost-bare shoulders. Her dress is a deep yellow vintage-looking number that hugs her upper body and flares out at her hips.

As she closes in on me, a shy smile on her lips, I see the blanket of freckles on her shoulders and nearly whimper. "You are stunning," I finally manage to say.

"Thank you," she murmurs. "You, too."

I give a low laugh. "Sweetness, I've got nothing on you."

Her eyes widen at the term of endearment, and she squeezes the small purse in her hands.

Unable to hold back, I lean forward to kiss her cheek. She smells exquisite, some kind of spice on top of her usual scent. I linger a beat longer than I should, and my dick twitches. Finally, I manage to pull myself together and straighten. "Ready?"

She grins and nods.

We go to one of the nicer restaurants in town, which isn't that fancy but is better than the burger joint on the square. As I turn off the engine, I look at her, and my breath leaves my body. "Stay there," I say, hustling to get out and open her door for her.

She looks up at me as she gets out, her hazel eyes looking green because of the makeup she's wearing. "Thanks," she says and smiles.

I put my hand on her lower back, keeping her close as we walk inside, only releasing her when we get to the table.

Jodi leans forward once the hostess leaves. "One of the Mom Group is here!" she hisses.

"The who?" I turn in my seat.

"Don't look!" she squeaks.

Grinning, I turn back. "Are you nervous about being seen with me?"

She blushes in the dim light and scoffs. "No."

The server appears to take our drink orders. Jodi orders a glass of wine and I do the same. Once the server leaves, Jodi continues.

"The Mom Group. You know, the moms and kids that come in. Megan and Mary Alice?" she prompts.

"Oh," I say, nodding. "Okay. Nice girls."

A shadow crosses her face. "Right. Anyway, the look of shock that Skim Milk Latte, Extra Hot, Extra Foam just gave me wasn't awesome."

I reach across to take Jodi's hand. "Don't worry about her."

She shrugs and picks up the menu. "I'm not."

I'm not sure I believe her, but I don't know what else to say right now. Is she ashamed to be seen with me?

"So, what's your favorite dish here?" Jodi asks.

It's obvious she's changing the subject, and because I don't know what else to do, I go with it. "Penne with Bolognese sauce."

She grins. "Mine, too."

I chuckle. "Of course it is."

"What's that supposed to mean?"

"It means it's one more reason why you're perfect."

This time, the blush seems to be full-bodied, covering her cheeks, neck, and chest. I love it. *Wonder if other parts of her blush?*

The server reappears with our drinks and some water, and Jodi immediately takes a gulp of the water. We both order the penne, and once the server leaves, I lift my wine glass. "To first dates."

Her smile, so shy and sweet, lights up her face. "To first dates."

She tells me the latest on her place—three weeks in and the sheetrock is finally off, but still waiting on supplies before the town's only good electrician can get started—and polishes off the glass of wine as we talk. Like last time, she only gets more talkative and animated with the second drink, and as I ask her question after question, she blooms in front of me.

When the main dishes arrive, she tucks in like her life depends on it. "Oh," she moans. "So good."

My dick absolutely takes notice of the way her eyes just rolled back in her head, her chin tipped up just a smidge. To say nothing of the moan. I keep sipping the only glass of wine I'll allow myself and send a prayer for restraint up to the heavens. "Yep," I choke out. "It's delicious."

She eyes me. "You haven't even had a bite."

I grab the fork. "Doesn't matter. It always is, and your reaction was proof enough." Her reaction, which is seared into my brain and is already replaying in my mind, again and again, like my own personal gif. And it's a gift. A gift gif.

Conversation flows easily as we eat, and despite how tiny Jodi is, the woman puts away an impressive amount of the pasta, which is apparently a turn-on I didn't know I had.

We say no to dessert. As the server leaves with my card to handle payment, Jodi eyes me. "So, why are you single?"

"Why are *you* single?" I counter.

She shakes her head and finishes her wine. "Asked you first," she says after swallowing.

Seriously, why am I paying attention to her *swallowing*? I'm trying to be noble here, but my body wants exactly none of my nobleness.

"Price?"

"Sorry. Um, why am I single." I fidget. "I've been…on a journey of self-reflection."

She stares at me, her lush mouth tipping into an encouraging smile. "Go on."

I can't believe I'm actually telling her this stuff. "And, ah," I stop and run my hand through my hair. "I wanted to be, um, untouched. While I worked on myself." I clear my throat and reach for my water glass.

Jodi's reaches for her own water glass and fights a smile. "What?"

She shrugs. "It's just—I *knew* I was right."

I tilt my head, curious. "And what, pray tell, are you right about?"

"That there's more to you than meets the eye. It's like you show the world this whole puppy dog vibe, but that's actually not you. At all. Not that I presume to know you or anything, but…" Despite yet another blush that's crept onto her cheeks, she holds my gaze as she speaks.

I blink, rendered entirely mute due to my chest cracking open at her observation. I open my mouth, then close it again. "You…" I finally start. "How long have you been paying attention to me, Jodi?"

She looks away for a moment, but when she meets my eyes again, I see something new in there. Something a little braver. "A while."

"Define 'a while.'"

She grins. "Longer than you can imagine."

I want to kick myself for being oblivious to her for so long. But there's no point in wallowing in it. Resolved, I lick my lips, and she follows the movement, her chest heaving. When I lean toward her, she comes closer. Then I gesture for her hand, and when she lays it in my palm, I use a finger to stroke the inside of it. My voice is low, meant only for her. "Maybe I'm single because I've been waiting for the right person."

She blinks, then blurts out words that I have never, so help me, *ever* in my life heard uttered by a woman in my presence: "I'm a virgin."

Pretty sure a record just scratched.

Did she just say…?

"What?"

"Oh, god." She yanks her hand back and covers her face. "Oh god. I can't believe I said that *out loud*. To *you*."

Yeah, I'm kind of having a moment over here, too. But I get my shit together fast, because this is not the time for me to have an existential crisis. The other day, the shyness I saw? Now I know what that was about.

Thankfully, the server returns with my card, so I scribble on the receipt and stand, holding my hand out for the gorgeous woman who's trying to disappear into thin air. "Come on, sweetness. Let's go home."

She peeks up at me through parted fingers. "Did that really just happen?"

"Oh, yeah," I say, smiling gently.

She takes my hand and stands, eyes on the floor. "This is so embarrassing."

"Hey." I crowd into her, trailing a hand down her back and using the other to tip her chin up to meet my eyes. "There is absolutely nothing to be embarrassed about."

She snorts softly. "Uh, *yes*, there is."

I press my hand to the small of her back and barely suppress the groan at how well she fits against me. Her eyes flare at the contact, and because there is only so much I can take, I pull her against me and lean down to press my lips just below her ear, hungry for her skin. "No," I insist, my voice rough. "There isn't."

She inhales shakily, and I lead us to the car.

## CHAPTER 18
## JODI

*I* CAN'T BELIEVE I told him.

I'm blaming the wine. I should never have two full glasses. I'm a short person. Short people shouldn't get served two full glasses of wine. *Note to self: no more drinking wine around Price.*

He's quiet on the ride home, and I'm certain I've freaked him out. I mean, why wouldn't I have? The man is thirty-four years old. What is he supposed to do with a twenty-seven-year-old virgin?

Nothing.

He is supposed to do nothing, and I've killed any shot I had at, well, *anything* with him by blurting it out. Crap.

Where is a shovel? I need to dig a hole and jump into it.

We pull up to the inn and he palms my knee, stilling it. I didn't even realize how fidgety I was, but that's what happens when I get nervous. I look up at him.

"Stay here."

He kills the engine and rounds the car to open my door. I catalog everything, knowing this is the only time I'll ever have this and banking it all for when I'm an old woman, sad and alone. The way his butt looks in those black jeans, the absolute thirst-trap of the way he's rolled up his light-blue button-down sleeves to show off his forearms. And his beard! His soft-as-hell beard that tickled my skin as he whispered in my ear at the restaurant. The way he smiled at me across the table. The way he's looking at me now.

Wait. The way he's *looking at me now*.

His eyes are definitely tracking my entire body as he opens the door, trailing from my legs to my chest and finally meeting my own. He was quick about it, but not so quick that I didn't catch it.

It's probably the wine.

But when he tucks me into him as we walk to the house, his hand splaying across my lower back...that's not the wine.

And inside, the way he guides me to the dimly lit living room, sitting me down on the couch, kneeling before me to unstrap my heels and cradle each foot in his warm hands. That is most definitely not the wine.

Price straightens, his knees still on the hardwood floor, my own knees spread much farther apart than the Baptist preachers would prefer, and as he licks his lips, I watch hungrily. He's done that move more than once tonight, and he knows exactly what he's doing, except this time his eyes aren't flirty when I meet them. They're dark, his pupils so wide that I can see only the barest sliver of dark gray around them.

His fingers trail up my calves, and I hitch a breath.

"Jodi."

I swallow hard. "Y-yes?"

"Can I kiss you?"

The air whooshes out of me. "Please."

He cradles my head as he leans in and makes a noise in the back of his throat. We're so close, trading breaths, and he studies me. After what feels like a lifetime, he speaks. "You are such a treasure, Jodi. And I—"

I close the inch between our lips, crashing mine onto his, unable to take it one second longer.

It's all he needs. He takes control immediately, yanking my hips to the edge of the cushion and wrapping his arms tight around me. His tongue flicks at my lower lip, and I open my mouth for him.

I don't recognize the moan that comes out of me at the feel of his tongue slicking against mine, but then again, I have never felt this way in my life. Those college boys were just that—boys —who clearly never knew enough to do to me what Price does by simply existing. Could I have found someone else before now? Sure. But holy hell, am I glad I waited.

My entire body buzzes, and there's an aching throb between my legs. On instinct, my hips thrust forward, meeting the hard plane of his stomach, and his arm snakes behind me to press me harder against him.

My hands are everywhere I can get them, feeling the way his back muscles roll and tense as I drag my palms over his shirt, and heavens, this man. Then I've got my hands on Price Joseph's ass and I think it might be the most perfect thing I have ever had the pleasure of touching.

I whimper.

"You want my shirt off?" he asks.

I meet his eyes and nod before I can overthink it. Then I start to scoot back and allow him room, but he gives a tight jerk of his head.

"Stay."

Entranced, I watch as he moves his hands to the top button of his shirt. Slowly, achingly slowly, he undoes it. I bite the inside of my lower lip and he growls, undoing the second button.

Finally, on the third, the shirt starts to fall away and allow me a view. I'm breathing so heavily it's a wonder I've not passed out, because this man's chest is the kind you see on romance covers. And I have never been this close to his skin and my god, he smells so good, clean and so exquisitely Price.

"Holy fuck," I whisper.

"Touch me, Jodi."

I swallow hard and snap my eyes up to his.

His voice is low. "I need you to touch me. Can you do that?"

I nod, raising a hand to his chest and letting it rest there as he unbuttons the shirt the rest of the way. He stills for me, and I hold my breath as I push the shirt off and watch it fall.

"Harder, sweetness," he says. "Please. I like to be touched hard."

My pulse racing, amazed at how free he is with voicing his desires, I press my palms against him, squeezing his perfect shoulders, watching the muscles ripple in the low light. His pecs are next, free of hair, but I feel the stubble beneath my palms. I drag my thumb over a nipple and his breath catches. When I get to his abs, I'm the one licking my lips, and he grunts as our eyes meet.

Gently, he traces the side of my face with calloused fingers, then brings them to my mouth. I relax, pliant, as he lowers his lips to mine once more, losing myself in the kiss. When his hand falls to my breast, I breathe out a sigh of relief, not realizing how much I needed it there.

He whispers a curse and trails his other hand up my calf and onto my thigh. My legs widen on instinct, and he deepens the kiss, his tongue plundering my mouth like it's the treasure he said I was.

"Will you let me touch you?"

Goose bumps race across my body at the question, and I nod.

His eyes meet mine, full of tenderness and something else I can't name. Restraint, maybe? "I need you to say it, Jodi."

"Yes."

His lips tilt up. "Good answer."

He pulls me back to him for a kiss, ramping up the intensity as though someone flipped a switch, and I am here for it. My body thrums, and I widen my knees as his hand moves higher up my skirt, the throbbing ache between my legs intensifyng.

He palms my center and I inhale sharply.

"Good?"

I mew in response and he squeezes me. My hips thrust forward.

He moves his lips to my ear, his palm still pressing against me, easing the ache as my lower body moves of its own accord. "Are there polka dots for me under this dress, Jodi?"

Heat flares across me and I whisper, "Yes."

His lips trail over my neck as he pulls his hand away. Before I can protest, he's pressed his thumb against my clit, and his fingers trace the seam of my silk panties.

Oh my god.

"You're wet for me, Jodi, aren't you? Do you feel it?" He circles his thumb, adjusting the pressure as he does it.

My eyes roll back as I breathe out a *yes*, the excitement at his dirty mouth adding to my pleasure.

Not stopping, he grabs the couch pillows with his free hand and stacks them behind me. "Lay back," he says and guides me down. "Let me make you feel good."

I relax against the pillows and he leans over me, his breath hot against my skin.

"There you go," he murmurs, trailing his lips to my chest as his fingers work absolute magic on me. "I can't wait to taste you, Jodi. Can't wait to put my tongue on your pussy and feel you." He shifts his fingers again, palming me once more and squeezing.

My hips buck, and I gasp. "Your *mouth*."

His voice is low, gravel crunching at midnight. "You like me talking dirty to you, Jodi?"

My hips swirl, chasing his touch. "Yes."

"Good, because I want you to listen to me. This is only the

beginning. I'm going to learn everything about your body, and I'm going to give you so much pleasure. I'm going to make sure you know how exquisite you are, and I want to watch you fall apart for me. Over, and over, and over."

Spikes of heat swirl and gather as he keeps whispering, urging me on, never moving the panties but staying on top of them. I squeeze my eyes shut.

"No, Jodi. Look at me. I want you to look at me when you come."

With effort, I open my eyes and meet his. They're dark, hooded, and watching me so intently that it pushes me even closer. My movements are frantic now, and I grasp his arms, needing something to hold on to.

"Fuck," I whisper.

"There," he says, his hand matching my urgency. His voice is low, and he doesn't stop talking and praising me, and it's the hottest thing I have ever experienced in my life. "You're right there, baby. So close. You can do it. You want to come for me, don't you?"

"Yes. *Yes*. It's coming," I say, wonder laced through my words. I'm racing to the edge, and the world stops, then tilts, swaying back and forth, before I finally tip over. "Oh god. Price. *Price!*" I meet his eyes and scream as I come, my entire body tingling as my core pulses intensely with the climax.

His gaze never strays from mine and he talks me through it. "Perfect, sweetness. You are exquisite. So good. You are so good. Keep going. There."

His words keep going as the orgasm wanes, and finally I go utterly limp. With one last press of his palm against me, he pulls his hand away. My eyes flutter shut.

"Watch."

The command is soft, but firm. I force my eyes open again as he brings his fingers up to his nose and inhales. When he puts them in his mouth, his eyes clamped onto mine as he sucks them, I lose my breath.

"You smell so good. I can't wait till these fingers are covered in your wetness. Till I taste you."

The sound that comes out of me isn't even a word.

He stands, and before I can make my body do the same, he leans down and picks me up, cradling me against his bare chest, and I…wow.

I still can't function. My brain isn't working.

He plants a kiss on the top of my head as he walks, taking me through the darkened house and into his room, where the only light is from the moon peeking through the curtains, striping onto his bed.

Still holding me—bless this man's firefighting workouts—he says, "I want you to stay with me tonight."

I nod wordlessly.

He tilts his head to kiss me, then lays me down on the bed. He rounds to the other side, and with a few swift movements, he's pulled the covers down and tucked me in, fully dressed. Standing in front of me, he undoes his jeans and shucks them.

And my brain grinds to a halt. I think I moan.

Because he's tenting red boxer briefs, and those briefs are losing the battle.

More of his stomach is on display than I have ever seen, even more than during the Fall Festival when he gets into the dunking booth, and I am positive my fantasies never imagined this. He is positively ripped, and so toned that my mouth literally waters.

Suddenly I am *very* aware of my virgin status, and every part of me tenses.

He must notice, because in seconds he's gotten into the bed with me, and he's curling me against him, little spoon to big spoon.

"Relax, sweetness," he murmurs, running his hand over my arm. "I just want to hold you."

He's so warm, a personal heater I never knew was available. His voice lulls me into submission, his lips on my shoulder a sweet caress. There's no mistaking how hard he is as he pulls me closer to him, securing my butt firmly against his dick. And even though I'm fully dressed, make-up on, teeth not brushed, I let the darkness sweep over me, and fall into a deep sleep.

*L*IKE ALWAYS, I wake up at 4:30, without the help of an alarm. Monstrous, I know, but that's what years of six a.m. firefighter shifts will do to a guy.

Instantly, I'm aware of Jodi beside me. She fell asleep almost immediately last night, and I spent a good half hour listening to her breathe, smelling her hair and skin, and wondering how the fuck I'd managed to stumble onto this gem of a woman.

A virgin. I have never been with one, not even as a pathetic teenager getting my own cherry popped. I'm still having trouble wrapping my head around how hot-as-fuck Jodi has maintained this status all these years, but at the same time, I kind of get it. I'm the asshole who didn't notice her until I saw her legs in the midnight of my kitchen, so, yeah.

The blackout curtains let in just enough light for me to see her as I rise up on my elbow. She's dead asleep, and happily, on her back. Her bra straps have slipped down and her dress is rumpled, but her chest is on display, rising and falling, nearly putting me into a trance.

Part of me knows she's too precious for me to have. The other part—the part that's absolutely winning the battle this morning—is certain that if anyone is equipped to walk this woman across the line, it's me.

Another thought rises, one about being worthy for maybe something a little more than sex, and I'm nearly desperate for it. But I let it fall away.

I slide a hand under the covers to check the situation. Her yellow dress is bunched around her waist, and without hesitation, I palm her hip.

She doesn't stir.

Beneath my hand, I feel the silk of her underwear. My dick twitches. *Sorry, buddy. You're on lockdown.*

I lean forward, my chest against her arm, and kiss her shoulder. She smells incredible, like warm sleep and the leftovers from her perfume. She's all shadow and light in the dark of the room, but I easily find and kiss the freckles on her chest.

She inhales, coming out of deep sleep. I whisper a *shh* and keep kissing up to her neck and over to her lush lips. She kisses me back, still not quite awake, and the tiniest noise comes out of her.

I laugh softly, tracing the side of her face. *I want this always.* The thought is startling, but I let it linger. "Good morning, Jodi."

She moans against my lips.

I move beneath the covers and settle my hips between her legs, clenching my jaw at the delicious heat between them. "Will you let me go down on you?"

She moans a yes. Trailing kisses down her chest, I scoot down to press my lips against her stomach. Her hands find my hair and thread through it. Her skin is velvet, warm and soft. I want to bury my face between her legs, but I make myself go slow.

Hooking my fingers into her panties, I pull them off one smooth leg, then the other. It's only now that I think to curse the lack of light, because I can't tell what color polka dot her underwear is. Kneeling, I bring her leg up to rest on my shoulder and meet it with my lips. She inhales sharply.

"I told you I would learn every part of your body, Jodi. That was a promise." I trail my fingers up her leg and bend it, licking and kissing my way over her knee to the inside of her thigh. Finally, I let her leg go, resting it against the mattress.

She's breathing hard now, whether from arousal or nerves I don't know, so I crawl up to check in. Before I can say a word, she's pulling my face to hers and kissing me deeply.

*Turned on. Got it.*

"Baby," I tell her between kisses, "if I don't get my head down there, I might die."

She groans. "Price." Her voice is scratchy, hoarse from sleep, and sexy as hell.

I give her one last kiss, then scoot down to heaven. Otherwise known as between her legs. "Spread for me, beautiful."

She obeys. I curse the darkness again, unable to see the details of her, but it doesn't matter. I'll map her with my tongue. I take my thumbs and press them against her folds, matching her quick inhale with one of my own, and spread her. I lick up her center, then find her clit.

"Oh my god," she says, then moans.

Fuck me. She sounds otherworldly, and I'm so hard that it hurts.

I keep at her, listening to her mews and gasps to learn the pressures she likes and the way she wants me to swirl my tongue. She's sweet, so damn sweet, and it's driving me crazy.

"You taste so fucking good, Jodi."

"Jesus Christ."

"He's got nothing to do with it. Say *my* name," I command, sucking her clit.

"*Price*, oh my god, right there, Price." Her hands grab onto my hair and pull.

I push my tongue inside her. She is so tight, swollen and

wet. I keep fucking her with my tongue, feeling her grip on my hair and the way her hips are swirling.

She moans and gasps. "Oh my god, whatever you're doing, I'm—" she breaks off and moans again.

I lick back up to her clit and suck, then push in the tip of my finger.

She swears and her hips thrust up, taking a bit more of my finger on their own. I keep it there, moving in and out, then work her with my tongue.

Her legs tense and she loses her words. There we go.

"I want you to come on my tongue, Jodi. Can you do that?"

"*Price*, oh god oh god oh god," she chants, pulling even tighter on my hair.

I bear down on her, letting her take as much of my finger as she can, and cover her with my mouth. Her legs clamp against my ears, and she shouts as she comes, her inner muscles pulsing. Before she finishes, I pull my finger out and thrust my tongue into her, and her cries intensify.

She is exquisite, keening and rolling her hips, and I'm certain I'm unwrapping the most incredible gift of my life with her.

Finally, she quiets, and she melts into the mattress. I kiss my way up her stomach, lifting over the dress and finding the freckles on her chest once again. I lick up her neck, feeling her shiver, then bring my lips just above hers.

"Kiss me, Jodi. I want you to taste yourself."

She squeaks, but opens her mouth for me. My tongue plunders her, and she threads her arms around me and squeezes. Right now, in her embrace, I am the king of the world.

# CHAPTER 20
# JODI

’M PRETTY SURE I'm still dreaming. Because there is no way that I'm in Price's bed, kissing him in the pre-dawn of the morning.

But as he eases up on the kiss, humming and stroking my hair away from my face, I realize that this is, in fact, absolute reality.

And that the orgasm he just delivered was even better than the one on the couch. He rocks his hips gently against me, and I feel just how hard he is. How big. Am I supposed to get that thing inside me? The pressure feels so good, and I rock with him, my hips dancing with his on instinct, and it's both a relief and a wonder all at the same time.

"Thank you," I whisper.

He chuckles, his laugh soft and kind in the dark. "The pleasure was all mine. And before you spiral somewhere in that beautiful head of yours, no, we are not doing anything else this morning."

"So—"

"So this hard-on will go away and I'll be fine," he finishes. He kisses me again, his hips still moving, and his mouth is gentle but commanding. He controls every part of it, his tongue slicking across mine, deep, then shallow, then deep again.

I can't stop the moan that comes out of me or the spikes of aching heat pulsing between my legs. I thrust against him, hard, and he groans, and it feels like a triumph. I do it again.

He swears, grabs my hand, and pulls it between us. "Feel that," he says, molding my palm against his dick. His voice has an edge to it. "*That* is what you're doing to me."

"You're huge."

"And *you're* driving me crazy."

"Come with me." I don't even know where the words have come from, only that they've escaped my mouth, and suddenly, it's imperative it happen. I squeeze him again, but I can't move my hand because he's still got his clamped around my wrist.

"Is that what you want?"

"Yes." My hips are thrusting harder now, and I'm desperate for the friction of his dick against me. "*Please*," I beg. "I need to come again."

"Fuck, you're hot," he says. He doesn't release my hand, instead sliding it up above my head and holding it down. His other tightens around my breast and squeezes, and I nearly levitate off the bed at the sensation. "You like that?"

I moan a yes.

He leans to take a nipple into his mouth, and I yell. Holy *shit* that feels good.

His thrusts against me get faster, and I meet him, again and again. "Oh, your tits are sensitive, aren't they, sweetness?" He pinches my nipple, rolling it, and I don't know my name anymore. "I bet I can make you come just by playing with your nipples. Maybe we'll find that out later. I can't wait to sink my cock into you. But not yet. Right now, you're going to come against my cock, aren't you?"

Urging me on, he whispers more filthy words and praise, and I'm racing to the edge. "Price," I gasp. "With me."

His grip on my wrist tightens and I explode a second time, a Milky Way of stars bursting behind my eyelids as I arch against him, my body shuddering as something like a sob escapes my throat.

"Fuck," he groans as he makes one last thrust and holds it against me. I feel his release, hot and wet, against my stomach.

He hangs his head, his lips against my ear. "You are going to be trouble, Jodi."

I can't do anything but hum in response. My entire body tingles.

"The absolute best kind of trouble." He releases my wrist and trails his fingers down my arm, tracing the side of my breast and coming to rest against my waist.

I'm still mute, unable to form coherent sentences.

He chuckles, nuzzling my ear and kissing me sweetly. "Come on. We both have work." He's out of the bed and walking to the bathroom in moments, and he angles the door just enough to let light into the bedroom without blinding me.

Through the crack, I watch him step out of his briefs, revealing once more the whitest butt I have ever seen. Maybe it's because my brain is absolute mush from the two—*two!*— orgasms I've just had, but I start giggling and can't stop.

He pokes his head out. "You want to take a shower with me?"

My giggles come to a halt. *Yes. Yes, I do.*

He disappears back behind the door and I undress. When I enter, Price's eyes flare with appreciation, raking over me hungrily. "C'mere, beautiful," he says, holding his arms out.

I step into them, too wrapped up in the feel of him to be shy about standing naked in the light, and we linger outside the shower for a moment, skin to skin, as he takes a deep breath. Releasing it, he tips my chin to meet my eyes, and his own are soft. "Let's get you ready for work."

He is as attentive in the shower as he is in bed, soaping me up and taking care with every part of my body. It's a wonder I'm not shy about it, but Price makes it feel like it's the most natural thing in the world to be naked in a shower with him. The amount of time he spends washing my hair is obscene, but it feels so good I can't bring myself to tell him to stop. Finally, it's my turn, and once again I'm marveling at how beautiful he is. The broadness of his shoulders, the way they taper to slim hips and muscular thighs.

His dick.

Have mercy.

It's not at full attention, but it's not exactly relaxed, and when it's time for me to wash it, his lips tip up in a grin.

"You can touch it, you know. I'll behave."

The smile that crosses my face is devilish. "But will I?"

He laughs, the sound echoing around the bathroom tile. When he quiets, he gathers me close and kisses me, the suds trailing between our bodies. "I'm all yours," he says as he pulls away.

I lather my hands and take his dick into them, feeling the way it begins to stiffen as I do. It's velvety, thick and long against my small hands, and I run my fingers over the head, feeling the edge of it and how it nestles against my palm. Price's breath comes quicker as I cup his balls.

I've read enough romance novels to know what I should do with my hands next, if I want to, but I keep going, moving my hands around to his butt and continuing to wash him.

"Taking it easy on me, I see," Price murmurs.

"Something like that."

As we're drying off, he says, "Want to ride to work together?"

I wrap my towel around me and take in his expression, the sweet hopefulness that radiates from his gray eyes. I would do just about anything this man wants. So riding to work together? "Absolutely."

*D*arius is on me like white on rice as soon as I walk in. Because of course, I'm late. Only by five minutes, but judging by the look on his face, he absolutely saw Price kiss me outside the shop before walking down the block to the station.

"Tell me everything."

The blush that spreads from my chest to my face is instant.

"Oh my god." He holds his hand up. "Never mind. I can't hear about it. I don't think my heart can take it."

I giggle, and he sighs.

"If you don't text your girls for an immediate summit, I quit."

"You threaten to quit at least once a day."

"This time, I mean it."

"Then lucky for you, they already plan on coming here later." I join him behind the counter and grab a yellow polka dot apron to wrap around my waist. "No way were those two going to let me go longer than twelve hours without hearing about my date with Price Joseph."

Darius steps in front of me, his hands in prayer position. "Just tell me one thing: Was whatever happened as good as you wanted it to be, or better?"

"Better. So much better."

He smiles. "Then that's all I need. If I know any more, I might hate you."

And with that, our day kicks into gear.

Ceci and Devon show up early, as expected. Devon teaches English at the middle school, and Ceci handles the admin side of her husband Rick's machinery repair shop. Normally, Ceci and Rick's twins would be around as well, but Ceci waves my question away before it comes out of my mouth.

"They spent the night with their grandpa. Probably torturing him right as we speak," she says, a gleeful smile on her face.

I shake my head. "I almost feel bad for your dad."

"He spoils them rotten. He deserves what he gets," she replies. "But enough about them. How did last night go?"

I push their drinks at them and we all head to our favorite corner in the shop, where a set of comfy, velvet-covered chairs surround a low table. Ceci's got her double shot half-pump vanilla latte, Devon has her usual cold brew, and I've got regular black.

Devon settles in and sighs, tucking a strand of her short, dark blond hair behind her. "I gotta say, it's really nice to not be the one we're talking about."

Rolling my eyes, I take a heavy sip of coffee and wait on the real shark of the group to attack.

As if sensing her sacred duty, Ceci leans forward, a gleeful look on her face. "Did he eat you out?"

Devon nearly spits out her coffee. "Jeez, Ceese. A little restraint, maybe?"

Ceci waves the idea away. "Please. Since when have I ever been known to have any of that? Answer the question." Her blue eyes are steely with determination.

"Yes." No point in hiding it. Plus, the way my face is blazing tells me I wouldn't have kept it a secret anyway.

They squeal. "Really?" Devon says. "Oh wow, this is fun. Details, please!"

I've never told them my sexual status, mainly because it's never come up, but if I'm being honest, because I also didn't want Ceci embarking on some sacred quest to find a guy to do the deed. But now, I don't see a way out. Not if I want to be entirely open about it.

"Hellooooo, earth to Jodi," Ceci sing-songs. "Did you get lost in memories of how delicious his tongue was?"

That snaps me back to reality. But, yeah, actually, his tongue between my legs *was* delicious. Miraculous, even. Ruined me for life. "I'm a virgin." May as well just lay it out there.

"The fuck?" It looks like she might say more, but no words come out. Ceci has finally been rendered speechless.

Devon, on the other hand, is not, and rolls with it. "So this is a really big deal for you, isn't it?"

I smile gratefully at her. "I had wine with dinner, and normally it doesn't go to my head as much as I guess it did last night, but it's hard not to be drunk on Price himself, right?"

Devon grins. "Right."

"So I kind of…blurted it out at dinner. Told him what I just told you. And he took me home and he—" I pause. How much do I tell them?

"Oh, no fucking way are you stopping now." Ceci's back and she snaps at me. "Continue."

Devon swats at her knee. "Be *nice*," she hisses.

The way he kneeled before me, his eyes hooded and focused on mine, his lips parted, as he brought me to orgasm on the couch. "It was the hottest night of my life," I manage to get out.

Devon smirks. "Glad to know the Joseph brothers have some things in common."

Ceci extracts the rest of the night's details out of me, and by the end of it, I'm pretty sure all of us want to jump into beds with our respective men. She looks at her watch and stands. "I've gotta go. Just remembered that Rick, ah, needs something at the house."

Devon makes a face. "Do not say anything else. You're married to my brother."

Ceci waggles her eyebrows. "Hell yeah I am."

As the two of them head out, my phone buzzes.

JESS

You up for a visit from your little sister?

My chest tightens and dread floods my veins. The only time Jess reaches out is when she wants something.

"What's that look on your face?" Darius asks. "Also, Mom Group, incoming."

I don't have time to answer Jess. Shoving the phone in my back pocket, I beam a smile at Megan, the first one in line. *Please don't let her ask about Price.*

"Good morning, Megan! Caramel latte with two shots of espresso?"

# CHAPTER 21
# PRICE

"**I**'M STARVING." HANGING up my turnout gear, I look over at Zach, one of the newest members of the team. "Keep Chief occupied while I grab my sandwich upstairs."

I don't give him a moment to respond before I'm taking the stairs two at a time out of the engine bay and up to the kitchen, where my delicious sandwich sits on the counter, untouched from where I'd been mere seconds from eating it before the alarm went off.

Palming it, I shove it in my mouth and chew around a groan of happiness. Pastrami on rye. God bless Mrs. Withers and the other old ladies at the historical society for their constant stream of sandwich meat and homemade bread. I finish half with a second bite, and I head back downstairs with the remainder in my hand.

Chief and Buck glance up from where they've initiated the post-call checklist. Buck's a grizzled motherfucker, well past his prime firefighting days, but don't tell him that. Dude might slug you. He raises a judgmental brow at me, his eyes flicking to my sandwich and back, before saying, "Who said you could get out of post-call?"

I flash him a shit-eating grin. "Didn't say I was trying, Buck. Just need to keep this spectacular body of mine fueled."

He huffs and turns away, and I inwardly cringe at what I've said. *This* is the kind of shit I need to stop doing. I resolve to do better. Besides, what I should have done is asked Chief to help with the post-call checklist.

Later, when I'm playing the latest Formula 1 on the gaming console and trying to keep my mind off a certain barista and the things I'd like to do to her, Aaron and Mike drop onto the other couch and look expectantly at Chief and Will, who've come in behind them. It feels very intervention-like, so obviously I ignore all of them. Besides, I'm driving the Dutch dude and I'm winning.

"How was your date with Jodi?" Chief asks.

Aaron says, "I thought we were here to discuss his pastry efforts."

"And to beg him to stop," Mike puts in. Mike is another paramedic and is Aaron's partner. We've all got basic EMT skills—it's part of the firefighter training—but Mike and Aaron are more highly trained.

Sighing, I pause the game and put the controller down. "Are we really doing this?"

Will grunts.

"So, that's a yes." I lean back and stretch my arms along the top of the couch. "Let's have it."

"Stop making the pastry. It's terrible."

"Damn, Will," Aaron says.

I shrug. "I know it's terrible. I'm working on it."

Chief steps forward. "Son, it's not just terrible. Some of the stuff you've been forcing on us is damn near inedible."

"It's not *that* bad," I say. At least, I didn't think it was. "Is it?"

They answer in unison. "Yes."

"Why are you even doing it?" Aaron asks. "You're already

handling the bed-and-breakfast, plus all your trips out of town doing whatever."

"Don't want to eat too much of it and ruin your good looks, either," Mike jokes.

They all laugh, and my stomach clenches. As usual, no one takes me seriously. Then again, I basically made the same joke about myself earlier. "I'm more than a pretty face, you know."

More laughs.

"I'm taking over the baking," Will announces.

"You're what?" I ask.

He folds his bulky arms across his chest and stands tall. "I'm taking it over."

"You can't order me to stop in one breath and decide you're going to be the pastry guy in the next," I sputter. I stand up, tired of being on my ass while the rest of them look down on me. Literally *and* metaphorically.

Will grunts and flicks his eyes to Aaron.

Aaron steps forward, clearly happy to be the one on the inside with Will for once. I wince. It was always me and Will taking care of our little brother Aaron, until it wasn't. And apparently, we're on the *wasn't* side of things right now.

"You'll have a bake-off," he announces.

I didn't hear him right. "A bake-off?"

He and Will nod. "We'll get Jodi to offer the pastries at her shop for free. People vote on which one tastes better. Winner takes pastry rights."

Chief nods approvingly. "Sounds fair."

I look at Mike, hoping he's a neutral party in this, and as such, will realize that this entire idea is nuts.

"I like it," Mike says.

Damn it. "Fine. We'll have a bake-off. But I think this is stupid."

"Because you're going to lose," Will says, his lips curling up with way too much satisfaction for my taste.

"You know, I don't think I like you very much right now,"
I say.

"I kind of like it over here," Aaron says. "Is this what it feels
like to be the middle brother?"

I shoot him a rude gesture, and he laughs.

"This has been entertaining, but I've got paperwork to do,"
Mike says, jerking his thumb toward the office and heading
that way.

"Good. Now we can talk about you and Jodi." Chief grins like
a fool and rubs his hands together. "I hear you two went out for
a fancy dinner last night."

*Thank god that's all he heard.*

"I don't think that's a good idea," Aaron says.

I look at him sharply. "Excuse me?"

He shrugs. "She's a good girl. You're...well..."

My neck heats and the urge to punch my little brother is
very, very strong. "What the fuck is that supposed to mean?" I
growl.

"Oh, come on." He smirks. "You're a total player, aren't you?
I'm just saying that Jodi isn't someone you sleep with and move
on. She's special."

So both my brothers think I'm unworthy. Great. Closing my
eyes and clenching my fists, I take a deep breath and try to parse
the hundreds of responses going through my head. Anger,
shame, hurt, and fear roil together.

"Unless maybe she's into you?" Aaron says doubtfully.

I snap my eyes open and step toward him.

"Whoa." Will moves like the fucking cheetah he is, getting
between me and Aaron before Aaron can feel what it's like to
take a fist to the jaw by a pissed-off older brother. "Aaron.
Apologize."

Aaron's eyes are big. "Wait a minute. You actually *like*
her?"

I lunge again. Will palms my chest like he's bored. Letting

him hold me up, I glare at Aaron. "Is it so unbelievable to you that she might like me?"

Will raises his eyebrows. "Are you asking?"

"So you like her," Aaron says.

"Is this how you three are with women?" Chief asks.

"Shut up, Chief," we all say.

Chief laughs.

Will pushes me upright and I roll my neck.

"Sorry, Price," Aaron says. "I didn't know."

Shaking my head, I say, "I can't believe *you*, of all people, think those rumors about me are true."

"You mean they're not?"

I flop back on the couch, defeated. "No, man. Like I told Will, everyone thinks I sleep with every woman who so much as looks at me, and I don't. I never have. I'm not saying I've been an angel, but shit, give me a *little* credit."

Aaron holds his hands up. "You never said anything."

I blow out a disbelieving breath. "Because I used to not care what people thought. And because I didn't know I needed to defend myself to my brothers."

"Enough," Will says. "Aaron, use your brain. If all the rumors were true, he'd have slept with half the women in the entire state of Alabama."

I snap my fingers and point at Will. "Exactly. Glad you've joined my side of things."

Then Will turns his steely gaze on me. I think of Jodi's nickname for him and she's right: He really can be Mr. Scary. "Price. You never confirmed or denied the rumors, which isn't that much better."

I flatten my lips. "Come on, man."

"Can we get back to whether Price and Jodi actually like each other?" Chief asks.

And immediately, I shut up.

Will grunts.

Aaron looks at me, then Will. "Well?"

"Well what?" I ask, stalling like the champion I am.

"Do you like her? For more than—" he stops.

I'm flooded with memories of Jodi. The way we've grown close over the past few weeks, how we talk so easily with each other, how she treats me like I'm more than my face and body. The feel of her in my arms, the silk heat of her as her thighs wrapped around my head, the lushness of her mouth, the look on her face as she came.

"Yeah," I croak. "Yes. And it's..." It's terrifying. Because I have never felt this way about anyone, and to be realizing it in front of my brothers and Chief isn't optimal. But there's nothing to do but own it at this point, and so I stand back up. "I do. I like her."

Chief's smile is wide enough to crack his face.

But all Aaron says is, "Oh."

I huff out a disbelieving laugh. "Oh? That's your response? *Oh?*"

"Sorry," he says. "Give me a minute. I'm with you, I swear. I'm just trying to recalibrate literally everything I know about you."

I know he means well, but right now, every word out of Aaron's mouth is breaking me. Because all it's doing is confirming my worst fears. No one has ever expected much of anything out of me. I'm the hot firefighter. Good to look at, but not good enough for anything long-term. And despite firefighters needing to actually be smart and know a hell of a lot more than most people seem to give us credit for, most people assume I'm dumb. They always have. As though my looks automatically mean I can only be good in bed and nowhere else.

And I'm so fucking sick of it.

I run my hand down my face. "Are we done here?"

"She likes you, too, you know."

Chief, Aaron, and I all swivel our heads to Will. After a beat, I manage to say, "What?"

So much for me being smart.

"I'm guessing for years," Will continues. "She's got stars in her eyes every time she looks at you. Like you hung the moon or some shit. Always has."

"I'm sorry. Where has Will gone?" I say. I know the look he's talking about—I've finally been paying attention—but to hear that Grumpy Gus, of all people, has also noticed? That's a whole other thing.

He quirks a rare grin. "Someone has to be the one to tell you."

"He's right," Aaron says.

"What the hell, man?" I raise my hands and let them fall.

Aaron laughs. "Dude, you *really* weren't paying attention to her. Because I have known for years."

"And you didn't think to tell me?"

He tilts his head, considering. "Would it have mattered?"

I open my mouth to say *yes*, but realize that's not true. "Honestly? I'm glad I didn't know."

He nods.

"But I'm ready for her now. I just..." Her words from last night, where she admitted she'd watched me for 'a while' come back to me.

"Just what?" Aaron prompts.

I really, *really* am not a fan of being this vulnerable with a fucking audience. Sighing, I admit what's been eating at me. "I don't know if I'm worthy of her."

All three of them grin at me. And frankly, it's terrifying.

"You aren't." Aaron looks like he has hearts for eyes. "None of us are worth the women we love."

"We'll help," Will says.

Chief rubs his hands together again. "Oh, this is gonna be good."

# CHAPTER 22
# JODI

E'RE IN THE pre-lunch lull when my phone buzzes. When I see who it is, I'm tempted to ignore it, but it'll only come back to bite me in the butt. So I wave my cell at Darius and accept the call as I step out from behind the counter.

"What's up?"

"Hi, favorite sister!" Jess's voice is sultrier over the phone than in person. She wields her words like a weapon, and it worked every time when we were growing up.

I make a fist, then force my hand to relax. *Breathe.* "I'm your only sister."

She laughs, oblivious as always. "Why didn't you answer my text earlier?"

"Because some of us have jobs."

"Ouch," she says, laughing again. "So, did Mom tell you about the demo I recorded?"

I push the door to step outside and let the April sun shine down on me. It's a little chilly, in the low sixties, but the rays feel incredible on my shoulders and back. I close my eyes and bask in them.

"Hello?" Jess prompts. "My demo—did Mom tell you?"

I sigh. "She did. Did *she* tell *you* about my apartment catching fire?"

"What? No! Oh my goodness, Jodi—are you okay?"

Surprised, I look around as if I'm being pranked. My sister actually cares? "Um, yeah. I'm fine."

"Is there anything I can do?"

I keep looking around. None of this tracks. I'm used to my mom being the way she is, and hearing that she didn't tell Jess is par for the course. But Jess asking if there's anything she can do might be the most surprising thing I've ever heard in my life.

"Jodi? Are you there?"

"Sorry. Yeah, I'm here. And, no, there's nothing to do. It's getting handled."

"No wonder you didn't respond to me asking about a visit," she says. "But, um…I kind of don't have a place to stay right now?"

And there it is: the real reason she's pretending to care. I shove down the kernel of hope that'd popped up at her concerned tone. "Jess…"

"Maybe I can, I don't know, share a hotel room with you or something?" Her voice kicks up a notch.

I pinch the bridge of my nose and will myself to be strong. "I'm not at a hotel, I'm at a bed-and-breakfast." I regret the words the instant they're out of my mouth.

"Ooh, there's a B&B in town now? Where?"

I've officially screwed myself. And because it's too long of a story to explain and she'd zone out anyway because it doesn't involve her, I simply say, "A few blocks from work."

"Perfect! We can share the bed."

*Hell no we can't.* The thought is iron-hot.

"…Or I'll sleep on a couch. Do they have another room open? Maybe I can get a used-to-be-local discount or some-thing? Because girl, let me tell you how broke I am." She laughs.

"I've got enough to pay for gas to get down there. I can't wait to see you!"

"I didn't say—"

But she's gone.

I glare at the phone, willing it to light back up with an active call so I can tell her that I didn't agree to anything, that no, she can't stay with me, and no to anything else she might have up her sleeves.

Even though I'd never say any of those things to her. That's not how it's ever worked. Not before Jason, and certainly not after Jason, when I was somehow the glue holding the family together.

For all the good it did me.

I look up and blink rapidly, refusing to let even one single tear come and ruin my make-up.

"Jodi!"

I swipe beneath my lashes, sniff, and turn. Brook is jogging over from her shop, a book in her hand.

"A little early for your afternoon coffee, isn't it?" I smile.

"What's this I hear about you and Price Joseph on a date?" Her eyes sparkle. "Is it true?"

I pause. "You know, I've never been the subject of the town's gossip network."

"Word is you two got so hot and heavy in the restaurant that he slung you over his shoulder and ran out, and everyone could see your leopard print panties."

My mouth drops open. "Seriously?"

"Time to correct the narrative, Jodi. Give it to me." She tucks a stand of chestnut hair behind her ear and grins. "You know you want to."

I shake my head, flabbergasted. "This is how it starts, isn't it?"

"Obviously." She motions her hands in a *spill it* gesture.

"Yes, we went on a date, and no, he did not toss me over his shoulder." *And I wouldn't be caught dead in leopard print panties.* Not that she needs to know that.

She leans in and whispers, "Did you kiss him?"

I tilt my head, trying to remember if anything happened with the two of them. "Didn't you and he—"

"Nope," she interrupts. "Never. We did go out once, but it was ages ago, and he was an absolute gentleman. Honestly, *I* was the one who was trying to maul *him*." She giggles, a faraway look in her eyes. "But he just gave me a hug when the night was over. Told me he had a great time and that he'd see me around at the bookstore. Nicest let-down I've ever had."

"I knew our gossip mill was enthusiastic," I say, "but I always assumed it was truer than not when it came to Price."

Brook shrugs. "I did, too, until our date."

Huh. I tuck this piece of information away to examine it later, because it isn't remotely close to what I would have expected. Not that it surprises me, and I should have known better. At this point, I'm not sure learning *anything* about Price would surprise me.

"So?" she prompts.

"Yeah," I say, smiling. "He kissed me." No need to give her any more than that.

Brook swoons. Like, actually bends backwards and has to hold onto the bike rack to keep herself upright. "Is his beard as soft as it looks?"

I laugh. "Yes! Yes it is."

She laughs with me. "I'm so happy for you. I'll be back later for my afternoon dose. Looks like Mr. Buchanan is making his way into the shop, ready to give me hell for not stocking enough James Patterson. See you later!"

I wave as she jogs away and crosses the square to the bookshop.

I'm exhausted by the time Darius and I close up. Price never came in today, but I'd heard about the call they'd gone on from

Chief when he swung in for a round of muffins for the crew. Apparently Mrs. Sweeney's boa constrictor had gotten out and shown up in the new neighbor's garage a few houses down, looking to help itself to the pet rabbits quivering in the cage. The new neighbor, a transplant from Atlanta, had been less than thrilled to find a ten-foot snake about to eat the kids' rabbits, and was minutes away from taking a shovel to it when Mrs. Sweeney herself showed up in her dressing gown and not much else, having heard the screaming on her way to get the morning newspaper.

The old ladies in this town are going to be the death of us all.

As I lock up and prepare to walk back to the inn, I hear my name and turn to see Aaron strolling toward me.

"Want a ride?" he asks. "I have to go by there anyway."

"Sure. Want a pastry as thanks?"

He grins. "I don't, but I appreciate you teeing that subject up for me so well."

I follow him around the back of the station to where his pickup is parked. "I don't understand. You needed to talk to me about…pastry?"

We get into the cab and he starts the ignition. "Yep."

"I'm scared to ask, but…"

He pulls onto the street. "Price is convinced he can get better at making pastry if he just practices more. Will and I are convinced he's wasting his time."

My heart flares with a surge of protectiveness. "That's not very nice."

Aaron glances at me and hums thoughtfully before looking back at the road. "*Anyway*, we decided they'd have a bake-off. Both of them bake a certain pastry, and you offer it free of charge in the shop. The customers pick the winner."

"And if Price wins?"

Aaron scoffs. "He won't."

Again the instinct to protect Price flies around my chest. "But if he does?"

"Then he can keep baking. But *when* Will wins, they agree that Will takes over the baking."

"So Will bakes now? What's next—you gonna start tightrope walking?"

Laughing, Aaron says, "Don't give Devon any ideas. And hell if I know what Will does when he's not working out. I'm just enjoying not being the one getting ganged up on for the first time in my life."

I look at him and see the absolute joy in his eyes, and I take it back. It's not going to be the old ladies that take this town down. It'll be the Joseph brothers. Because only these three could decide a bake-off is the way to resolve something. Although I guess it's better than fighting.

"Fine," I relent. "But I pick the pastry."

We get to the house, and I put a hand on Aaron's arm. "Thanks," I say.

"For what? Being awesome?"

I blink, caught off-guard at the similarity between his and Price's eye color. "Wow, you guys really *do* have almost the exact same eyes."

He arches an eyebrow. "You been staring into my brother's eyes, Jodi?"

I blush and swat at him. "Shut up."

He chuckles and we get out of the cab. He grabs some boxes and follows me in, setting them down inside the foyer. "Listen, Jodi."

I turn, holding onto the banister as I'm about to go upstairs.

He grips the back of his neck. "You and my brother," he starts.

I hold a hand out. "I don't—"

"He'll hurt you," Aaron blurts.

I blanch and pull my hand to my chest.

"Not on purpose," he continues. "God, nothing like that. He's great. But he just…." He shrugs. "I don't want you getting hurt. That's all."

I bite my lip and study Aaron, choosing my words carefully. "You don't give your brother enough credit. I don't think anyone does, about anything, really. So I appreciate your concern, but it's not warranted." I pause, and part of me wants to keep going, to lay into Aaron for the decades of injustices he probably unknowingly piled onto his brother, but I don't. It's not my fight.

To his credit, Aaron nods and holds my gaze unflinchingly. "I'm sorry. You're, ah, you're right."

My throat tightens with unshed tears, and it's so surprising that all I can do is nod back and say, "I am."

As Aaron takes his leave, the women Price has dated flit through my head. Brook, Megan, Mary Alice, and more. Did he love any of them? Did *they* love *him*? I shake my head, trying to push away the doubts that swirl. Because it's true that no one seems to have given him any credit, but at the same time, I have no idea what I'm doing. Am I just setting myself up for heartbreak?

I'm tucking myself into bed with my e-reader, the latest romance novel from my favorite author loaded and ready to go, when my phone dings.

PRICE

I missed you today.

Sorry I didn't get a chance to come over.

My smile is so wide and instant that I'm glad no one is around to see it. How does he manage to erase all of my doubts with just a few words? I type back.

> Missed you too.

PRICE

I know you're about to go to bed.

If it's possible, the grin gets wider.

> I am

PRICE

But I need to know something.

> What's that?

PRICE

Are you wearing polka dot pajamas tonight?

I laugh.

> Of course

PRICE

What color?

Biting my lip, I consider not telling him. But Price has unlocked something inside of me. Something I can't exactly name, but that I'm only too happy to explore. So I take a deep breath and answer.

> Red.

> To match.

Three dots appear and disappear and appear again. Finally, the response comes.

PRICE

Pretty sure you just exploded my brain.

I laugh again, drunk on the knowledge that Price Joseph is into me.

To be clear, the red is to match my hair.

And not the hair on my head.

PRICE

Jesus

Fuck

You are not playing fair.

Never said I would.

PRICE

I have never hated being a firefighter until this exact moment.

I squeeze my legs together as thoughts of what Price would do run through my head.

PRICE

What are you doing?

Lying in bed.

I type the next part before I lose my nerve.

Tell me what you'd do to me if you were here.

PRICE

Oh, are we doing this?

Feeling dizzy, I type.

> We are definitely doing this.

PRICE

> Answer your phone.

Immediately, the FaceTime notification alerts and I practically jump out of my skin. But I do as asked.

Price's face fills the screen. He's walking, then shutting a door behind him and sitting down in a dimly lit room. The bedroom, I'm guessing. His eyes darken as they take me in. "Sweetness, you are killing me over here." His voice is low.

I wave at the screen. "Hi."

"Let me see you." Another command.

I gulp. "What do you want to see?"

"Pull the covers back and let me see everything you're wearing."

Clearly, I've never done anything like this before, so I'm certain that my movements are anything but sexy as I push the covers down to reveal the promised pajamas.

Price growls. "Are they silk?"

Suddenly I'm glad I'm out from beneath the covers, because my skin is on fire. "Yes."

"Unbutton your top."

I put the phone down.

"Jodi."

I pick it back up.

His mouth is hooked up in a grin. "Baby, I'm gonna need you to do it one-handed. I want to watch." He pauses, and the intensity in his eyes lifts. "Is all this okay?"

Biting my lip, I nod. "I've always, um." My pulse races. "I've always wanted to do this."

At my confirmation, he growls. The man is actually smoldering at me.

I swallow hard and admit, "I like doing all of this with you. It's what I've always wanted."

A flash of tenderness crosses his face. "You want me there with you, don't you?" His voice is gravel, scraping across my skin.

"Yes." My voice is barely my own.

"Undo your top."

Angling the phone so he can see, I unbutton the shirt. I keep my eyes on the screen, but his attention is focused on my hand, and on the skin that each undone button reveals.

"Beautiful," he says softly. His eyes meet mine. "I want to see more."

I push the panels of the shirt to the side, giving him a full view of my breasts. My nipples peak in the air, and another low growl comes from Price.

"Touch yourself."

"How?" I want to give him exactly what he desires, but I want the instruction, too.

"Remember how I touched you?"

I nod, an ache pooling between my legs.

"Did you like it?"

I nod again. "Yes." My voice is hoarse.

"Touch yourself like that."

I grab my breast and squeeze.

"Good. Now your nipple."

I obey, and my eyes roll to the back of my head. It never feels this good when I'm by myself.

"Talk to me. Does that feel good?"

"So good."

"What do you want to do next?"

I squirm, and his eyes get even darker.

"Are you turned on for me, Jodi? You are, aren't you. Good. I want you soaking wet for me. Look at you. You're gorgeous. And the way you touch yourself...fuck." He breaks off.

"I need to come," I say. I almost can't believe the words have left my mouth, but the way he's looking at me makes me feel so powerful, so in control, even though I'm doing what he tells me to.

"Slide your shorts down. Let me see."

Without hesitation, I lift my hips so I can push the fabric down. For a moment, I consider telling him about the toy I have in the nightstand next to me, but something primal comes out of his mouth as he looks at me through the screen, and the words fall out of my head.

"Beautiful," he says. "So beautiful. I want my mouth on your pussy so bad, sweetness. I'm so hard for you."

My breath hitches.

"Touch yourself. Show me how you make yourself come."

I slide my fingers down to my clit.

"Spread your legs," he orders. "Let me see everything."

So I do.

He growls. "Jodi. Sweet lord."

"I'm so wet," I whisper, my fingers gliding into my folds and again finding my clit.

I keep my eyes on Price, and his eyes are glued to my fingers, watching as I pleasure myself.

"God, baby, the things I'd be doing to you if I were there," he growls.

"I want you so bad," I answer. "I want you to fuck me." Again, the words are out before I can fully register them.

"Fuck, Jodi. I'll give it to you," he answers. "I'll give you whatever you want. Always. Just let me see you come, baby. Are you getting close?"

My hips undulate in time with my fingers, and I can feel the swirl of pleasure begin to tighten. "Yes," I hiss. "Price, *yes*."

"Almost there. Keep going. I wish it were my tongue, my fingers on you right now. I'd drink you up. You taste so good, Jodi. You are perfect."

More words of praise spill out of him as he urges me on, and my fingers fly, and soon, so soon, my eyes roll back into my head as everything comes roaring to the edge, and I groan, my hips stilling as the orgasm pulses through me, waves of ecstasy crashing on top of each other.

"There you go. Yes, baby. Yes," Price croons as I come.

I go limp, sinking into the mattress with a satisfied hum, and manage to peel my eyes open to look at the screen once more.

Price's hair is sticking up, like he's run his hands through it, and his eyes are the darkest silver I've ever seen them as he drinks me in. He shakes his head, the expression on his face one of pure wonder.

"I can't believe I just did that," I say, almost bashful now.

A low laugh escapes him as he says, "I wish I was there."

Spent, and chilly now, I pull the covers over me and tuck onto my side. "Would you cuddle me if you were?"

He gives me a wicked smile. "Baby, we'd just be getting started."

My pulse spikes and I squeeze my thighs.

"Two more nights," he says.

I nod.

His eyes soften. "We take this at your pace, sweetheart. You know that, right?"

"I know. But—" I break off.

He waits for me to say more, his eyes steady and full of tenderness.

I lick my lips. "I don't want to wait." What I don't say is, *I'm a twenty-seven-year-old virgin and I'm tired of it.* Even though that's true. Instead, I say the truest, scariest thing I can imagine. "I want you, Price. I always have."

He blows out a breath and pins me with his eyes. "Good. Because I'm all yours."

## CHAPTER 23
## JODI

*I* BLAME THE orgasm for the way I look at Price when he comes in for a coffee the next morning. I'd fallen into the deepest sleep of my life last night after we hung up, and the creases in my cheek from the pillowcase are only now starting to fade at ten a.m.

Remember those old-school cartoons when a character is so hungry that when they look at another character, all they see is dinner? That's me. This man sauntering into my shop is a freaking roast turkey leg, and I can't wait to sink my teeth into him.

I have no idea what has happened to me. I'm still technically a virgin, but in the span of forty-eight hours—less than that, actually—Price has turned me into a sex-obsessed woman with only one thing on my mind. And that is the snack in front of me.

"Good morning, Jodi." His smile deepens as I grin back at him.

"Hi." I practically purr the words.

His eyes light up with an amused expression on his face. "You're in a good mood."

"You have no idea."

He barks out a laugh, and I remember that there are more

people around than just us. Like Darius, who is hip-checking me and snickering as he gestures the next customer forward.

I clear my throat, well aware of how my cheek is now pillow marked *and* redder than my hair, and ask, "What'll it be?"

Now it's Price's eyes that darken, and validation punches through my chest. It's not just me.

"Vanilla oat-milk latte and a round of pastries for the station," he says, his voice thick.

My lips curl up in a smile, and I start to make his coffee without another word.

I feel his eyes on me as I work, and sure enough, when I let myself look up as the oat milk is frothing, he's watching me. The look I see there—possessive, wanting—warms my entire body, and I almost feel drunk with it. His hand brushes mine as he takes the cup, and my knees go weak.

"How do you want—I mean, *what* kind of pastries do you want?" I shake my head and try to focus, because I was about to ask this man how he wanted me in front of everyone. And not only are the Moms watching our every interaction with more than a little interest, but Megan just winked at me and Mrs. Withers is straight up aiming a cell phone our way. There's no doubt we'll be front-page news on the town's social media page.

The hunger in Price's eyes is unmistakable.

And maybe it's because I'm new at this, or maybe it's because some inner sex goddess has finally been unleashed (unlikely), but I decide to give everyone a show. So after I fill the box of pastries with Price's choices, I plate a croissant and a few fresh strawberries and motion for him to follow me.

He follows, sitting without hesitation.

"Hungry?" I ask, taking a seat at a table in a corner with my back to the shop.

He grunts. "You tell me, kitten."

My eyes widen at the term, and I have to clench my thighs together. Price smirks.

Determined to get the upper hand, I grab a strawberry and pull it to my mouth. For all I know, I'm going to look like a total idiot, but judging by the way Price's eyes track the strawberry like it's going to save his life, I suspect I won't. Holding it between my fingers, I put the berry to my lips and slowly suck it halfway in, letting my lips stay circled around it for a moment before biting into it and chewing. Price's eyes stay glued to my lips, so I dart my tongue out to lick the half-eaten berry before putting the rest in my mouth and discarding the leafy top on the plate.

Price shifts in his seat and his forearms flex.

Next, I tear a piece of the croissant off and raise it to my lips. After I swallow the bite, I suck the flakes off my thumb and fore-finger, then grab another strawberry.

He watches my every movement as I eat the fruit, his breathing shallow, and there's no question he's just as turned on as I am. I nip the pad of my thumb, then swirl the tip of my tongue around it.

Price swears softly, his gaze never leaving my face. "You are…" He chuckles darkly and shakes his head.

I look up through my lashes, my breath coming fast and nervous. "I am…what?"

He angles toward me, his hands cupped. "Not at all what I expected. But I need you to know something."

I lean forward, my heart thumping so loudly it's a wonder no one can hear it, and sink into his gaze, the food—the game I'm beginning to think I might be pretty good at—forgotten.

His eyes hold my own, and I read everything in there. Desire, yes, but also playfulness, sincerity, and something else I can't name, but is so unmistakably Price. He reaches a finger out to stroke the inside of my palm, then up to my wrist, and goose bumps erupt. "What you're doing here, at this table?"

I swallow, torn between the intensity of his silver-blue eyes and watching the way his finger circles the tiny blue veins beneath my skin. "Yeah?" I whisper.

"It's working." He smiles then, wide and open, like he's having *fun*, and I nearly swoon at the sight of it. To have this man's complete attention is a heady thing.

He stands, and I rise as well, walking into his outstretched arms in a daze. He pulls me tightly to him, and my breasts press into his chest. I have to tilt my head to meet his gaze, and I swear I'm the safest I've ever been. As though here, in his arms, I'll never know insecurity of any kind. Something inside of me glues together, something I didn't even know was cracked, and I take a deep breath.

"Kiss me?" he asks.

"Always," I reply, smiling against his lips as they meet mine.

He leaves, pastry box and latte in hand, and I practically float back to the counter.

Darius whistles low. "Damn, girl. No wonder that man's a firefighter—you need an extinguisher once he's left the room!"

I blush, but it's light. "He's...yeah."

Darius chuckles and looks at me affectionately. "You're falling fast, aren't you?"

Shrugging, I say, "How could I not?" Because it's always been him. And the way he looks at me, the kindness and acceptance and safety I feel with him, it's everything I've always wanted, in the man I've always wanted.

# CHAPTER 24
# JODI

IT SHOULDN'T BE a shock when Jess saunters into the Daily Dose the next day after lunchtime, but it is.

"Jodi!" she squeals, drawing the notice of absolutely everyone in the shop.

As usual, she's made certain to be worthy of the attention. Jess is the epitome of Nashville new country chic, with honey-blond hair falling in luscious waves down her back, and her face made up and contoured to within an inch of its life. She's wearing a short flowy dress and cowboy boots that I'm willing to bet are super-pricey Luccheses, but on her arm is the same canvas tote she's carried since her senior year of high school. It's the tote that makes my stomach unclench, because it reminds me that underneath this hardly recognizable exterior, she's still my baby sister, even if I want to strangle her oblivious self sometimes.

"Hi, Jess." I walk around the counter to give her a hug. She smells like expensive perfume, fruity and breezy, but to be fair, she's *always* smelled like that. Before I can stop myself, I default to the sister I've always been. "Did you eat? I only have muffins at this point in the day, but they're yours if you want them."

She smiles, but it doesn't reach her eyes. "Honestly, I could use a nap. Could I go…?" She gestures upstairs.

I fight the annoyance that flares. "It's a disaster up there, remember? Electrical fire?" I prompt.

Her shoulders slump. "Oh. Right. You told me that. Well, what about the other place you're staying? I can go there?"

"Is that Jess Bristol?" Kerry jumps up from the Mom table and bolts over. "Oh my goodness, I didn't even recognize you!"

Jess transforms in front of my eyes, a veneer of gloss seeming to move over her like a waterfall as she turns from me. "Kerry, oh my god!"

I back away and let them reconnect, knowing they'd gone to school together.

Darius raises an eyebrow when I return behind the counter. "*That's* your sister?"

"Sometimes I forget you didn't grow up here," I say. "But yeah. That's Jess."

He watches her thoughtfully before finally sucking air through his teeth. "Okay."

"That sounds ominous," I joke.

He shrugs. "I'm not going to talk bad about your family, but I *am* going to say that now I understand a lot more."

I narrow my eyes. "A lot more about what?"

He shrugs again and gestures at me. "You."

I gape at him. "What's that supposed to mean?"

He ignores me and smiles at the customer who's arrived.

After a while, Jess comes up to the counter. "So, can I go to wherever you're staying? Please?"

I hold out a piece of paper with the inn's address on it. "They're technically not even open yet and they're letting me stay there out of the goodness of their hearts," I say. "I don't know if Will is going to be there, but if he is, tell him you're my sister and that you're just there for the day."

"Who's Will? And why would I lie to him—I'm staying indefinitely."

My back straightens. "Indefinitely?"

"We'll talk later," she says, plucking the note from my hands with a snap of her gum.

As the door shuts behind her, Darius mutters, "Like I said."

I don't bother responding. It wouldn't matter. Because when it comes down to it, Jess is my sister. And I'll keep my mouth shut and do whatever it takes to keep my family happy. We've had enough sadness to last us a lifetime. So sure, it's not great that she's here, but that's okay. I'll help her get back on her feet, send her on her way, and everything will return to normal.

*I*'M EXHAUSTED, BUT nothing—and I mean *nothing* —is going to keep me from seeing that sweet woman's face when I get off-shift in thirty minutes.

Will and I have been more like passing acquaintances these past couple of weeks, now that we have a guest and Chief is starting to realize that we're serious about wanting to have a real go at making the bed-and-breakfast successful.

I get the feeling that Will wants it more than I do. My passion, the thing that I wake up and get excited about every single day, is being a firefighter. Becoming Assistant Fire Chief, and eventually, when Chief retires, being Fire Chief. But I don't think that's Will, and he's the one with the Assistant Chief title. The more I watch him, especially when he thinks no one is paying attention, the more I realize that this isn't his calling.

Doesn't mean I'm not going to crush him in the bake-off, though. I head to the fire house "gym," which is really just a room off the engine bay that we've thrown every kind of exercise equipment into that can fit, and speak of the devil. If the devil likes to chill in the Talladega Fire Department's gym.

"Hey, Hulk," I say to Will. Then I turn to Aaron and grin. "Hey, Not Hulk."

Aaron shakes his head. "You do realize it's never going to be funny, right?"

I pistol my fingers at him and increase the wattage of my smile. "It's always funny. You two just don't appreciate my humor."

Will grunts, curling a weight that I'll never do in my life and glaring at his reflection in the wall of mirrors like it's pissed him off. "There's another guest at the inn."

"Jodi's sister," I respond.

He lifts an eyebrow and assesses me through the mirror. "How'd you know?"

Aaron looks at him. "Will."

"What." He basically snarls it.

"He took Jodi on a date. Don't you think that maybe it means they're talking to each other regularly? That she would have cleared it with him?"

Will drops the weight and spins on me. "Why didn't you tell me?"

I hold my hands up. "About the date or the guest? Because you're looking like you're about to legit Hulk out on me, and I'd at least like Aaron to know the proper means of death to put on my headstone."

The humor works, because Will shakes his head. "How are you related to me?"

"You love me."

"You have to run these things past me when they happen," he shoots back.

I open my palms. "Honestly, I'm still not sure what *did* happen. Jodi texted that her sister needed a place to crash, and that she was heading to the inn. I told her we'd figure it out. But that was yesterday, and I've not really talked to her since then."

It was an absolute lie. We'd talked last night, and it'd been so stilted that I nearly crawled out of my skin. But I'd assumed it was because her sister was on the couch next to her. Reason number 593 why I wanted to get home to Jodi as soon as possible.

An alarm blares in my head at the way I thought of that. *Home to Jodi.* I shove it down. Now is not the time to inspect little boy Price's hopes and dreams.

Will grunts. "She needs to pay if she's staying."

"Quit being a growly bear. Let's figure out what's going on first. We're technically still not open for business."

"We will be in another two weeks. We have guests coming for the race."

Ah, Race Weekend. I loved those as a kid. People can say whatever they want about NASCAR, but the majority of those folks are hard-working, big-hearted people who just want to have a good time. And talk about seeing literally every type of person imaginable in one spot. As an adult, and as a firefighter in particular, things were a bit more…interesting. The track had its own crew, but they usually tagged crews in from around the state on a rotating basis, partly for extra bodies but also to spread the experience around. Let's just say that while we'd not had to put out literal fires, we'd done our share of metaphorical firefighting, especially at night in the pit once the racing was done. Shit got wild, and wasn't even close to family friendly.

"We'll get it sorted before the race," I say.

Will picks the weight back up to curl with his other hand and doesn't respond, his version of agreement.

With that settled, I decide against running on the treadmill and turn to go.

"Hold up," Aaron says, following me out.

I pause.

"Listen." He grips his neck and gives me a hangdog look. "I need to apologize for what I said the other day. About you and Jodi."

I raise my eyebrow. "Devon giving you shit?"

"More like Jodi," he says.

A burst of warmth spreads through me. "What'd she do?"

He blows out a breath. "Let's just say she told me where I could stick my opinions."

I laugh. "That doesn't surprise me at all." Over all our conversations, I'd learned Jodi was a hell of a lot more forceful than people gave her credit for. At least, she was with me, and I was inordinately proud to hear she'd been that way with Aaron.

"She definitely put me in my place," Aaron says with a grin. "But seriously. I'm sorry. I stuck my nose where it shouldn't have been, and was promptly called on it."

Clapping his shoulder, I say, "No problem, bro. We're good."

"Cool. Now to the next thing: Devon won't stop squealing about possible double dates."

I chuckle. "One thing at a time, Aaron." My phone rings and I check it. I point to it and wave goodbye at Aaron, then answer. "Monica?"

"Hey, Price," my agent says. "I know you said you were done modeling."

"I did, and I am," I say.

"Fair enough. I've always gotten the feeling you kept it pretty quiet, so that's why I'm calling."

I grab my duffel and sling it over my shoulder. "You're right. What's up?"

"One of the romance covers you did is rocketing up the charts."

I still. "What's that mean?"

She laughs. "It means we should've asked for a portion of the profits. But what it really means is that your face and chest are getting way more attention from American readers than ever before."

"Okay," I say, heading to my truck. "How bad could it be?"

"Oh, you sweet naïve boy," she chuckles. "The author has already reached out and asked if you'd be interested in attending one of the country's biggest romance novel conventions."

"Is that a thing?"

"It's absolutely a thing," Monica says. "But because most of your work has been in foreign markets—at your request, I'll remind you—it means that there's not been a huge audience state-side for you. Plus, you've always been clear that this is a side hustle."

"What are you getting at?" I start the engine. *Jodi, here I come.*

"I'm not sure how secret your secret is going to stay."

"Oh."

She laughs. "Yeah. *Oh.* Anyway, I just wanted to give you a heads up. You might have some readers at home who recognize you. That's all."

My stomach clenches at the thought. People have never had high expectations for me. They'd always taken one look and dismissed me as nothing more than a pretty boy who was good for one thing only, and treated me accordingly. If they found out I was a romance cover model, no one would ever take me seriously. Never mind the shit I'd get from my brothers and the guys at the station. And would any of it get in the way of my goal of eventually becoming Fire Chief?

"I gotta go," Monica says. "Call me if you change your mind."

She ends the call and a wave of cold fear crashes over me. *Jodi.*

What if Jodi finds out?

But I stop. What *if* Jodi does find out? So what? If anyone would give me the benefit of hearing me out, of not judging me, it's Jodi.

It'd still suck, but maybe...not as bad?

Feeling a little better, but still not great, I kill the engine and walk into the inn. And there, lounging on the couch, is my girl. Whatever doubts that had lingered absolutely vanish as she catches my eye and smiles. Because she's looking at me like she actually sees the person I am, and even better, she likes it. Whatever this thing is between us, I want more of it.

"C'mere," I say, practically growling the words as she unfolds herself from the couch to come toward me.

"Hi," she says, her tone shy but her hazel eyes telling an entirely different story as they eat me up, from shoes to face and back again.

I gather her into my arms and inhale her coffee and vanilla scent. Even on her one day off a week, that smell never quite leaves her skin. I'll never get enough of it.

"I missed you."

She wiggles in my arms, the laugh that escapes her hitting my neck in a puff of air. "I missed you, too."

"Jodi, where's the—oh, hello."

I turn and see who I figure must be Jodi's sister. I give her a friendly smile and extend my hand. "Jess, right?"

She closes her mouth and nearly stumbles down the stairs, but catches herself on the banister and grips it tightly. We shake and she says, "Um. Yeah. Yes, hi. Jess. You know that already. Sorry—I'm, Jesus, you're hot."

I bark out a laugh and look at Jodi, whose expression is unreadable. So I pull her to me, draping my arm over her shoulders, and as she glances up at me, I hope my eyes tell her that I'm hers and hers alone. Out loud, I say, "Thanks, but I'm taken." Then I squeeze Jodi to me and look back at Jess.

Jess points at us. "You two...?"

Jodi finds her voice. "Oh, we're not—I mean..."

Nope. No way am I letting her wiggle out of this. Especially when her sister is giving me the once-over. "We don't have an official title, but Jodi and I are definitely something."

Jodi coughs and reddens, and Jess's face clears. "That's amazing," Jess says. "Treat her like the angel she is," she tells me, her tone playful.

"I plan on it."

"Wait," Jess says. "You're *Price Joseph.*" Her eyes widen and she looks back at Jodi. "Holy shit, is he the guy you always—?"

"Okay then," Jodi interrupts her and claps her hands, "Now that we've covered introductions, let's move on." She glares at Jess, her mouth pinched and eyes blazing, and some kind of silent conversation flows between them that I can't figure out.

Jess must back down, because she gives me a bland smile. "So we were just talking about dinner. We'll cook here?"

"This is my first day in the house in a few days, so I have no idea what's here," I say. "Why don't we go to the burger spot in the square?"

Jess's face falls, even as Jodi is nodding. Jodi notices, and immediately backtracks. "Let's eat here. I'll whip us something up. I think Will went to the store yesterday."

Jess brightens. "That sounds great! I'll go upstairs and you just let me know when dinner is ready."

I stay with Jodi in the kitchen, the two of us moving around in it as though we've been doing it for years instead of mere weeks. I grab a beer and pour her a glass of the wine she prefers —something else I've learned about her—and do whatever she tells me.

But she's quiet. Too quiet. Normally, she'd be chattering away, telling me about her days at the shop or asking me about mine. Instead, she only speaks up when she's giving me a direction about the food.

Part of me wants to shake whatever it is loose and pull it out of her. But the other part of me holds back, wondering if maybe I spooked her with the way I acted earlier. *Aren't* we something?

I study her, how she concentrates as she sears the chicken, biting her lower lip in one moment and then blowing a strawberry-blond curl out of her face the next.

She glances at me. "What?"

I lean against the island counter and rest my palm in my hand. "You're pretty. And amazing," I say. Because I don't think she's ready to hear what I really want to say. Which is, *I like you. A lot. And I want to be something. I hope you do, too.*

She blushes. "Thanks."

We eat, and Jess dominates the entire conversation, talking about Nashville and the music industry and all the trials and tribulations, waving her hands to emphasize points and seeming to suck up all the air in the room. Beside her, Jodi grows even more quiet, shrinking into herself and becoming someone I don't recognize at all. The confident, bold woman I've come to know is nowhere to be seen. I hate it.

At the first chance I get, I say, "Jess, you have friends here, don't you?"

She pauses, her fork halfway to her mouth, and her eyes dim a bit. "Y-yes. I do."

I nod encouragingly. "And maybe you can go see them tonight? We've had an early dinner, after all."

"Well, it's Sunday," she hedges.

I wave it away. "You're young! What's a Sunday but just another day ending in Y? You should reach out. Go have fun."

Jodi watches me, her expression again unreadable.

*Come on, Jess,* I urge silently. *Leave.*

"Besides," I continue, "nothing fun is happening here. Definitely no fun. Bo-ring, is what we are."

Jodi finally seems to pick up what I've been laying down, and says haltingly, "He's right. What about Kerry? She's definitely at home."

"Clearly you two want me out of here," Jess huffs. "So fine, I'll go." She stands and pushes her chair back, dropping her napkin on her plate. "Don't wait up."

I watch her go, noting that she didn't even bother to clear her place at the table, and look over at Jodi.

Jodi exhales and slumps against the chair, sending a wave of protectiveness surging over me.

"You don't even have to say it. I know," she says, her voice dull.

And with that, Jess just took the number one spot on my shit list. But I put that aside and focus on Jodi instead. "Say that you are a goddess among women and that I don't deserve to be in the same room as you?"

Her lips tilt up.

"Say that your cooking is divine and that I'm just the lucky bastard who gets to eat it?"

"Price."

"That your oat-milk vanilla lattes are the absolute best thing I have ever put in my mouth?" I leer at her. "Other than you?"

She laughs and covers her face with her hands. "Oh my god, stop."

I stand and pull her to me, still laughing, and tip her chin up to give her a kiss. "Keep me company while I clean up from dinner?"

She nods and something in me shifts. I don't know the deal between the sisters, but the way that Jess seemed to make Jodi shrink into a fun-house version of herself tells me I'm not a fan of Jess.

# CHAPTER 26
# JODI

*I* TRY TO help him with the dishes, but he's not having any of it. So I perch on the island and watch him work, and damn if it's not the sexiest thing I've ever seen. Yes, I've seen him in turnout gear, but watching him clean the kitchen and load the dishwasher is a huge turn-*on*.

"So. Jess," Price says, looking over at me.

"Yep. Jess."

"Baby sister?"

I nod.

He scrubs a plate. "You know I'm the middle kid, too, right? Same as you."

A flash of heat forms behind my eyes and I clear my throat. I'm usually really good about not missing my brother, but with Jess blowing into town and being…Jess…the hole he left is bigger than usual tonight. Jason was the only one in my family who actually *saw* me. Actually gave a crap about me. "It's different," I hedge.

Price looks at me, his face open, gentle. "Tell me how."

My throat closes up. I swallow, over and over, trying to find the words. But I don't have them. How do I explain the feeling, the utterly unreasonable pressure to be the easygoing one no matter the cost, because the last time I let my emotions fly, it exploded in my face? The responsibility I feel to keep Jason alive in my heart, because no one else in my family wants to talk about him? How do I look at this man who has never let a person walk all over him, and confess that on top of everything else, Jess has always made me feel as though whatever is going wrong in her life is either all my fault, or is something that only I can help her fix?

Instead, I shake my head and shrug. "It just is."

He tilts his head. "Okay. Another time, then."

*Not if I can help it.*

Then I blink, and blink again, followed by a snort, because Price is wiggling his butt and looking over his shoulder at me to get my attention. "What in the world are you doing?" I ask, giggling.

He shuts the dishwasher and is standing between my legs in two strides, the heat of his hands on my hips instantly making my body take notice. "Trying to get you to laugh," he says, his eyes scanning my face. "And it seems it worked."

I cup his jaw, the softness of his beard tickling my palm, and stare into his silvery-blue eyes. "You know, all you have to do to make me laugh," I pause for effect, "is show me just how white your butt is."

His jaw drops and his eyes glitter. "Are you making fun of my ass?"

I suppress a laugh. "Nope. Just stating facts."

"Oh, that's it." So quickly I don't realize what's happening, he flips me over his shoulder and carries me through the house to his room.

I try to straighten my back and laugh. "What are you doing?"

He gives my butt a gentle pop. "Reminding you whose ass you're talking about, missy," he answers, his voice full of mirth.

In the bedroom, he bounces me into a seated position onto the bed, then braces his arms on either side of me. "What's this about my white ass?" His lips are tipped up in a smile.

But the nearness of him, feeling the mattress beneath me, smelling his unmistakable scent, all of it is scrambling my brain. "Um," is all I manage to say.

He quirks an eyebrow and leans away from me. "Is this okay?"

My head moves like a bobblehead. "Absolutely."

"Are you su—"

I put a finger on his lips, and his eyes flare. "Yes," I say. And even as my pulse is ratcheting up so high that he can probably see my heartbeat in my neck, I continue. "I want everything."

He kisses my finger, and as I let my hand fall, he leans forward to nuzzle my ear. "In that case, tell me how, exactly, you're aware of how white my ass is."

The sound that comes out of me is a laugh and a whimper. "The shower."

"Why do I think there was another time?" he says against my neck.

"When you, ah, kissed me that night in the kitchen...*shit*," I gasp as he nips my earlobe.

"Keep talking," he murmurs as his tongue snakes down the column of my neck. Then he sucks lightly on the hollow base of it, and I nearly come out of my skin. He chuckles softly, moving a hand up to my breast and swiping a thumb across my still-covered nipple.

My eyes roll to the back of my head, the ability to think straight quickly leaving. He is so fucking *good* at this. "I came down here, I don't know why."

"Liar," he says, and pinches my nipple.

I hiss in a breath at the painful pleasure he's delivered. "To see if you were as worked up as I was."

"Better. Keep talking." His lips are on my neck and his hands are unbuttoning my shirt.

"And you were…" My entire body is on fire. What are words?

"Jerking off?" he finishes, his voice low. He pushes the shirt off my shoulders, then tosses it on the floor.

"Mm-hmm," I manage. Is this happening? It's happening.

He kneels in front of me and pulls me to the edge of the mattress. "Fucking polka dots," he growls, burying his face between my breasts. "Did you hear me say your name, Jodi?" Then he folds the fabric of my bra down and closes his hot, wet mouth around my nipple.

My hips jerk forward. "Yes, oh god, yes," I breathe. I push my hands into his silky hair to hold him at my breast. "Don't stop."

His hands snake around to unclasp the bra and he pulls it off, still attending to my nipple, the feel of his tongue and teeth doing things to my body I didn't even know were possible. "And then?" he murmurs, popping off one breast and moving to the other.

"And then you got up to go to the shower, and I saw you —*fuck*, Price, that feels so good."

He chuckles darkly. "I knew I heard something that night. Don't you know you're not supposed to watch something like that without consent?"

He bites harder at my nipple and I yelp, then moan as he soothes it with his tongue. "You should apologize."

I don't hesitate. "I'm sorry."

He bites the other nipple, sending a spike of delicious heat to my center, then soothing once again with his tongue.

"*Price.*"

"You like that?"

"So much."

"Good."

Still kneeling, his hands slide down to unzip my skirt, the pads of his fingers rough with callouses. Wordlessly, I lift my hips and he pulls it off, along with my panties, and he lets out a soft curse.

"You are the most beautiful creature I've ever laid my eyes on," he says, then reaches back to pull his shirt off in one smooth motion, revealing his sun-kissed and inked chest.

Licking my lips, I say, "Right back at you, Price."

He hums in approval and runs his palms up my calves, then spreads my knees. His gaze snaps to what he's revealed, and he sits back. After a moment, he says, "Kitten, you have the prettiest pussy." Then his eyes meet mine. "Everything?"

The ache between my legs is so intense I think I might cry. "Everything," I say with a nod.

"Fuck me," he whispers reverently. Then he lifts my legs, bending them so my feet are on the mattress. "One word from you, and I stop. Understood?"

I lean back on my elbows. "I'm yours, Price."

His eyes darken. "And I'm going to make you forget your name." With that, he descends.

I've dreamed of this, fantasized about what it would feel like to have Price between my legs more times than I can count. And I've already learned my fantasies have nothing on reality, and I'll want this—want him—the rest of my days. With the first touch of his tongue flattening against my folds, I cry out in relief.

"Watch," he directs. "Watch me eat your pussy."

A bolt of heat spikes through me at his words, and I do exactly as he says. Holding my gaze, he licks up to my clit and swirls his tongue around it, and immediately I tense at the incredible sensation. This is nothing like the vibrator I have in my nightstand. He keeps going, moving his tongue all over, making it soft and then hard, flat and then pointed, and my legs shake with the effort of staying up.

"Let them fall, Jodi," he says.

So I do, spreading my legs and baring myself completely to him.

He grunts in approval, his eyes again meeting mine. "Beautiful." Then he redoubles his efforts, and I keep watching, even though his own eyes are closed as he works me. Again and again he licks, his tongue pleasuring me beyond anything I have ever known.

He pushes a finger into my entrance, and I hiss in pleasure.

"You're so tight," he murmurs against me. "But so wet for me, kitten. I want you to come."

"Yes," I gasp. His finger pushes in just a little more, and it feels as though it can't go farther, but he thrusts it in and out in time with his tongue, and I lose all sense of time and space. My walls clamp down as the orgasm rises, and he doesn't stop, his tongue still on me, and then he covers my clit with his mouth, sucking at the same time his finger thrusts. I detonate.

"Price!" I yell as the orgasm takes over. Wave after wave pulses through me, and I gasp for air as he works me through it. My entire body tingles, and a small laugh escapes me at the release. "Holy shit," I whisper. My limbs are heavy.

He stands, still very much dressed, and gazes down at me hungrily.

My blood singing, I push farther up the bed and rise on my elbows. "Let me see you," I say, my voice soft.

Wordlessly, his eyes hooded, he undoes his pants. They fall to the ground, revealing navy boxer briefs. He pushes those down, his cock springing free, and my mouth goes dry.

He chuckles. "You definitely know how to make a man feel good, looking at me like that."

I tear my eyes away from his cock to meet his gaze. "White ass aside, you are without a doubt the most beautiful man I've ever seen."

The laugh that bursts out of him is full of genuine surprise. He throws his head back, his abs tight as he shakes with laughter, his pretty penis just bobbing away, and I can't help but laugh, too. When he looks back at me, his eyes are bright and cheery, and I lose my breath. Because there he is, an absolute dead sexy specimen of a man who's just given me an orgasm, and he's laughing and happy to be here, with me, and the whole moment is so incredibly *Price* that my chest squeezes at the rightness of it.

I'm also absolutely certain, beyond any doubt, that I have fallen head over heels in love with this man.

Still smiling broadly, Price pulls me to my feet so he can pull the covers back, then he guides me back onto the cool, soft sheets. He crawls in and covers us, and briefly I panic that he's going to try to make me go to sleep before we do anything.

He must read it on my face, because he says, "Just warming you up, kitten," while snuggling close.

Sure enough, I do indeed have goose bumps all over, but I think we've established that the world could be coming down around me and I wouldn't care, as long as I was naked with this man.

I cup his jaw and bring him to me for a kiss, tasting myself on his tongue. It's not what I expected—none of this is—and then Price's hand is gripping my breast and our legs are tangling together, and I feel the silk of his shaft against my belly.

I breathe in, our tongues slicking across each other, and I don't think I'll ever be as happy and content as I am now. Here, on the same precipice that millions have beheld, I am so grateful it's him.

"Talk to me," he says, pulling away to gaze at me. He trails a hand lazily down my stomach and pushes into my folds, and I moan.

"I want you," I say.

"More."

"Your mouth is magic, your fingers..." I break off on another gasp as he breaches my entrance again. "So good." I reach down to his cock, exploring it. It jumps beneath my touch, and I grip it, all while Price's own fingers are buried between my legs. My hold on his cock tightens and I pump up and down, and a sound breaks from him. "Good?" I ask.

He kisses me lightly. "Any touch from you is good, Jodi." He shifts then, rolling over to grab a condom from the bedside table.

"I want to watch," I say.

He nods, kneeling on his haunches to open the foil packet. I watch, fascinated, as he rolls it on, then meet his eyes. They're a deep silver now, the irises blown. He settles himself between my legs.

"Oh," I breathe out. Because my fantasies never dared to get to this point, to imagine the glorious, solid weight of him as he cages my head with his arms.

He smiles, his face so close to mine he's blurry. "You okay?"

I nod. "Absolutely."

He takes my mouth with his, giving me a deep, passionate kiss while one hand squeezes my breast. He trails hot kisses down my neck, pausing to give each nipple a kiss, then continues down my belly until his head is again between my thighs, his tongue lapping at me, and I'm panting. Need, desperate empty need, burns through me in moments. He pushes a finger into me, and it goes easily. "More," I say between whimpers. "Please."

Another finger, stretching me, and it's good, so good, but I know there's more to be had, and I buck my hips in a rhythm I have no control over.

"Fuck, kitten," Price says, then kisses his way back up to me, his fingers still inside me.

I pull him to me, needing his lips on mine desperately, and as we kiss, I feel him position himself at my entrance. I spread my legs wider, the ache so intense that it's almost painful. "Now," I say, not even knowing what I'm asking for. "*Please.*"

His forehead resting on mine, he pushes in just a little.

I gasp.

"Breathe, Jodi," he urges.

I inhale, then on an exhale, he pushes in a little more.

"So tight," he grits.

And it is. There's a burning sensation at being so stretched, but at the same time, it feels good. "More," I say, holding his gaze.

He gives me what I want, pushing in farther, squeezing his eyes shut for a second before ripping them open and meeting mine once more. We breathe together, then he pulls out and pushes back in, going a little farther. And again, bit by bit.

"Give me all of you," I whisper.

"I'm trying not to hurt you," he says, his voice tense with the effort.

I thrust my hips up, and I take a little more. "It's okay." Because it is. There's some discomfort but the ache of need overrides it. "Give me your cock, Price. I need it. I need *you*."

His eyes widen appreciatively and he nods, then he kisses me. And as his tongue slicks across mine, he withdraws, then thrusts.

I gasp into his mouth as a flare of pain ricochets inside me. "Price," I hiss, squeezing my eyes shut.

"Look at me, Jodi," he whispers.

I open my eyes. His gaze is tender, even as his arms shake with the effort of holding himself back. The pain subsides as my body adjusts to him, and I nod, biting my lip.

He pulls out a bit, then pushes again, and my hips rise to meet him, the burning sensation easing. He curses softly as he buries himself to the hilt.

I exhale and my eyes flutter shut. "Yes. God, yes."

"Kitten," he grits out, then begins to roll his hips.

I moan. I'm so full, so incredibly full, and something deep within me pulses.

"*Fuck*," he says. Then he pulls out and pushes in, again and again.

On instinct, I pull my knees higher, changing the angle, meeting his thrusts. It's incredible.

"Good?" he asks, his lips tilted up.

I bob my head, all pain gone. "Now I see what all the fuss is about."

He chuckles. "There's a lot more to do." He pushes in and I groan. "And I intend to show you all of it."

He buries himself in me again, and sounds of pleasure break from my throat. I grip his back, feeling the muscles ripple, and slide my hands down to his ass. He nips at my neck, then raises up. "Watch," he commands.

I look down, taking in where we're joined, how his cock disappears into me again and again, and it's the hottest thing I've ever seen.

"Touch yourself, Jodi. Show me what you like."

Again I obey, moving my fingers around my swollen clit. I hitch a breath and curse in pleasure.

"There you go. Look at you. Look at how you take care of yourself. You're so tight, so perfect, baby. Do you think you can come for me? Can you do it?" His voice is low, dark, and sensual.

I whimper. I've lost all language. All I know is pleasure, and Price, and the tautness of his stomach as he's thrusting into me, the dirty words he keeps whispering, the fullness I feel, the intensity of it, and suddenly I'm there again, the swirls of feeling all tightening, swirling, condensing into a ball before exploding. "Price!" I yell his name as I come, and I'm gripping his back as his own rhythm speeds up.

"Yes, yes, yes," he croons, soft and gentle even as he fucks me through my orgasm and chases his own. Within moments he finds it, pushing into me and holding, gritting his teeth and cursing, his eyes still never leaving mine.

Afterwards, we lay there, the only sound our breaths mingling, our chests heaving into each other, and the emotion that overtakes me is so sudden that I'm surprised when a tear threatens to fall.

Price frowns. "Did I hurt you?"

I grip my arms to stop him from moving. "No," I say. "No. You did the opposite."

He relaxes, but his eyes search my face.

I try to find the words, searching for a way to tell him that he's changed my life irrevocably, and he's the best thing that has ever happened to me. That I'm so glad he's the one I did this with first, and that I will always want him to be the only one whose body touches mine. That I have fallen for him, and I keep falling, so much faster than I should because I have always loved him in some small way, and now it's growing so quickly that it's terrifying, but beautiful all at the same time.

He waits patiently, the roughened pads of his fingers gently tracing my face as he studies me.

And that's the other thing. His patience, quiet and steady thoughtfulness, and his tenderness, and…all of him.

Finally, I say, "Do you have any idea how incredible you are?"

Surprise moves across his face, but his lips quirk up. "That is not what I expected you to say."

I grin, then wince a little as he shifts on top of me.

He's rolling off me in a flash. "Figured that might happen."

"I'm fine, I swear! Just a little sore." Physically *and* emotionally, but I don't tell him that.

"Don't move." He sits up, but before he stands, he admonishes, "And no making fun of my white ass, either."

A laugh bubbles out of me, and it turns into a wheezing cackle as he walks to the bathroom, shaking his butt as he does so. But I quiet when he returns with a warm washcloth and tucks me back into the bed.

I still as he cares for me, luxuriating in the comforting heat of the cloth between my legs.

"We'll still need a shower," he says, "but I thought this would feel good."

This man. I am so in love with him. "Thank you," I whisper, then pull him to me for a kiss.

## CHAPTER 27
## PRICE

*I* COME AWAKE with Jodi snuggled against me the next morning, sleeping soundly, her body rising and falling with every deep breath. With a glance at the bedside clock, I know her alarm is going off any moment, so I will my eyes to see more than what the dark allows. There's nothing but shadows, so I use my imagination, seeing the pale creaminess of her skin, the way freckles scatter across her chest and down her stomach, not so many that I can't count, but enough so that, with time, I can learn their numbers. Make constellations. Lick and kiss and worship each and every one of them.

I can barely believe my luck, that this astonishing woman gave herself to me. I'm absolutely certain I'm not worthy of her, of the trust I see in her eyes, but I'll do everything in my power to be worthy going forward.

She sighs, a tiny whimper escaping her, and throws an arm across my chest. I trail my fingers up her bare skin, knowing by the way her breathing changes that she's waking up.

The alarm on her phone dings, and I reach to shut it off as Jodi stretches against me. "Good morning," I whisper, then kiss her forehead.

"Mmm, good morning," she responds, her voice breathy and sexy as hell with sleep.

I shift us, putting her back against the mattress and lying on my side, letting my hand move up and down her silky, warm skin. "How are you feeling?"

"Sore, but in a good way," she says.

I'd suspected as much. My girl had pulled me to her a second time last night, and I'd been powerless to resist her. I tip my head, finding her lips and kissing them, taking the invitation to go deeper as she opens her mouth to me, soft and sweet. Her arms wrap around me, and the sound that escapes the back of her throat makes my dick jump against her leg.

She pulls away with a soft giggle. "Sorry."

"Don't ever be sorry for that," I admonish.

Another noise, this time a tiny whimper. "I want to stay in bed all day."

I kiss her. "You *are* the boss. You could make it happen."

She scoffs, her small hands sliding down my chest and around my back, tracing my body, learning it the same way I'm learning hers. "I own the only coffee shop in at least five miles. The townsfolk would riot."

"You might be right."

"So, kiss me one more time."

I slide down the bed and spread her legs. "Oh, kitten, I'm doing more than that." And the gasp that escapes her as I put my mouth on her is one that will live in my head all day.

FTER SHE LEAVES to open the coffee shop, I lace up my shoes. The early April morning is crisp, and as I

settle into the rhythm of a three-mile run, I can't help the broad smile that seems plastered across my face. *She's mine.* She'd come out of nowhere, and yet it was like she'd been there the whole time, waiting for me to get my head out of my ass and see her.

Remembering what my brother said, I suspect that's exactly how it went. Warmth unfurls itself inside me, curling around my heart and squeezing. I'm the luckiest bastard in the world.

I wave to Mrs. Withers, who's probably on mile four of her near-daily speed walking routine, and she waves back, giant sunglasses and a broad-rimmed hat covering her face. She's dressed in her standard 1980s gear of windbreaker and parachute pants. "Morning," I say as I near her.

"Good morning, young man," she says, a smirk on her face as she gestures at my chest. "Thank you!"

I chuckle as I pass her and throw "You're welcome!" over my shoulder.

It's a joke between the two of us that has gone on for years, ever since she got a little tipsy at the bar one night and confessed she felt she needed to thank me for all those years of running shirtless around the town. I'd laughed and responded she could start saying it from then on, and damned if she hadn't, no matter if we were bundled up in winter gear or if I was indeed running around shirtless. Today, she'd gotten an eyeful of t-shirt.

My usual route takes me past the Daily Dose and fire station, and Aaron is stepping out of the coffee shop as I approach. He waves me over.

"Good morning," I huff.

He gestures to his phone. "Is this you?"

Instantly my heart rate kicks up even higher, and it has nothing to do with the fact that I've been running. "Is what me?"

"On the cover of this book." He aims the screen toward me.

*Shit.* It's me, all right, ravishing a swooning Adriana. The scene was meant to be a nod to 90s-era Regency clinch covers, so I'm in a gauzy, unbuttoned tunic that's falling off one shoulder, and pants that leave nothing to the imagination. I didn't know which shoot the cover was from, and knowing it's one with a former flame just made things a lot more uncomfortable. I shift on my feet.

Then I look at the title and nearly choke.

"It *is*, isn't it?" Aaron says, his eyes wide. "Holy shit."

I wipe the sheen of sweat off my face and pin him with my best glare. "Don't. Say. *Anything*."

He zooms in on the photo. "Oh, this is so good. Wait till Will sees this. Did they airbrush your abs?"

I tug him away from the coffee shop windows. "You will not tell Will. You will not tell anyone."

He gives me an assessing look. "Care to tell me what the hell's going on?"

I sigh. "How'd you find that?"

He shrugs. "It was an ad when I was looking for something. It was impossible to miss your ugly face, so I clicked it."

Shit. How many more people were going to see this?

He continues. "Jodi knows, right?"

My eyes widen. "No one knows."

Instantly, his demeanor changes. "Why not." It's not a question.

I lean closer and lower my voice. "Because what am I supposed to tell her? Or tell anyone, for that matter?"

"I don't know, Price. You tell me." Then realization seems to dawn. "So *this* is how you had the money to buy Gigi's place and turn it into a bed-and-breakfast."

I nod. "And now I'm done. No more modeling."

"Modeling? So you've done this for more than just the one book cover?"

I grip the back of my neck. "Yes."

"All the trips—that's what you were doing?"

"Yes. Are you done with all the questions?" I ask.

"Not even close," he says. "I'm impressed you were able to keep it a secret this long. Not when you love a good piece of gossip as much as the next person in this crazy town."

"Okay, one, that's not true. And two, this is my life we're talking about, not some random piece of gossip I heard at the coffee shop or somewhere else."

He's not letting up. "How much money have you made doing this? It's pretty perfect for you. Why bother doing anything else?"

"What's that supposed to mean?" I growl.

He pulls a face. "Oh, come on. All the peacocking you do, this is perfect for you. I'm just saying I'm not surprised, is all."

My chest hollows out. My own brother still doesn't see me for who I really am. "We're done here."

I turn away, but Aaron grabs my arm. "Hang on. Jodi."

I stop. "What about her?"

"She is my friend. Whatever it is you've been doing with her—"

"Watch it," I say, gritting my teeth.

"No," he shoots back. "Because this is bullshit. You shouldn't be hiding this from her. And to think that me and Will and Chief were rooting for you. Did you fuck her?" He points at Adriana.

My pause is all he needs.

"*Dammit*, Price. How many side pieces do you have? Is Jodi just the nice one for when you're in town?"

Rage floods my system and I step close to him, going toe to toe. "Don't you ever insinuate something like that again. I would never, *never*, cheat on anyone, least of all Jodi. And it pisses me off that you think so little of me that you'd even consider it."

Surprise flickers across his face. A beat later, he raises his hands. "Fine. You're my brother. This is your deal. But Jodi is a *good girl*. Don't you dare fuck this up."

Without another word, he turns and heads to the station.

I pull my phone out and pull the book up. Why did the cover have to be one with Adriana? We'd seen each other off and on, but I broke it off last year when I started focusing on improving myself.

Zooming in closer, my stomach sinks. The book has seventy-five hundred reviews. Out of who knows how many purchases.

Shit.

$\mathcal{P}$RICE, WILL, AARON, Chief, and Matt all watch as I set up the competition pastries on top of the display case. "Will's are here"—I point to the right—"and Price's are here," I finish, pointing to the left. Then I lay out the pencils and notepad and jar for votes.

"No favoritism," Chief says. "Just because this one here's your boyfriend, don't go telling people to vote for him."

I cough, not knowing how to respond to Chief's declaration, but a glance at Price tells me he's not in the least concerned about being called my boyfriend. In fact, judging by the warm smile he's shooting me, I'd venture to say he likes it.

Belatedly, I realize they're all staring at me and waiting on a response. "Oh. Sorry. No favoritism. I promise!"

I'd assigned them what I thought was a pretty even competition: two pastries, banana nut bread and lemon poppyseed muffins, both of which were standard offerings at the shop. Over the last week, the bed-and-breakfast's kitchen had seen a near-constant stream of activity, because whenever one of them was off-shift, they were baking.

Unless Price was ravaging me, which happened. A lot. I manage to suppress a groan at the memory of him above me this morning, whispering the dirtiest things in my ear while he brought me to orgasm.

"When will we have a winner?" Matt asks, dragging me back to reality.

I shrug. "They baked enough pastries to get me through at least two days. Today's offerings are the lemon poppyseed, and tomorrow we'll do banana nut."

"Who's watching the votes?" Will asks.

I shoot him a smile. "Darius."

On cue, Darius emerges from the back. "Don't worry, boys, I'll make sure everything's nice and fair. No cheating."

Will grunts and glares at Price, who winks and smiles in return. "Quit being a grumpapotomus, Will. Do you need a hug?"

"Fuck off," Will grumbles. "This is serious."

"Nope. That's it. I'm coming in." Price latches onto Will, who immediately disentangles himself with little effort. Price smiles as Will shakes him off, but I see the shadow that crosses his face. My chest squeezes at the thought of my sweet Price, just wanting hugs and love.

*My sweet Price.* I am a goner. If it were middle school, I would have doodled his name all over my folders.

Ha. I *did* doodle his name all over my folders in middle school. Honestly, it's a wonder no one other than my sister has made the connection between my little girl crush and the sinfully hot firefighter in front of me.

The door to the shop opens and Jess walks in. All the guys swivel to her as one, and she stutters to a stop, her gaze landing on each of us in turn. "What?"

"She can be the first one to vote," Price says.

"Come on up." Chief waves her up. "How you been, Jess? Nashville needed a break from you?"

Her eyes flit away. "Something like that."

I fight the urge to press her for more. Not here. She's not

said anything this past week, and has managed to make herself scarce anytime I think I'll be able to actually talk to her.

"Get back to work, guys," I say. "No one wants to vote with an audience."

Price catches my eye and jerks his thumb to the side. As the men start to disperse, I step out from behind the counter and into Price's solid arms. He inclines his head and I tip up to meet him for a kiss, his soft beard tickling the skin around my lips.

"How's it going up there?" he asks, indicating the renovations on my apartment above us.

I exhale. "Slowly. Larry's going as fast as he can, but there's only so much he can do when the electrician's still working."

"You can stay with me as long as you want," Price says, squeezing my hips.

"Yeah, I think your brother's getting tired of it," I say.

"My brother will deal with it." Price's eyes glint as he speaks, and I've learned that means he's dead serious.

I smile and accept the kiss he gives me. "Get back to work."

He rolls his eyes. "It's slow."

I swat at his taut stomach. "That's a *good* thing."

"It is, but it gets boring when there's nothing to do. It's much more fun to kiss you." He grins and steals another kiss. "Like that."

I giggle, stepping out of his arms and shooing him back to work. He leaves, and as I start back toward the counter, I realize Will and Jess are still here. Jess is biting a nail and eyeballing the pastries, while Will is simply being Will.

Meaning he's scaring the shit out of my sister and doing a good job of intimidating me as I near him. I'm not *as* scared of him as I used to be—seeing him in Christmas pajamas in the kitchen has helped—but he's got the same look he had that first day we talked about payment for me staying at the inn.

I nod at him, knowing he'll say whatever he needs to say without me inviting him to do so.

"The race is next week," he starts.

I take my place back behind the counter and Jess stays off to the side, a fresh nail in her mouth.

"And the room she's been staying in is booked. Starting in two days."

"You can't kick me out—" Jess starts.

Will raises a singular eyebrow in her direction, and she shrinks back. "I didn't say I was. But that room is booked. And you haven't paid for the week you've been in it, either."

She squeaks and looks at me. "I thought it was no charge, since," she raises a palm. "You know." Her arm drops.

"There is no *you know*," Will intones, then shifts his attention back to me. "Full rate for this one, and she needs to be out of the room tonight."

Jess turns pleading eyes on me. I swallow. "I'll pay for it, Will. But separate from anything else." I don't want Price knowing I'm paying for her. I can't face his wordless acceptance. Not when I can't accept it myself.

Will narrows his eyes. "Explain."

I scramble. "For the insurance," I say, hoping he'll buy the vague term. "Just let me pay for her room when I get there after I close the shop."

He nods, then turns and leaves without another word. I almost sag against the counter.

"He's scary," Jess says.

I narrow my eyes at her. "What is going on, Jess?"

She flushes. "Nothing."

I stare at her.

She presses her lips into a thin line and looks away. "It's nothing. I'm just…going through some stuff. Okay? I don't want to talk about it."

I scan her, taking in her limp hair and the purple shadows beneath her eyes. She's not nearly as glossy as she was a week ago. But something in me stands up and screams, and it's loud enough for me to say, "Either tell me what's going on, or leave. You're not staying with me."

Immediately, her eyes glass up with tears. "You can't do that."

I cross my arms. I actually *won't* do it, but I refuse to let her see that. "I can, and I will. You tell me you're coming to visit, then you get here and suddenly it's not a visit, but you're staying indefinitely. What the fuck is going on?"

She flinches at me cussing at her. "I just need time. Okay?"

"No."

"Jodi," she whines.

This is normally where I'd relent, but I envision telling Price, and my resolve strengthens. "Either tell me what's going on, or pack your stuff and go."

She stares at me as a tear rolls down her cheek. When I don't speak, she finally says, "I didn't...I didn't actually record the demo."

I knit my brow. "But Mom sent you money."

"I, um, I used it to pay my back rent."

My brain skids to a stop. "What does that mean, Jess?"

She wraps her arms around herself, shrinking in front of me. "It means I'm a total failure. It means I'm totally broke, and the only things I own are my guitar, my clothes, and my piece of shit car." She laughs bitterly. "I'm a walking country song."

"But weren't you doing something else? Some other job?" I prompt, still not understanding how all this could have gone so badly for her.

"I got fired."

The beginning of a massive headache starts to form behind my eyes.

"So I'm here," she continues. "Because I literally don't know what else to do, and you're my sister, and I thought..."

She doesn't finish the sentence, but I know what the implication is. *Be the non-confrontational girl. Do whatever it takes to keep the peace.* I sigh, the fight sagging out of me. "Okay."

Her face clears. "So it's settled. I'll move into your room."

I give her a tight smile and fight the nausea that roils in my stomach at the way I just rolled over.

She points a pert finger at the cut-up pastries. "Free?"

I want to ask her if she would have had the money to pay if they weren't free, but instead, I lift the glass toppers. "Try a bite of each, then vote for the one you like best." I'm at least getting that out of her.

She does as I ask—easy for her to do now that she's gotten her way—then wheedles Darius into a latte.

I watch her leave, seemingly without a care in the world. How is it that she can turn her emotions off and on like that, and I'm the one who ends up being the one feeling crappy?

Sighing, I pull out my phone.

"Jodi?" Mom says when she answers.

"Everything's okay," I say, keeping my words smooth and calm. Mom's hated us initiating calls with her ever since Jason died.

"Good," she breathes, the fear leaving her voice but the concern still there. Probably because I never call her; I usually text.

"How are you?" I ask. "How's Gran?"

"We're fine. Gran's up and moving today without too much pain. Thinking of walking to the beach in a little while."

She doesn't say anything else. Doesn't ask how I am, or how the renovations are going on the apartment. Doesn't ask anything. The disappointment is bitter, but honestly? I should know better. "I wanted to ask you about Jess," I say.

I hear the sharp intake of breath and can almost see her straighten, see the way her pale blue eyes widen behind her glasses at the mention of her precious youngest daughter. "Is she okay?"

I can't help but wonder if Mom ever has this kind of conversation with Jess about me. But I know the answer before the thought even finishes: no. Never. I check my feelings and aim for what I called Mom for in the first place. "What I mean is, she's done a whole bunch of nothing since she got here."

"What do you mean, got there?"

My eyebrows lift in surprise. "Jess is living here. She didn't tell you? Came to crash with me a week ago and has no plans to leave."

Mom titters. "I'm sure you're mistaken."

I blindly scrub at the counter with a towel, knowing if I don't do something with my hands, I'll throw something. "Pretty sure I'd know if my sister was living with me, Mom," I say dryly.

"But she just recorded that demo—I sent her the money." She sounds almost terrified, as though she's facing demons only she can see.

I open my mouth to say it. To tell Mom that Jess didn't record the demo, that she supposedly used the money to pay off her rent before rolling over and giving up. I want to say so many things, not just about Jess but about Dad, and Mom, and Jason, and how unfair all of it is, even though I don't even know what 'it' is. But the words stick in my throat, and I press my lips together, hoping the bile stays down.

"Are you sure?" Mom prompts.

I swallow and take a steadying breath, letting go of the towel and hanging my head. "She is living here, with me."

"Well, I'm sure everything is fine," Mom says. "She's just visiting you. Not *living* with you, for goodness' sake. Why would she do that? She's just waiting on the demo to get picked up like she told me. Maybe saving some rent money, working with you at the shop. There's a process, you know? And it'll all be great. Did you know she met Faith Hill in the grocery store?"

I grip the phone, with absolutely no energy to pick apart everything in Mom's response that was pure fantasy. I don't think she'd listen, anyway. "When was the last time you talked to Jess?"

"When she called about making the demo," Mom answers.

I do the math. At least a month. Meaning there had to be more to this than what Jess was telling me. Or she'd run out of options before finally coming home.

"I should go," Mom says, her voice clear as a summer blue sky.

"Right." And before I can tell her I love her, she disconnects.

*S*WEAT BEADS ON my brow as I tap out a beat against my uniform pants. Darius stands in front of us, the pink envelope in his hands holding the results of the pastry vote.

The past two days had been torturous. Absolutely the worst. I'd been on-shift, which meant no Jodi. I'd gotten to the shop and FaceTimed with her a few times, but just like the last time I was on-shift, she shut down a bit and seemed to withdraw. I think it's got something to do with her sister, but until I get some time with her, just the two of us, I won't know.

On top of that, Talladega residents were mostly managing to stay safe and healthy and we'd had longer than usual gaps of downtime between calls. I'd offered to help Will organize the station's HR files, but he'd looked at me like I'd grown a second head. His position as Assistant Chief meant most of the paperwork fell to him, and I knew he hated it. Even Chief, who heard the entire conversation, didn't say a thing. If I want to be the chief one day, then I have a lot of work to do, starting with getting someone to take me seriously. Which means I need to talk to Chief himself.

Darius clears his throat and Jodi, standing beside me,

threads her fingers into mine and squeezes. Her smile is relaxed, easy. The opposite of me right now.

"And the winner is…" Darius looks at all of us in turn. Jodi, me, Aaron, Chief, and Will. Then he pulls the paper out and studies it like he wasn't the one who wrote on it a few minutes ago. "Will Joseph!"

Figures.

Jodi tightens her grip on me and I shoot her a quick grin, holding back the disappointment because there, on my brother's face, is an honest to god smile. Will looks *happy*. And what am I supposed to do with that? Sighing, I hold my hand out. "Congrats, broseph."

Will keeps smiling as we shake. "You had me worried," he says. "I tried one of your test batches, and you've gotten a lot better."

"But not enough to keep baking," Aaron makes certain to say.

I roll my eyes. "You ever going to stop acting exactly like a younger brother?"

"Where's the fun in that?" Aaron counters. "It's way more fun torturing you."

I study Will, shoving the disappointment at losing down another few feet. His shoulders are relaxed, and he's not as broody as he normally is.

Aaron, on the other hand, has spent the past week glaring at me nearly every chance he gets. He's waiting on me to tell Jodi about the cover model thing, and I know I need to.

To make matters worse, I got a text yesterday from none other than Adriana. "Just checking in," she said, to see how the sudden fame was treating me. I'd shut the conversation down as quick as possible. I wasn't interested in talking to her about anything, least of all the cover.

I need to speak to Jodi. I know that.

Suddenly, it all clicks. First, I'll talk to Chief about taking on more responsibility at the station. Once I've got him on board, then I'll tell Jodi. I want something for her to be proud of, something that I've done with my head and not my body. And maybe winning the pastry competition wasn't going to make her proud of me anyway, but doing more at the station? That definitely will. And it'll ease the sting of me not telling her about modeling.

Jodi wraps her hand around my waist, pulling me back to reality. "I still like your baked goods," she says, her eyes mischievous as she tugs me down for a kiss.

I snort. But then I inhale her scent and lose myself for a few seconds as her soft lips meet mine, amazed at how it takes so little for her to make me feel better.

I shake it off. Moping won't do me any good, and besides, I have Jodi smiling up at me, the shop's about to close, and I'm officially off-shift.

"So now what?" I ask Will.

He grunts, quickly returning to his usual self.

"Are you the official B&B baker? The pastry maker extraordinaire for Shirley's Inn? Are you going to start walking around with flour in your hair?"

"One time," he counters. "*One time* last week I had flour in my hair."

God, he's fun to rile. "It works for you—the pastry chef thing."

"I'm making them for our customers. That's it." His tone shuts the conversation down, and even though I want to see just how serious he is about baking, I let it drop.

The bell dings over the door as someone walks in. Given how close it is to closing, I expect Jodi to tell them she's done for the day, but she says no such thing as the customer nears.

"Let's go, guys," Chief says, rounding everyone up to head back to the station. He claps me on the shoulder. "Tough break, Price."

I almost say a joke about how all the baking would be bad for my figure, but manage to keep my mouth shut. *Making progress.* "Thanks, Chief. I'd like to talk with you about something."

He gets serious. "You're not quitting?"

"No way." I shake my head. "The opposite, actually."

He nods and says, "Well, you know where to find me. Not like you need an appointment."

The woman walking in makes eyes at Aaron and Will before turning to me, and it's easy enough to see where this is about to go. I tense.

She continues her advance toward the counter. "Hello there," the woman purrs at me.

There was a time I'd have preened under this kind of attention. But now? No. Especially not with Jodi watching. I nod at the woman, hoping the disinterested look on my face is enough to shut it down.

Instead of ordering, she saunters closer, absolutely confident in the blonde bombshell package she offers. She stops a couple feet from me, too close for my taste, and I take a step back. She smirks. "I'm Layla. You're a firefighter?"

I nod again, still giving her nothing.

"Can I get you a drink?" Jodi's voice rings almost too loud in the empty shop.

Layla slowly turns her head to Jodi, still not moving, and says, "Caramel Frappuccino, please."

Jodi scowls. "This isn't Starbucks."

Layla sighs. "Fine. Something like that, then." She waves her hand at Jodi dismissively before turning her full attention back to me. Grabbing a lock of long hair in her hands, she twists it in what I guess she thinks is a sexy move, then says, "What's your name?"

"Not interested," I say. I step around her, my skin crawling, and make way for my sanctuary: Jodi.

Jodi, who has her back turned, and who is hopefully putting

a laxative in the woman's frozen coffee drink. She ignores me as she finishes the drink and gives it to Layla, whose name is probably not Layla at all, and collects payment.

Undaunted, Layla strides to me, frozen drink in hand, and holds out a card. "You should call me," she coos. "We'd have a lot of fun."

My stomach turns, and I shove my hands in my pockets. "No thanks," I bite out.

She raises a perfectly arched eyebrow. "I'll leave it here if you change your mind." She drops her card onto the display case and leaves.

Jodi still doesn't look at me, but walks to the door. "You should go."

I tilt my head, considering. Then I meet her at the front, wrapping my arms around her stiff body and waiting patiently for her to cave in and look up at me. When she does, I see unease written across her face. I cup her chin and run my thumb lightly over her lips, the red lipstick faded enough to show the freckles beneath. "I love these, you know."

Her brow knits.

"Your freckles. The ones on your lips, especially. Although the ones on your neck are pretty spectacular, too." I give her a light kiss, and she returns it, but I still sense the wariness. "Actually, I love all of them. I love that every time I'm close to you, I find new ones. That I can make up my own personal constellations with the ones that no one but me sees."

She rolls her eyes. "They're just freckles, Price."

I run a finger down her neck and trace her collarbone. "But they're mine," I whisper.

Finally, she smiles. "You're claiming my freckles?"

*I want to claim you.* "You know you don't have anything to worry about, right?"

A light flush sweeps across her face. "She was gorgeous, and confident, and I'm—"

"Perfect," I interrupt. "You are perfect."

She snorts and ducks out of my embrace, heading back to the counter. Not facing me, she says, "Hardly."

Darius emerges from the back. "I'm out. See you tomorrow, boss." He tosses Jodi a smile and salute, then nods at where I stand in front of the door. "Lock this behind me?"

After he's gone, I go behind the counter and through the swinging door. I've never been back here. Shelves line the front part of the room, lined with neatly stocked coffee cups and beans and all manner of supplies. Nestled against the far wall is a metal desk that's probably older than the two of us combined.

Sturdy.

Able to withstand…all kinds of things.

Jodi stands in front of it, her back to me, small and unassuming, and the need to show her what I feel is overwhelming.

"Still here?" she says over her shoulder, then starts to untie her polka dot apron.

I close the distance between us and stop her hand. "Wait." My voice is low, strong. Meant to be obeyed.

She stills.

I don't speak. Not at first. The air in the room goes thick with tension as I finally move her fingers away from the fabric, placing each palm on the desk in front of her. Stepping closer, I lean against her, not an inch between us, and shift her braid to the side as I put my lips to her ear and wrap an arm around her waist, bringing her close. "You are the only woman I want, Jodi. Only you."

She shivers, and goose bumps rise along her bare arms.

I tighten my grip and her breath quickens. "Everything you are, inside and out, is what I want. No one else comes close. I will never want another person. I will only ever want you. Do you understand?"

She hesitates.

So, fine. I'll show her with my body instead of words. "Jodi,"

I murmur, then begin to untie her apron. I'm slow, letting my breath hit her neck. Finally, I pull it over her head and toss it to the side.

"Tell me, kitten, what color are you wearing?" I whisper against her skin.

"Green."

I nuzzle beneath her ear, trailing a hand up her arm and across her chest, dipping again to the collarbone, then up her neck, pressing just gently enough to force her chin up. "Spread your legs."

She obeys, her pulse ratcheting up beneath my fingers. "Whatever you're about to do," she breathes.

"Yes?"

"That's my answer," she responds. "To whatever it is you want to do." She twists to face me wholly, her eyes shimmering, excited, without a trace of fear in them.

I manage to shut my mouth from where my chin hit the floor, then give her a wicked smile. "Is that so?"

She reaches down and cups me, then growls, "Yes." Then she turns around and resumes the position: palms on the desk, legs spread. She tosses a thick braid of hair to the side and smirks over her shoulder at me. "Any time, Price."

I wipe a hand down my face. *Fuck.* She completely turned the tables on me, going from the possessed to the possessor…and I love it. This woman is going to be the death of me. I take a moment to savor her, the anticipation making her arms shake just a little, and the tiny wiggle of her hips. Hips that are clad in a cotton, curve-skimming skirt that she innocently swore was comfortable when I saw her earlier, but that I'm now certain she'd donned simply to torture me.

Without a second thought, I smack her butt cheek. She whips her gaze back to me, eyes wide.

I smack the other.

Her eyes get bigger, even as she bites her lip and a flush blooms across her face.

"Face forward," I say.

She does, turning completely away from me, and I raise her skirt, revealing inch after inch of lush skin, until finally her ass is uncovered, bare except for the slip of green polka dot silk and lace framing her cheeks perfectly. Instantly I kneel, pressing my tongue to the back of a knee, and she hisses, still turned away from me. I suck at the delicate skin, gently, and she moans my name softly.

I lick my way up slowly, savoring every sound she makes, until I'm biting her ass, pulling the reddened flesh into my mouth and nipping and licking at it. I give the other side the same attention, trailing my hands along her legs and up and around her curves, never allowing myself to get close to her center. Not yet.

"Price." My name a plea on her lips. "Please."

I chuckle darkly. "No."

Then I straighten and press my hips against her. She moans, arching back, seeking pressure. I let her grind on me for a moment, then lay my palm on the base of her spine. Wordlessly, I push up, guiding her down until she's splayed, stomach down, on the desk, her arms spread wide, her head against the cold metal, her entire body heaving with every breath.

"Good," I say.

She doesn't speak.

I pull the thong down, my fingers skimming her calves as I go, and inhale. She smells fucking delicious. "On your toes."

She obeys, and I spread her ass, angling her so I can lick her pussy. I dive in, all sense lost, and bury my tongue in her.

"Fuck, Price," she groans.

I worship her, licking and sucking, until her legs are trembling and she's not speaking, only gasping and mewling.

Standing, I pull her upright and turn her to me, then pick her up and position her on the desk. She's flushed, her hair falling out of her braid and her hazel eyes shining a gorgeous blue as I bury my face in her again, focusing on her swollen clit. Instantly she shouts, and I push a finger into her, needing to feel her muscles clench around me when she comes.

I look up at her, meeting her eyes. "You're almost there, baby. Let go. Fuck my face." And I push another finger in as I suck at her. She loses control then, her hips bucking up, and I bear down.

"Price!" She nearly screams my name, and then she's coming, her inner walls tightening and loosening with every pulse of the orgasm.

I soothe her down, but don't give her much time to recover before I straighten and pull her upright. Her eyes are glassy and unfocused, and she lets me yank her shirt off as she sucks in one breath after another.

And I nearly lose my mind.

So help me, I will never look at polka dots the same again. Because this isn't just her standard silk bra, but instead is some kind of lacy confection that also has tiny silk bows—fucking *bows*, like a damn present—at the top of each breast. And there, displayed for me as though they haven't a care in the world, are her nipples, an innocent shade of pale pink, poking out between dual panes of forest green fabric. I clear my throat. "Kitten," I say, managing to drag my eyes up to her face, "did you wear this for me?"

She smiles shyly, and I want to drop to my knees in supplication. "Do you like it?"

My mouth is a desert. "Yes."

She licks her lips. "The thing is," she looks away, then squares her shoulders to meet my gaze again, "My shirt has been rubbing against them all day, and, um."

I fist my hands to keep control of myself. "You've been wanting to be fucked for hours, haven't you?"

Her face reddens. "Yes."

Wrapping a hand around her waist, I pull her to the end of the desk and step between her legs. "Did you think about me? What I'd do to you when I got you to myself?"

She grips the metal edge and swallows.

Then I put a thumb against each nipple, circling them lightly. "Your nipples are so sensitive, aren't they? But you never knew, and now that you do, you wore this little thing to get yourself hot."

She nods. "Y-yes."

Something like a growl comes out of me and I grit my teeth at the fantasies that begin to form in my head. "Oh, kitten," I grit out. "We are going to have so much fun, the two of us. Now, watch," I command. When her gaze drops, I increase the pressure of my thumbs. My mouth, no longer a desert, waters as her nipples tighten. She inhales sharply, and as I pinch them, her thighs clench.

"I need your skin," she says, her voice hoarse, and she reaches for the hem of my shirt. I yank it off and she pulls me to her, her mouth hot against my chest.

But I need those nipples more, so I bend and take one in my mouth and suck while I reach down to part her folds.

"Fuck," she breathes. "So good, Price. You're so good."

"Goddamn right I am," I say, my teeth around a nipple. I push my fingers into her pussy.

She chokes out a groan, her hips writhing.

"Cock," she says. "I need your cock inside of me, Price."

"Listen to that filthy mouth," I say, straightening and unhooking her bra as her hands dart to my pants, undoing them and pushing them down.

Her eyes widen. "You didn't wear any underwear?"

I raise an eyebrow. "Maybe you're not the only one who wanted to be all hot and bothered today, kitten."

Without a word, she grips my shaft and pulls it toward her. "Now," she growls.

Heat flaring inside me, I step away from her and flip her back around. She pushes her skirt down from where it'd bunched at her waist and kicks it off, and I grab the condom I'd put in my wallet.

"Get yourself ready for me, baby," I say. "Chest on that desk. Arms and legs spread."

"Yes, please, god yes," she answers, following my instructions.

I line myself up, eyes on her ass, and push in slowly, letting her get used to me. "You are so fucking tight, kitten," I gasp.

"Because I waited for you," she says, circling her hips to take me in farther.

"You—?" But I can't finish, because stars explode behind my eyes and I nearly black out with pleasure as her walls clench around me.

"Price." She heaves a breath.

"Hang on," I grind out, because I might detonate if I don't get my shit together. I gulp air in, willing the dizziness to go away, then I pull out and push in again. "Fuck, Jodi."

She circles her hips, and the picture of her sears into my head and brands me, absolutely ruining me for life. Spread before me, her pale skin dotted with constellations of freckles, her thick braid undone, the tips of her fingers white as they press against the desk. A sex goddess coming into her own, and I'm the lucky bastard who gets to go along for the ride.

I thrust into her, gripping her hips and beginning a steady rhythm, going deep, her walls so fucking tight that I can barely see, and she sobs in relief.

"Yes, Price, please, yes," she chants.

"You take it so good, baby. Take my cock. You need more, don't you? Tell me. Tell me what my good girl needs."

"More. Deeper."

I push harder, sweat beading off my brow.

"More, Price. *More*." Her voice is guttural, unlocking something primal within me.

*Mine. Mine. Mine.* It's all I think as I move inside her.

But it's still not enough. "Price!"

"Goddamn, kitten," I exhale. "Put a knee on the desk."

She does, and I change my angle, thrusting so hard into her that the metal legs scrape across the floor.

"*Yes!*" she shouts. "Right there, Price, more, more, *more!*"

I'm going to die. I piston into her, the desk screeching as it inches toward the wall with every movement, the lamp already gone, crashed to the floor I have no idea how long ago, and I'm slick with sweat.

"Don't you fucking stop, Price Joseph. Don't you fucking— oh *god*. Shit. Yes, yes, *yes!*"

I give her everything I have, growling in relief that the desk has finally hit the wall. The resistance is all I need, and I bend my arms beneath her hips to raise them, changing the angle again. "Hold on," I bite out, the base of my spine tingling as my balls tighten.

She grips the metal and I pound into her, lost to everything but the feel of her muscles beginning to flutter around my dick. With a shout, she starts to come, and my own climax is right behind, and I thrust through it, unable to control anything. A strangled sound comes out of me and finally, I push into her and stay, my dick twitching inside of her as she goes limp.

"Oh my god," she says.

Still dizzy and closer to blacking out than not, I tug her knee off the desk and guide her leg to a standing position. I pull out and collapse onto her back, not caring that I'm a sweaty monster.

"You," I manage to rasp out. "You are going to kill me."

She laughs throatily. "Sorry not sorry."

"Fuck," I groan. *I love you.* The words are on the tip of my tongue, but I keep them in. "You are amazing." I kiss her neck, which is just as slick as my own, and manage to pull myself to standing on shaky legs and dispose of the condom.

Jodi straightens, her eyes tender. She doesn't say the words, either, but they're written on her face. "So are you."

Suddenly it feels like my blood is fizzing, and the blackout that threatened moments ago is back. "Oh wow. I think I need to sit down."

She sits on the desk and pats the space next to her, and as I plop beside her, she starts giggling.

"What?" I say warily.

"It's just…you just fucked me into oblivion, *here*, in my storage room."

I smile. "Probably gonna need to wipe this down."

She leans her head against my shoulder, her body shaking with quiet laughter. "Yeah, I think so."

I kiss her forehead. "Look at it this way. At least it's memorable."

She loses it, throwing her head back and laughing so hard that tears begin streaming down her face. "I—I swear, Price," she wheezes, "I don't know why it's so funny. It's *not* funny, it's wonderful and you're my dream come true, but—" She breaks off, holding her stomach and laughing.

I want to laugh with her, but her words. *Dream come true.* Shit, that's a lot of pressure. I remember what she said earlier, too. *Because I waited for you.* The monumental realization of what I've stepped into finally dawns on me, and another wave of blackness threatens to overtake me.

I shake it off. I'm just hungry. And madly in love with this woman, who won't stop laughing.

I peel off the desk one butt cheek at a time and put on my pants, then grab her panties. Kneeling before her, I help her step into them as she, too, peels herself off the metal.

Wiping her eyes, Jodi finally settles and wraps her arms around my waist. "This…what this is…"

I cup her cheek, her hazel eyes tethering me to the earth, and wait.

"It's something, right?" she finishes.

I nod. "It's everything, Jodi."

Her eyes soften. "Good."

She pulls me to her for a kiss, and as her soft curves press against my skin, a peace settles inside of me, soothing all the cracks and rough edges I've carried for so long. With her in my arms, I know that everything will be okay.

# CHAPTER 30
# JODI

$\mathcal{I}$T'S RACE WEEKEND, which means I keep the coffee shop open on Sunday because there are plenty of tourists—and locals—who need the caffeine ahead of each day's festivities at the racetrack. The inn has been bustling all week, with actual guests other than me and Jess, but that hasn't stopped Price and me from grabbing every second we have together. I've found that I have muscles in places I never knew existed.

And I love every minute of it.

Jess has spent the week in my room, as Will wanted, but I've spent the nights with Price in his room when he's off shift. Turns out, he and Will actually share that room, which explains the looks Will gives me every time I see him. I was mortified at first, but Price explained that he and Will had agreed to always change the bedsheets and bathroom towels before going on shift at the station, meaning that Will has not, in fact, been sleeping in our sex sheets.

"And the scowls Will gives me?" I'd asked.

Price had shrugged and smiled. "*You're* the one who calls him Mr. Scary."

And maybe it's all the sex, or maybe it's that I'm trying to grow a spine—or at least be able to force words out of my mouth when it matters—but I've also roped Jess into working the weekend at the coffee shop, giving Darius and me a much-needed pair of extra hands. Even if they might be more trouble than they're worth.

"Sorry!" she says, dodging me with a rustle of individually bagged pastries to hand to the women at the end of the counter. There's five of them, all wearing matching shirts that say *Raise Hell, Praise Dale* on them, in honor of Dale Earnhardt. I smile at them and keep going, because the line of people needing caffeine stretches out of the shop.

Mrs. Withers and Miss Betty are up next, and I scribble their orders down on the order pad for Darius. Race Weekend is the only time we can't keep up, so sticky notes it is.

"Busy morning," Miss Betty says. She's dyed her hair an almost natural looking lavender, and in her pale pink sweater set, she looks like Easter personified.

Mrs. Withers sniffs. "It's always like this on race weekend, Betty." Then she peers up at me, her watery brown eyes owl-like behind thick lenses. "You and Price are a hot item now, huh?"

I redden and cough. "We—"

"Leave the poor girl alone!" Miss Betty elbows her. "You know they're together; Devon told us that already. It's too busy to chitchat. Sure wish you'd have taken me up on the offer to sell my lemon bars. You could have used them." She directs that last bit to me.

Darius, bless him, appears next to me with the old women's coffees, and I've never been more grateful for his interference in my life. "Mrs. Withers," he smiles, "here's your cappuccino, no time for a pretty leaf on top, I'm afraid. And Miss Betty, girl, that hair!" He kisses his fingers. "Your English Breakfast." He winks at me and slides back to the espresso machine, pulling off the two handles and dumping the grinds in one graceful move.

The women pay and toddle off, and the line keeps growing.

Finally, after four solid hours of coffee orders, we run out of food and I flip the sign to *Closed*. Jess leans against the counter and shoots back an espresso, then grimaces like she's just taken a shot. "How do you two deal with this every day?" she asks.

Darius snorts. "We don't. This is insane."

I point to the overflowing tip jar. "*That's* insane."

Darius whistles. "I see more than one twenty-dollar bill in there."

Jess's eyes widen and I feel a twinge of guilt. Because of course I do. "Jess can have my third."

Jess gives me a side squeeze. "You're the very best sister in the whole wide world. Split it up for us, Darius?"

Darius makes a show of giving me a healthy dose of side-eye, but nods and pushes off the display case. "Let's get this over with so I can go home and get horizontal."

Jess squeals and claps her hands, and we set to it.

As Darius leaves, his pockets bulking with cash, Price saunters in, and my pulse kicks up a few dozen notches. He's in his station uniform of navy pants and shirt, and holy moly. I think he's gotten hotter. Is that possible? Or is it all the sex altering my brain chemistry?

Nah. He just got hotter.

He stops in the middle of the shop and strikes one silly yet sexy pose after another. There's a Superman pose, his chest puffed out and hands on his hips, then there's a series of poses I can only describe as weightlifter poses, complete with over the top grimaces and grunts and growls. I can't decide if I should laugh at his antics, or climb him like a tree. The man knows how to show off his assets.

"Ahem," Jess says, waving her hand in front of my face. "I'm still here."

I swat it away as Price nods at her.

She nods back, and I can feel the coolness seeping from both of them. They rarely talk. Not at dinner, or hanging out at the inn, or here at the shop. I don't know what to do about it. My stomach cramps.

"You know, it was…kind of nice today," Jess says to me. "Being busy," she clarifies.

"You actually helped?" Price asks, the surprise evident.

She cocks a hip out and crosses her arms. "Yes, I *actually* helped. You think I'm just going to mooch off my sister indefinitely?"

"Not like you've said anything to the contrary," Price says smoothly.

She huffs. "Whatever."

A wave of anxiety pushes through me, certain they're about to argue. But before I can say anything to head it off, Jess turns to meet my gaze and tilts her chin up defiantly. "I'm out." She swivels on her heel, grabs her purse, and tornadoes out of the shop.

I watch her go, and nausea joins the cramps inside of me. What am I going to do about her? What am I going to do *with* her?

Price tips his chin at the door. "What is her deal?"

"Don't worry about it," I mumble.

"But I am worried," he says. "Because you're clearly unhappy and it looks to me like it's all her fault."

"Yeah, well, she's my sister, so it doesn't matter." I turn and look for something to do. *There.* Tea boxes to straighten. I beeline to them and kneel in front of the open cabinet.

"Jodi, seriously." His tone is soft as he comes and squats beside me. "Talk to me."

I shake my head. "I'm fine."

"You're not fine."

A spear of heat joins the riot happening inside of me. "Don't tell me how I feel," I say, rising and stalking away, scanning the shop for something, anything to get me away from this conversation. In seconds, I find myself fluffing pillows in the area where Ceci, Devon and I always gather when they're here. Ceci sure as hell wouldn't let something like this happen to her. Even though I can't quite identify what 'this' is.

"I'm sorry," Price says, standing behind me. "But it seems like she's taking advantage of you."

I whirl on him. "Do you hear yourself? 'I'm sorry, but'? Don't apologize when it's not true. You're not sorry. Not at all." The anger, blind and indiscriminate, feels good.

His eyes widen. "Okay, wow." He takes a step back and says, "You're right. And I'm sorry. Truly."

I stare at him, my chest heaving, my throat and eyes burning with unshed tears, and I blink. What is wrong with me? I've lost complete control of myself, and of the situation. I don't let this kind of thing happen, not since Jason's funeral. That was the last time I got angry, and look what happened: my entire family, gone.

My chin quivers and I wipe at the tears falling down my face. "I'm sorry. Don't be mad at me."

He squints at me. "Jodi, why would I be mad at you? Come here." He's in front of me in three long strides, eating up the distance to wrap me in a hug, pressing me against his chest.

But I can't relax. I have to figure out how to fix all this. How to get my sister back on her feet without making her mad at me. How to get Price and my sister to like each other.

"Hey," Price whispers, cupping my cheek and caressing my temple with his thumb. "I'm on your side. Always."

I nod, silent.

"I can tell she drains you," he continues. "And I want to help. I'm here for you. If there's something going on, all you have to do is tell me. Okay?"

*Tell him. Tell him. Tell him.* The words are on the tip of my tongue, to tell him everything, but it's as though a literal zipper is closing across my lips, the metal teeth sinking into place one by one, leaving me silent.

"I'm fine," I say.

But I'm not. I'm not fine. I'm the exact opposite of fine. And I'm desperate for him to drag the words out of me, one by one by one. Because the only way I'm going to say anything is if he forces me. Only I can't make myself say that. I can't seem to say anything.

I meet his eyes and he smiles gently, even as a shadow of hurt sparks in his silver eyes. "Okay," he says.

# CHAPTER 31
# JODI

"JESS, COME ON."

Bleary-eyed and glaring at me from beneath a barely-lifted eye mask, Jess swears. "Jodi, I'm not one of your workers. You can't just boss me around."

I gape at her. I want to scream she's acting like a child, but I can't. I'm gripped by the familiar vise that's had a hold on me since my mom put a newborn Jess in my arms and told me that even though she was the mom, being a big sister was the most important thing I'd ever do. As an adult, I now know that's not true, but it's impossible to shake the decades of responsibility my mom managed to dump on me even as she simultaneously treated Jess like the golden child. Staring at her tucked into bed now, Jess's return feels like a chokehold that's going to suffocate me.

Suffocate or not, I'm the only person Jess has. Technically, she's got Mom and Dad and even Grandma. But do they count? When things went bad for her, it wasn't any of them she ran to. And sure, maybe she came to me because I've always seen past her bullshit, even though I've never done anything about it. But I still want to be worthy of that trust.

The whole thing scrapes at me, like an itch just out of my reach. As though there's something I'm missing.

I take a deep breath and steel myself before saying, "Jess, please. You've been living off my good graces and literally in my bed for weeks. So you may not be one of my workers, but you're working today." And before I can talk myself out of it, I open the curtains wide to let in the pale blue dawn. A small part of me wishes the sun was up high and aiming right at her eyeballs.

"Jesus fuck, *fine.*"

My pulse ratchets up as Jess flips the covers back and stomps past me to the en-suite bathroom, not saying another word.

I shake my hands out and breathe. *See? It wasn't so bad,* I tell myself. She's angry, sure, but I can handle her anger. It's my own that I have to keep in check.

We make it to the shop with minutes to spare, and Darius is leaning casually against the door, one foot against the bottom, scrolling his phone. He looks up. "Hey, boss. Hey...wow, late night?" he asks Jess.

"Is any coffee brewed?" she asks.

Darius laughs, then stops when he realizes she's serious. "The coffee's in there and we're out here, love. So no, there is not yet any coffee brewed." He throws me a wide-eyed look and mouths *What the fuck?* behind her head.

I twist my lips as I shake my head, unlocking the shop and heading straight to turn on the drip coffee machine. The sound of grinding beans immediately fills the air, and moments later, Darius has the music going. I catch the opening sounds of The Commodores' "Easy" and can't stop the smile that spreads over my face.

He comes back into view, crooning *"That's why I'm easy...I'm easy like Sunday mornin',"* and I laugh. He keeps singing loudly, and I join him on the next chorus, the both of us going through our standard opening activities on autopilot.

When we get to the bridge, singing about wanting to be

high, Jess joins in, belting it out with her show-stopping voice, and even though I'm internally jolted, I keep going. Darius holds his hand up for a high five, and Jess gives him one as she heads to refill the sugar.

I watch as I sing, hardly believing the change that's come over her so quickly. But the smile seems genuine, as if for at least a moment, she's set down whatever burden it is that she's been carrying. My heart squeezes, because this is what I want. I want my little sister happy. It's what I've always wanted: to be surrounded by my family, happy.

We had it for the longest time. And it wasn't perfect, not even close. Nobody but Jason saw me for who I really was, and I spent most of the time in the shadows, but we were whole.

I shake my head to clear the cobwebs of memory, coming back to the present right as the song ends. Another Commodores song comes on, and we all keep singing.

It's absolutely amazing.

Jess's smile stays on when we open, and she works for hours alongside Darius and I as though she's been here for months instead of days.

Maybe it's bravery when I broach the topic, or maybe it's stupidity, but I figure now's as good a time as any. "Have you given any thought to what you're going to do next?"

She plates the pastry and hands it to the customer with a smile, then turns to me, her smile falling. "Thanks for bringing up my failure in front of everyone," she says.

Adrenaline floods my body and my heart gallops. "I didn't say you were a failure, Jess." I keep my voice low. "I'm just trying to understand your next steps."

She faces me directly, her eyes flashing. "I don't know, Jodi. I don't have it all figured out like you, okay? Can you lay off me for one day? Just one day."

"I haven't asked you every day," I insist.

"Sure as fuck feels like it," she mumbles, then moves around me to help Darius.

Well, that went about as badly as it could have. As my pulse returns to normal, I remind myself that I'm taking baby steps with her. She sang for the first time in who knows how long, and she's working here. I need to be happy with that.

Ceci and Devon swing by a while later, Ceci's twins in tow, and luckily, the crowd isn't as nuts as yesterday. Most of the out-of-towners are firmly ensconced at the track, and will remain there until tomorrow morning. I make their drinks—low-temp hot chocolates for the twins, double-shot half pump vanilla latte for Ceci, and a mint tea for Devon since it's one o'clock and she swears she'll stay up too late if she has caffeine past noon—and we hole up in the area with the stuffed couches.

Ceci gets the kids set up with coloring books and Mad Libs from our stock near the Mom corner, then settles back in the couch. "So, dish. How are things with the second-hottest Joseph brother?"

Devon raises an eyebrow. "Who's the hottest?"

Ceci waves her hand. "Will. Obviously. You know I like them a little mean and growly." She leans toward Devon. "The other night, your brother—"

"Stop it. Stop it right now," Devon hisses, plugging her ears. "You know I never want to hear about you and Rick. Ever. *Never.* I want to go to my grave having heard exactly nothing about your s-e-x lives."

Ceci levels Devon with a look. "Are you really trying to spell sex around my kids? They're not listening, and even if they are, then good. They'll learn that it's a perfectly normal, healthy activity with nothing to be ashamed of."

Satisfied that she's put Devon in her place, Ceci turns back to me. "Speaking of sex." She waggles her eyebrows and takes an obnoxiously loud slurp of coffee.

I can feel how red my cheeks are, and even my chest feels like it's on fire. "We…"

"Oh, they definitely did," Devon says. "Look at how she's blushing. Wow, is that normal?" She laughs and peers at me. "I didn't know you could get that red."

"Shut up," I say, laughing in spite of myself. Looking around the shop, I see it's full of people, but none of the usuals who would have my news on the community social media page before I even finished a sentence. I scoot to the edge of the couch and lower my voice. "Yes. We have."

They squeal and clap, and because I remember all too well how Ceci behaved the last time she was extracting information out of me, I hold my hand up. They both lean forward, eyes shining, and Ceci makes an *out with it* motion.

I breathe deep. "How much detail do you want? I mean, your kids are five feet away."

Ceci rolls her eyes and Devon bites back a smile.

I hold my hand up and count off. "Bedroom. Against the door. In the shower. In the supply room. Positions I didn't know existed. Muscles I didn't know I had."

"That's what I'm talking about," Ceci says, holding her hand up for a high five across the coffee table.

Giggling, and still blushing like a school girl, I high five her and Devon.

"The supply room, huh?" Devon says. "Good for you."

"It was…intense," I say.

Devon studies me. "Wait. Did you two—you *did*, didn't you?"

"What? They what?" Ceci asks. "What are you talking about?"

"They told each other they loved each other!" Devon whisper-shouts, grabbing onto Ceci's arm and shaking it. "Holy shit I'm gonna have you as a sister in law *again*!"

Ceci swats at her. "Unhand me, woman! But are you?" she asks me.

My eyes bug out. "We have *not* said that! And there has definitely been no marriage proposals, Devon, get your act together."

"Just a matter of time," Devon says. "Because you do, don't you?"

No point in denying it. "Yeah," I say, feeling like a giggly schoolgirl.

They stand and I do, too, and they envelop me in a tight hug. "I'm so happy for you," Devon says softly. "Seriously. You deserve it."

Ceci nods, her hair tickling my chin. "Keep getting that D, girl."

I snort as I break the embrace. "Will do, Ceci."

I head back behind the counter. Another hour passes, the work steady and soothing, and then the bell dings. I look up as Price saunters toward me, the sun streaming in behind him, and he's gorgeous as ever in his navy blue uniform.

Will it ever get old? Probably not.

I smile and gesture for him to come to the front of the line, but he shakes his head and indicates he'll wait his turn.

Almost immediately, the bell rings again and Megan walks in. Her blonde hair falls in long waves down her back, and she's effortlessly chic in high-waisted pants and a shirt so tiny that Ceci's little girl could probably wear it. She smiles at Price, her eyes lighting up as she leans to give him a hug.

*Focus on work.* They dated. They *more* than dated, and Price is a hugger. Megan said she's happy for me.

But the way she won't stop touching him, how there's barely even an inch between them. She's married with a kid. Does her husband feel uncomfortable when she does this?

I clench my jaw and force a smile at the customer stepping

forward to place her order, her face buried in what looks like Instagram. "Can I help you?" I ask.

She glances up and smiles, her eyes meeting mine behind red heart-shaped glasses, and I look at her shirt. A stack of books lines one side, and the words *Good girl* are in hot pink font on the other. Definitely a romance reader.

After reading the menu board on the wall behind me, she asks, "Can I get the 'Dega, Baby'?"

I grin back. It's a triple shot blended latte, with whipped cream, caramel and chocolate sauce on top. In other words, plenty of caffeine and sugar to make a person feel like they're racing.

I process her payment, unable to help glancing back at Price and Megan. Yep, she's still all over him, and he doesn't seem to be doing much to stop her.

"This is just the cutest coffee shop!" the woman says as I start to make the drink. "Definitely need to put it on my socials." She opens her phone, holds it up and starts to video, murmuring as she does.

I start the espresso as the woman walks around, filming. Usually I enjoy the way some would-be influencers come into the shop and do their thing, but not right now. Will Megan just stop *touching* him? Shaking my head and trying to focus, I force myself to pay attention to the task at hand. I pour the espresso, milk and ice into the blender and run it for thirty seconds, then turn to grab the whipped cream.

"Holy. Shit." The woman is close enough to hear, and I turn to see if anything is wrong. She's holding the phone up at Price and gaping.

Megan has moved away, and Price is as still as a deer in headlights.

The whole thing has gone into weird territory, and all I can do is stand with a plastic cup in one hand and a can of whipped cream in the other.

"Are you—no way." The customer taps the screen, presumably to make the camera face her, and says, "Um, guys? I think I just found the models from Angel Breaker's viral book, in *Talladega*, of all places. There is a goddess and she is smiling on me right now."

# CHAPTER 32
# PRICE

*H*OLY SHIT IS right. This woman hit the nail on the head. I'm frozen to the spot as she comes toward me, holding her phone up to capture the entire conversation. Jodi stands behind the counter, looking at me, and all I can do is stare back at her and hope she understands.

*I'm so sorry.*

"You're him, aren't you?" the woman asks. "Price Joseph? The model from Angel Breaker's book *The Rake Who Railed Me?*"

A splash comes from behind the counter, and I look over in time to see whipped cream shooting into the air.

Jodi squeaks and turns in circles before managing to grab a towel and duck behind the counter.

I blink.

"Such a great title," the woman says, then leans in conspiratorially. "I mean, with a title like that, how could it *not* go viral, right?"

She knows my name. She knows the book. She's acting like she's my best friend. She's *recording*. Swallowing, I nod and give her a small smile. "Yeah." My voice doesn't sound like my own.

"This is amazing. Who knew I'd find the hottest man on the planet during Race Weekend in Talladega, of all places? I've even got your book with me—this is almost as good as meeting the author herself!" She digs into her tote and pulls the paperback out with a flourish, still managing to keep the phone trained on me.

"Would you sign it? Oh, I'm live, by the way—we're streaming. My name's Annie."

Around me, the shop has gone quiet, save for the sounds of Jodi cleaning up the spilled drink. This is bad. Very bad. But there's no stopping this Annie woman, because she's still talking, still filming this live of all things.

"You should say hi to the audience. We're up to five thousand," she says.

I nearly choke. "Five thousand?"

She smiles. "Yep! I've got a lot of followers. So, I see you're wearing a uniform. Are you a firefighter?"

I nod woodenly.

She nods back, and below the phone she makes a gesture that I think is supposed to mean *tell me more*, but my head is buzzing and it feels like I've taken stupid pills. "Um. Yes, I'm a firefighter for the Talladega Fire Department."

She must flip the camera back to her, because she looks at the phone and says conspiratorially, "This is a man who not only starts fires, he puts them out. He can heat me up and cool me down anytime, right?" To me, she asks, "There are a lot of questions streaming right now, but one keeps popping up. Do your abs really look like that?"

"What. The fuck. Is going on?" Ceci is standing two feet away, hands on hips and looking righteously angry.

And even though I'm sure she'll turn that anger on me eventually, right now it's directed at our mutual buddy Annie and I couldn't be happier.

Annie looks flustered. "Oh! Oh, hi. Um, I'm Annie, I'm a book blogger on Instagram and I've gone live with Price here. What's your name?"

"My name is get your phone the fuck out of my face," Ceci snaps. "Better yet, turn it off. Now."

Annie's head swivels between Ceci and me, as though she can't quite process what's happening and doesn't know what to do.

*Same, Annie. Same.*

"Now," Ceci growls. "It wasn't a request."

I make a mental note to ask Rick how he actually survives day-to-day life being married to Ceci, then watch as Annie signs off and shoves the phone in her tote.

"I'm sorry," Annie says, seeming unsure of where to direct her apology. "I just—you're Price Joseph. Do you have any idea how big you are?"

A younger, stupider version of me would have made a joke related to my dick right now, but Caught In a Massive Pile of Shit me realizes that now is most definitely not the time. Something about Ceci's fury has managed to pull me back together, so I say, "Annie, I really appreciate the attention. And I'll sign your book, but then I need you to go."

She nods and hands it and a pen over. I sign it—the most surreal thing I think I've ever done in my life—and she turns to leave. "Wait," she says, laughing self-consciously. "Coffee."

My chest constricts as I finally return my attention to the woman of my dreams, who's handing Annie a fresh drink with a dazed look on her face. Beside her, Darius seems to have figured everything out and is watching Jodi closely, ready to turn on me at a moment's notice. Jess is there, too, her gaze calculating.

Annie leaves and the noise level in the shop returns, and I'm one hundred percent positive that the entire town will know about this in under an hour. But that's not what matters.

What matters is the way Jodi is looking at me.

# CHAPTER 33
# PRICE

*I*'M AT HER side in seconds. "We need to talk."

She pulls her focus to me. "Clearly."

Jerking my chin in the direction of the storage room, I say, "Can we talk in there?"

Still quiet, she nods and turns, and I follow, aware of everyone's attention on us. The door swings behind me, giving us the only shred of privacy we're going to get.

"I'm sorry. I'm so sorry." It's all my brain is screaming. How fucking sorry I am. Along with how stupid I've been, and why didn't I tell her before now, and cussing.

She stands in the center of the room, her hair waving over her shoulders, her hazel eyes a bright blue as she studies me. She holds her arms across her stomach, and it's no longer love and acceptance I see written all over her face. It's confusion, and even worse, it's retreat. "You're—you're the guy on *The Rake Who Railed Me?*"

"I—yes."

She deflates, looking down at the ground. "I've seen the cover. Almost bought it. And I thought the guy—you—looked familiar, but then I thought there was no way it was you." She meets my gaze. "What about the woman?"

I wince. "Which…woman?"

She chokes out a broken laugh. "'Which woman.' God, Price. You really know how to make a girl feel special."

"Kitten, I'm—"

"The woman on the cover."

"Right." I blow out a breath. "She…" Jesus *fuck*. I meet Jodi's eyes, praying she can see how sorry I am. "We used to date. It wasn't serious."

Jodi laughs humorlessly as she throws her hands out before letting them fall. "Of course you did. Another one. I bet you're still friends, too, aren't you?"

A memory of Aaron's face, righteous with rage, flits through my head. "Yeah," I croak.

She leans against the desk and folds her arms as splotches of red bloom on her cheeks and neck. "So is this a thing? Do you have a ton of books you're on and a ton of women you're still friends with?"

"Jodi," I plead.

"How many?"

"I was going to tell you," I start. "But I wanted to make you proud of me first, and…" I take a deep breath. "I'm not doing this right. Let me start over."

She's silent, and I take that as my cue to begin.

"Seven years ago, this agent saw me and said she could book me jobs as a model. I, ah…" I curse and grip the back of my neck. *Get a hold of yourself.* "I thought it was a joke, but she was serious. Her name's Monica. My agent. And the whole thing felt, I don't know. Not wrong, exactly, but weird. Secret. So I didn't tell anyone. No one knew."

She still says nothing, just keeps holding herself quietly, almost as if she's afraid to say anything. My arms ache to hold her.

"Monica agreed to my terms: no big jobs, I had to be able to get to them and back in three days, and the first one she booked me was this romance cover shoot for a German publisher. Or something. Basically, I posed without my shirt on, made what felt like an obscene amount of money for three hours of work, and that was that. Suddenly I was a model."

Jodi presses her lips together, looking anywhere but at me. "You know what's crazy? I bet I've seen you on some of those covers. Because occasionally I thought, wow, that guy sure looks like Price, but there's no way. Guess I was a fool." Her eyes flit to me. "How many?"

My chest squeezes. "I don't know. I pose for a lot at a time, and—"

"*No*. How many women?" she presses, anger surging into her voice. Then she holds her hand up and closes her eyes, taking a deep breath and letting it out. When she opens them, she doesn't look at me, and all the fight seems to have left her. "Don't answer that. I shouldn't have asked and it's bad enough seeing the ones here…"

I flinch. We've never talked about the women I've dated, and clearly, that was a mistake. My stomach sinks. "Jodi," I plead. "I didn't—it wasn't like that."

She swallows and shakes her head. "I can't sit here and shame you for doing…whatever it was you did with women before we started dating. I just…" She breaks off and raises her tear-streaked face. "Why did you keep it from me?"

I have fucked this up so bad. The anguish in her voice, the absolute disappointment in her eyes. It breaks me.

My voice thick, I say, "Because I'm an idiot, Jodi. Because I was scared that you'd think less of me. And because—" I rake my hands through my hair—"because all I have wanted since you moved in was to be worthy of you, Jodi. To be the man you seemed to see when you looked at me. No one looked at me like that. Ever. You made me want to be more than I ever thought I'd deserve. And I didn't think modeling was worthy."

I curse again. "I quit a couple of weeks ago. My plan had

been—" But I break off. "It doesn't matter. The only thing that matters is I should have told you."

She searches my face. "Why did you quit?"

I step closer, because if I don't touch her I might lose my tether to this world. She barely reacts when I palm her hips. "Honestly?"

"Honesty would be good right now."

I flex my fingers against her jeans. "Because I was tired." I clear my throat. "I was tired of…being a body. It felt like that's all I was, and that feeling wasn't worth the money any more. And I was tired of the secrets, and tired of being, um, touched."

Her eyes flash as they meet mine. "Did something happen?"

"No, nothing bad. Well—being touched without consent is bad. But nothing more than that ever happened."

Her face clears. "Okay."

Dammit, I feel like a cat with tape on its paws here. How do I get on solid ground?

"Jodi." I bend my knees to get face to face with her. "Tell me what you're feeling. I don't know what I'm supposed to do."

"Me, neither," she says, her voice flat as she shrugs.

"Will you at least look at me?" I ask.

She hauls her eyes to mine, and instead of the usual spark, her irises are dull, her expression empty.

This is infinitely worse than having her mad at me. I think.

"I'm so sorry I didn't tell you."

She looks at the shelves behind me. "Okay."

"Okay?" I say. "That's it? Okay?"

She hauls her gaze to mine. "Yeah. Okay. I don't know what you want me to say, Price. You kept this a secret from everyone, not just me. Sure, we were seeing each other and yes, I would have thought you trusted me enough to tell me, but okay. You didn't. And you say you'd stopped anyway, so…okay."

Her eyes slide away again.

*Fuck.*

"I wanted to wait to tell you until I did something to make you proud," I say, repeating myself from earlier. "To, I don't know, move up at the fire station or something." I mumble the last part, entirely unsure of myself.

"Price, I—I need to get back out there." She steps out of my grip and is through the swinging door without another word.

Swearing, I run my fingers through my hair. What the fuck do I do now?

My phone pings with an alert, signaling all firefighters. I pinch the bridge of my nose, fighting the urge to throw my phone across the room and watch it shatter into a billion pieces, then take off.

The call was fucking brutal. House fire, likely caused by the unattended ten-year-old who was only trying to cook lunch for her little brother. The kids got out and were safe, but there was no sign of their caretaker as Aaron and Matt looked them over and draped blankets over their shivering, tiny shoulders. I wanted to rage against everything that could have possibly gotten those kids into this situation: poverty, drugs, divorce, all the above, or none of the above. I would never know. Donna, a very kind and overworked social worker I was unfortunately too familiar with in my line of work, showed up as we were packing up the rig.

She'd patted my chest and pointed over to where a neighbor was making her way over to the kids, and smiled reassuringly up at me. "Don't worry, Price. They'll be okay."

It was one more shitty nail in the coffin of today, and I still have my brothers and the rest of the station crew to deal with.

Back at the station, I help Chief and Buck with the post-call checklist, and I can feel Aaron staring at me the whole damn time. When we're finished and Buck wanders off, Chief beckons me over.

"You still want to help out more around here?" he asks.

I nod, my face serious. "Absolutely."

He jerks his chin toward his office. "Meet me up there in a bit. Pretty sure Aaron's about ready to chew his hand off for waiting to talk to you."

"Be there soon," I tell him, then turn to face Aaron. "Whatever it is, I really don't want to hear it."

"The fuck is this?" Aaron seethes, waving his phone in my face the same way he did when he showed me that fucking book cover.

I look. It's a series of texts from Devon about the scene at the coffee shop, in excruciating detail. I sigh, completely wiped. "It's exactly what you see. I don't think Devon missed much."

"So you never told her? Even after we talked, you just— what? Thought waiting was a good idea?"

"I planned on telling her!" I shout. I close my eyes and inhale through my nose, then out through my mouth as I open my eyes again. "I had a plan. Clearly, it did not go the way I intended it to."

"You think?" he says derisively.

"Aaron, all due respect, but if all you plan to do right now is shit all over me, then step off. I don't need it."

His eyes darken. "I told you she was too good for you."

I throw my arms wide. "What the fuck, man? I *know* that. But I also know she's the love of my goddamn life, and I'm going to fight like hell to fix this. So either help me, or get out of my way, but don't fucking make it worse."

His mouth opens. "She's the what now?"

My shoulders slump. "She's the love of my life, Aaron. She's it." And I haven't told her. Another mistake to add to the growing list.

"Holy shit. You're serious, aren't you?" He steps closer, inspecting me like I'm a foreign object.

My throat burns and I blink. "Yes, I'm serious. I'm putting a ring on her finger if she'll ever find it in her heart to forgive me. But right now, I have no idea what she's thinking. I'm stuck at this fucking station for another forty-eight hours in purgatory."

"Shit."

"Yeah, shit," I laugh sadly, burying my head in my hands. "I don't know what to do. I need her to know how sorry I am. I need her to understand that if I could take it back, I would go back and do it all differently."

"What can I do to help?" Aaron asks.

"You can stop busting my balls, for starters," I shoot.

"You should be thanking me for defending her," he returns.

"Maybe one day I'll thank you—but today's not that day."

"Fair." He shrugs. "Good luck, man. And if you need something, let me know."

I nod. "Thanks. That means a lot."

He tips his chin at me and pivots away.

I check my phone on the off-chance that Jodi's texted, but nothing. Sighing, I head upstairs and rap on Chief's door.

"Come in," he says. "Close it behind you."

I raise an eyebrow. I've been here long enough to know it's never good when he wants the door shut. "What's going on?"

He leans forward in his chair and turns the computer monitor toward me, and that damn book is pulled up on the screen. "*The Rake Who Railed Me?*"

I open my mouth.

"Tell me I don't need to worry about this shit."

I pinch the bridge of my nose and squeeze my eyes shut, wishing to god I never had to look at the book cover again. "You don't," I bite out.

"Care to explain?" he asks, closing the window and leaning back in his chair with his arms crossed.

"Not right now." I'm not interested in going over this with anyone else today. It's Jodi, or it's no one.

Chief tries to wait me out, silently watching me, his eyes boring into mine, but this man is a second father to me. I know all his tricks, and I have mastered many of them. "Fine," he says after a minute.

Thank fuck. That's one less thing I need to worry about right now. I briefly wonder if all of this is going to make it harder for me to move up at the station, but swat the thought away. "Is that why you called me in here?"

He shakes his head. "No." He clears his throat. "You meant what you said about helping?"

"Around here? Absolutely. I meant it when I said I wanted the Assistant Chief position, and I'll do whatever it takes to get there."

He nods thoughtfully. "There's no easy way to say this. We're...in trouble."

I straighten. "What do you mean?"

"I messed up. I swear I don't know how, but ever since Christine stopped helping with the books, things have been backing up, and, well..."

A cold sense of dread washes over me. Christine was a retired math teacher who'd volunteered her time here for decades. She'd kept this office in shape and handled the book-keeping, but we all assumed Chief was able to keep things going without her. "Christine passed away two years ago, Chief—what kind of mistake are we talking about?"

"A five hundred thousand dollar one. Your brother is going to kill me. It's why I called you in here first," he said, a thin layer of panic lacing his words.

I stand, unable to take this sitting down. How is my day getting worse? "Chief. Be specific. Actually, wait." I hold my hand up, then dial Will and put it on speaker. Then I put the phone on the desk between us. "Will is your Assistant Chief, even if the two of you barely act like it."

"I'm up to my ass in dirty laundry and one of our toilets is overflowing, so this better be good," Will growls in greeting.

"I'm here with Chief and we've got a five hundred thousand dollar problem that he was just about to tell us about," I volley back.

"Shit. Hang on."

We hear some rustling and banging, and a minute later, he's back.

"Start talking."

I gesture at Chief. "The floor is yours."

Chief sighs. "We owe the state five hundred thousand dollars. Apparently we used to receive a federal grant that the state administered—don't ask me to explain it, it's Alabama and it involves money and politics, so you know it's convoluted as hell—but the feds stopped paying once the grant ran out. Problem is, the state didn't update its records and kept on funneling that money on over to us. And now, the state's figured out it's shat the bed and wants us to give it back." He leans back again and laughs. "Us! A small little fire station. As though we've definitely got that kind of money lying around and can just give it back."

I don't do anything but gawk, and Will's voice comes over the speaker. "What does this mean?"

Chief shrugs. "Hell if I know. We're the only station on this side of town. They can't shut us down—least, I don't think they can—so I just don't know. Saddle us with a debt we have to figure out how to pay for the next twenty years, I guess."

I tilt my head back and look at the ceiling. "What did we use the money on?"

"Salaries, mostly. Benefits. Health insurance is a pricey thing. Probably some rig repair along the way, but I don't really know. I didn't track it in any way." He lets out a big sigh. "So, Price, welcome to unofficial management. You got any bright ideas?"

My mind whirs. "Not yet. But give me a day or two and I'll come up with some options."

"We're not taking your money," Will says over the phone.

"Everything's on the table, son," Chief says, his expression telling me he clearly disagrees with Will.

I wave the option away. "I don't have it to give, Chief. Sorry. I sunk most of what I had into the inn."

"I probably wouldn't let you do it," Chief says. "But I'm not above at least considering it."

"I need to go," Will grunts.

He hangs up, and I meet Chief's eyes. "Thank you for asking me," I say. "For trusting me enough to tell me, and include me in the search for an answer. It means a lot."

He lifts his brows and I swear I see them twinkle. "I remember your high school economics presentation, Price. I remember your GPA from college, too. And I've been watching you. I know I give you shit, but I see what you're up to."

I stare at him, not able to speak.

He stands up. "Get out of here. Go think with that brain of yours." Smiling, he waves me out.

I stop in the hallway and lean against the wall. I don't know what to do first, which way to turn. The entire day has been a roller coaster of one thing after another, and the only person I want to talk to is Jodi. But she's not having it.

I make my way outside to the back of the house, thankfully avoiding everyone as I go. I drop into one of the Adirondack chairs and tilt my head back, closing my eyes in an effort to calm my mind down.

I hear a bark, and open my eyes in time for Samson to jump his tiny, furry little body into my lap. I chuckle and he licks my chin before settling into my lap, content to let me pet him.

So I do. And I think.

# CHAPTER 34
# JODI

*I*'m slurping ramen noodles in my room when Price texts me that night.

PRICE

Can I call you? I don't like how we left things.

I swallow the bite and study the text. I'm not ready to talk to him. All I feel is numb.

Eating dinner with Jess.

PRICE

Later, then?

I know this is how it's going to go. I know he's relentless, but I need time. Time to process and figure out how I'm feeling.

Tired. Tomorrow?

PRICE

Tomorrow.

*T*HE NEXT TEXT comes as I'm unlocking the coffee shop door.

PRICE

Good morning, sunshine. I miss you.

Darius hears the ping and reads the text over my shoulder before I can stop him. He raises an eyebrow at me, but I flatten my lips and say nothing. He grunts and leaves me to stew.

I put my purse down in the back and type back.

Good morning.

The dots are instant.

PRICE

Okay if I swing by to say hello today?

Is it? I need to get over this, right? Or do I? I don't know. So I deflect.

You've never asked before.

PRICE

I'm asking now.

And because I don't know what else to do, I fold.

Okay.

*B*ut it turns out, I'm not ready to talk. So I hide from him when he comes in later that afternoon, and make Darius tell him I'm out. He leaves, and five minutes later, another text arrives.

PRICE

I get it. You're definitely avoiding me. But we need to talk. Will you come by the station after you finish your errands?

My stomach clenches. But instead of standing up for myself, I do what I always do.

Maybe.

A moment later, his response comes.

PRICE

I'm not letting you run away from this, kitten. We're talking.

## CHAPTER 35
## JODI

 *E*VERYONE IS TALKING about Price.

It's all I hear about. *Have* heard about. For the past day and a half, it's been Price this, Price that. Price on this romance novel cover, Price's abs on that romance novel. Price in Regency clothes. Price in almost no clothes. Price's body. Price's abs. Price's face.

I want to scream.

And the Moms. God help *all* of us, the Moms. There's Megan, of course, who smiles her sweet smile and orders her no-hassle latte and gives me a larger than normal tip, all while *not* talking about Price. The rest of them just keep giving me looks—and I can't tell if they're ones of pity, curiosity, jealousy, or maybe all three. And they won't ask me about it. No, they'll just buy my coffee and chat about nothing to my face, and then turn and whisper in their corner while they bounce their babies. Even Mary Alice, who I would have expected to say something a little off-color, hasn't said a word.

It's not just them, either: No one will ask me about it. Literally, no one. And I don't care about most of them, but Devon and Ceci? Darius? Hell, even Jess hasn't said anything. It's as though they've decided that this is A Big Deal and they're waiting to see how I react first.

"Jodi?" Devon searches my face from across the register.

I snap back to attention. "Sorry. What's your poison this morning?"

"Iced cold brew, please."

I nod and skirt around Darius. On her side of the counter, Devon mirrors me, moving one step for each of mine, her fingers tightening and loosening, and I know, beyond a shadow of a doubt, that she wants to say something.

I've not talked to Price. He's tried, but I've avoided him, and judging by the look on Devon's face, Price called in reinforcements. But only the friendly one, because I'm fairly certain Ceci wants his balls in a vise.

God, I love that woman.

"You got a minute?" Devon asks.

And there it is. "I really don't," I answer.

"Oh, sure you do," she says and grins. "Darius, you got this?"

Darius the traitor responds that he does, and Devon steps around to grab me and her drink the second I've got a lid on the cup.

"I'll take that, thank you." She holds her hand out for the drink, then takes a deep sip once it's in her hands. "You know, I can't decide if your coffee is so much better because you make it, or because it's free."

I twist my lips and scowl. "Maybe once I pay you back, I'll stop giving you free coffee sooner than expected."

She pops her mouth open. "You would *never!*"

I cross my arms. "Try me."

Her blue eyes dance as she guides me to our usual spot. "I kind of like this sassy Jodi. Come over here and spill." After we sit, she drinks her coffee and looks at me expectantly. "Well?

Come on. I've given you an entire day—which nearly killed me, by the way, but Rick swore he and Ceci would leave me with the kids for an entire week by myself if I didn't let you have time to process. Although I'm not sure Ceci agreed with him, but." She shrugs and smiles.

I blink. "Really?"

Devon squints at me. "What, did you think I wasn't going to say anything? Jodi, we *all* have been waiting on you, but you turtled on us. And it's been well over twenty-four hours. Tell me what the hell is going on."

I sit back, trying to reconcile her words with my own thoughts. "Even Jess and Darius?"

"Girl. Darius does whatever the hell he wants, but Jess? None of us talk to her. How long is she staying, anyway? Wait. Don't answer that. We're talking about Price."

"I—" I stop, not knowing how to proceed. "It's fine, I guess."

"What?" Devon leans forward. "It's fine, you guess? Are you serious right now?"

I blow out a deep breath. How do I explain that I can't get mad, even though I want to? That my best course of action is to just stay calm and basically ignore the whole thing? Because if I don't, I lose him. Even though him not telling me kind of feels like a betrayal, and kind of not because it's not as though we've been dating for a long time, and that I'm just really, really confused?

"I don't know," I finally tell her. "I—I don't know." I sigh, and hot tears spring up behind my eyes. I blink quickly, unwilling to let them fall.

Devon grabs my hands. "You're allowed to feel whatever you want to feel, Jodi. You know that, right?"

I twist my lips ruefully. "Am I?" Because I've never known that to be true. My feelings were always minimized in one way or another, always in favor of whatever my brother or sister needed. *You don't really mean that, Jodi. Quit being so dramatic, Jodi.*

Tummy aches dismissed for Jess's recitals; skinned and bloodied knees spattered with gravel left unattended while Jason's football game was still happening. The examples were endless, but small. And eventually, I learned to make myself small as well.

So now, when faced with something like this? I don't know how to act.

Devon furrows her brow. "Of course you are. Why wouldn't you?"

"Because it doesn't matter," I blurt.

"Um, hell yes, it matters," she responds. "What's going on, Jodi?"

I stand up, mortified the words slipped out of my mouth. "You know what? I'm fine. Really. I need to get back to work." I leave her staring after me and join Darius behind the counter once more. When he looks at me quizzically, I force a smile. His eyes search my face, not believing my lie for a second, but lets it go.

A few minutes later, Larry appears from upstairs. He's been a saint of a man, overseeing the renovations and watching my budget like a hawk, taking care to run everything past me before proceeding, and doing everything he can to get supplies quickly. Still, it's been almost two months since the electrical fire. I've not allowed myself to go upstairs, because I figure it'll just depress me.

"Need a refill?" I ask, stretching my hand for his travel mug.

He nods and takes the lid off before handing it over. "Wanna come upstairs and have a look around?"

"You know I don't," I say over my shoulder as I pour his coffee.

"We're close," he says. "Maybe another week or two." He lifts his mug in a salute and heads back upstairs.

Right as he disappears, Jess shows up, her mouth set in a determined line. I inhale and exhale slowly, preparing for battle.

Jess walks right around the counter and starts making herself a drink.

"You need to tamp the grounds down more than that," I say.

"It's fine," she says dismissively. "I just need some coffee."

I swallow as she notches the handle into place and starts the espresso machine. "It's not fine. The espresso won't taste nearly as good because the—"

"It's fine," she repeats.

Clenching my jaw, I say, "Okay, but until you do it properly, you can't make drinks for the customers."

She rolls her eyes but doesn't say anything. After the machine stops, she dumps the espresso into a cup of ice, then grabs the caramel sauce and squeezes an insane amount into the drink. Leaving the bottle on the counter, she pours almond milk on top of the whole thing. "I'm not trying to work here more than necessary, Jodi," she says, doing a crap job of screwing the top back onto the almond milk before tossing it haphazardly into the fridge at her feet. Finally, she takes one of the silver shakers, pops it on top of the cup, and shakes.

It's the worst technique ever, and I want to throttle her. "Please put the caramel back where it belongs."

She huffs and grabs it, sliding it into the vicinity of the others and turns back to me, sucking down the coffee and leaning against the counter. "Does Will walk around with a stick permanently up his butt? You should have seen him this morning, scowling at me and probably scaring the other guests half to death with what he thought was a smile."

"It's just Will."

"Well, *just Will* needs to just relax. But listen," she says, her face brightening. "I have an idea."

My stomach clenches.

"This place does a killing, right? So I was thinking you could loan me some money to get back to Nashville. I don't need much, like two, maybe? And then I can get the demo recorded for real. I heard from Joe," she says, bouncing on her toes, "and he's got a line on some labels who might be interested. I just need to get back up there and record the demo."

"Two?" I say. "Hundred?"

She makes a face. "No, of course not. Two thousand."

I blanch. "Are you serious?"

"It's not a lot of money, Jodi," she says, waving me off as usual. "Besides, your boyfriend is filthy rich, right? If you don't have it, maybe ask him."

I feel nauseous. "That's not—no," I manage. "No."

"You don't mean that. Think about it: you give me the seed money and I'll give you a percentage of my earnings."

*Give it to her and maybe she'll never come back.* The thought streaks through me, bathing me in cool relief, and a vile taste immediately fills my mouth. Is this what guilt tastes like?

My chest tightens. I turn away and say, "I need a break."

"Wait," Jess says. "I need to give Joe an answer—it's yes, right?"

And that's it. I whirl on her, blood instantly boiling. Hands shaking, I let it all out. "No more. I'm done. My apartment is being redone from an electrical fire, Jess. And this 'killing' you think the shop does? It's just enough to pay Darius, keep this place running, and buy groceries. My entire life, Jess. My *entire life* I have done whatever you asked, given you whatever you needed. And have you ever said thank you? Have you even noticed?"

Her jaw drops. "Jo—"

I keep going. "No. You *haven't* noticed. You *haven't* said thank you. And I know it tore our family apart the last time I bothered to speak up, but you know what? Maybe that's just what I do. Maybe that's my contribution. Either way, your answer? It's no. And not just no. *Hell* no."

Shaking, I turn away without another word, slamming into the back room and out into the lot behind the shop. Anger floods through my veins and I want to scream, but I don't. It won't help. Nothing will help.

# CHAPTER 36
# PRICE

*T*URNS OUT, TRYING to get a person in state government to talk to you about money is like screaming into the void. I've gotten exactly nowhere, which is exactly how far I've gotten with Jodi, too. To Chief's credit, he's let me run with every idea I've had, the first of which was to attempt to convince someone, *anyone*, that this was the State of Alabama's fault and that our little station shouldn't be held accountable for that.

Problem is, no one seems to know who I should actually talk to. I'm beginning to think I'll have to go to Montgomery and start knocking on office doors to get this sorted.

In the meantime, Will has finally shown up for his shift, which means mine is over. Before I can bolt to find Jodi, he jerks his head to the engine bay and tells me to follow him.

After ensuring no one else is around, we stand between the two apparatuses as he crosses his meaty arms and glares at me. "Explain."

And to think that for a moment, I thought I'd get away without having to talk about it with Will. I try anyway. "Don't suppose you've got any contacts in state government? Because let me tell you, I'm striking out left and right over here."

He shakes his head. "Mom called me, you asshole. *Mom.* Somehow, even she's heard about your little career prancing around shirtless."

"Nope," I say, holding my hand up. "That's not how we're doing this."

"Am I wrong?" he presses. "Because from where I'm sitting, that's exactly what this looks like."

"Oh, fuck you, Will," I shoot back. "You don't get to stand there and be all self-righteous when it was *my* money that allowed us to buy that house and turn it into your fucking dream."

His eyes flash. "You wanted to do it, too."

"Not like you. I wanted to invest in something, and this dropped right into our lap. It took all my money and then some, but I wanted to do it because of you."

"Don't put this on me," he says, shaking his head.

"Why not? You grabbed onto the idea of the bed-and-breakfast with the desperation of a man dying to get out of this place. But not me. *This* is my dream." I gesture around us. "I want this. And as for my *little career prancing around shirtless*, I kept it from you for this exact reason."

"And what's that?" he asks, still pissed and unwilling to concede.

"The way you're looking at me," I say. "Like you're disappointed. Like it's what you expected. Like I'll never live up to your expectations, but that you never figured I'd live up to them, anyway."

"The fuck are you talking about?" he growls. "I expect plenty."

I scoff. "Like what?"

"Like you'll have my back. In a fire. Around this station. With Mom. With Aaron. In *life*, Price."

"That's loyalty. Fucking golden retrievers have loyalty, Will.

I'm talking about up here," I say, pointing to my head. "When have you ever expected anything from me here?"

He starts to speak, but stops, thinking. Then he pierces me with his eyes. Eyes that are so similar to mine, but I only see our dad when I look at them. Which, I realize with a start, is a problem.

He holds his palms out. "Price. I'm your big brother. It's all I know how to be with you. When Mom left, it was just the two of us trying to take care of Aaron, because Dad was…Dad. And then he died, and Mom dropped all her shit on us, and it was all I could do to keep us all moving in the right direction. I needed to know you were in the boat with me. And you were. You were always with me, every step of the way. I don't know what I would have done if you weren't. All I know is I wouldn't have come out on the other side without you, asshole. Whether that comes from your head or your heart, I don't know."

I study the chrome behind him, my throat tight, and I exhale a curse. "I'm sorry." I look at him. "Clearly, I'm working through some stuff."

He grins. "No shit. And listen."

I raise an eyebrow.

"I'm sorry, too. I get what you're saying. I'll do better."

I nod. "Thanks, bro. Hug it out?"

He rolls his eyes. "Like you ever give me a choice."

We slap each other on the back, and he clears his throat. "There's one more thing."

"Yeah?"

"Your girl."

"I know."

"You need to make it right."

"Believe me, I'm aware." I push off the rig. "I was heading there before this."

He nods, satisfied.

"And Will, while we're being honest?"

He glances up.

"You really, *really* need to shave the 'stache." I toss him a salute and grin, backing out of the bay into the sunlight as he scowls.

*I* find Jodi wearing a path in the back lot of her coffee shop. She doesn't see me, and my heart swells with affection as I watch her pace and mutter in the gravel, gesturing and stomping for emphasis. Her wavy hair is pulled back in a braid, and she's wearing a pair of too-big jeans and a form-fitting shirt beneath her red polka dot apron.

*I love her so damn much.* The thought continues to bowl me over. How she's been right here, under my nose, the whole time. But I wasn't ready for her. I'm ready for her now, and even more importantly, I'm ready for the hell she's about to put me through. I step into her line of sight.

She stops mid-mutter and comes to a halt in front of me, her eyes widening in surprise. "Price."

I smile. "Hi, kitten. Figured I'd better come to you." I glance around us. "Darius told me where you were. Until the electrical fire, I never even knew this little spot existed."

She nods slowly.

I close the distance between us and can actually *see* her grow small. I've seen her do it with her sister, but now it's happening with me. Her shoulders hunch the tiniest bit, the corners of her mouth pull in, and her normally bright eyes dull by the smallest fraction. To a casual observer, it doesn't look like anything has happened. But I'm anything but casual.

"I see what's going on here," I say.

Her eyes spark. "I'm not doing anything."

I shake my head. "One minute ago, you were raging through here, wild and alive, and it looked like nothing was going to stand in your way. Then you see me, and you change."

She shrugs. "So what."

"So what?" I repeat. "So what? So *what* is that I want you to give it to me, kitten."

"Give you what?"

I pat my chest. "Your anger. You're pissed—clearly. Otherwise you wouldn't have been giving this parking lot what's what. So, give it to me. Tell me you're mad. Come on."

She twists her lips. "I'm not mad."

"Yes, you are."

Wrapping her arms around her stomach, she turns away from me. "I need to get back to work."

I hustle to move in front of her. "Oh, no you don't. No more running."

She stops and stares at my chest. "I'm not running," she insists. "I just need to get back in there." She tries to step around me, but I move again.

"Jodi. You're mad."

"I'm not mad."

I poke at her arm, lightly. "Yes you are. You're pissed. Tell me about it. C'mon." I poke again.

She swats at my finger. "You're acting like a child. Stop it."

"There we go," I say, poking again. "You're mad, aren't you? Are you mad at me? Your friends? Your sister? Or is it something else? Tell me."

A flush spreads up from her chest, splotching her neck and cheeks. "I'm not. We're fine. I'm just—could you please move?" She keeps trying to go around me, but I've got years of football feet on her, and I block her every turn.

I poke her with my other hand. "You're getting even more mad now. Look at those angry splotches on your neck and face.

You're pissed. Tell me why." *Come on, kitten. Give it to me,* I plead silently. She needs so badly to explode. "I've watched you. I didn't realize it at first, but now? I know you, Jodi. Whether you want me to or not, I do. I don't think you ever learned how to fight. So we're fixing that. Let's fight. It'll be fine. Because I see how you hold it all in, shove it down, laying those bricks one on top of the other, building this thick wall that you think no one can get around. But guess what, kitten? I scaled that motherfucker. And I'm on your side of it now. Right beside you. So c'mon." I poke both arms and lower my voice. "Go boom."

She yells, a guttural sound so deep and raw that goose bumps fly up my arms, and pushes me. I'm so startled that I stumble back, and she pushes again, putting all of her weight into it, and I let her move me.

"There you go," I say. "Do it again."

So she does. Eyes flashing, again and again she pushes at my stomach, growling and yelling. I let her walk me across the lot until she has my back against a tree.

"Good—how's that feel?" I ask.

"I hate it!" she yells. "All of it! All of *them*, all of *you*, fucking no one sees me! Ever! And I'm over here, just Jodi, the one who's always fucking here and no one bothers to notice. Those moms. *My* mom. She doesn't see me, she never has! My brother. My sister. This whole goddamn town, Price! Even *you*! For *years!*"

She pivots on her heel, swiping hard at the tears streaming down her face. "My whole life, it's never been about me. Ever. Then you come along." She turns and stalks back to me. "You. You finally notice me and you make me *feel* things and make me feel like I'm seen, and you, you," she takes a breath, "are fucking everything I wanted, Price. You were everything." Her voice breaks.

I straighten off the tree. "Jodi."

"I'm not done," she snaps. "Not at all. You opened this fucking box so you just stand there and shut up, pretty boy."

Her arrow hits its mark, and I wince. "Don't say that," I say quietly. She can't believe that I'm just a face. Because I will crumble.

A flash of uncertainty crosses her face, but she presses on. "Almost every day, someone you dated comes into the coffee shop. And they're all so *nice*, and they're *beautiful*, and I've got no chance comparing myself to them. But you made me feel like I was different. That you felt something for me."

"I do—"

She speaks over me. "How could you make me fall for you, get me to open up to you, when the whole time you were holding back? Do you know how proud I would have been?"

"Bullshit." I can't help it. "That's bullshit and you know it."

"Don't tell me what I would have thought. You have no idea."

"I know the pride wouldn't have been your first thought, Jodi. It would have been insecurity. A fuck-ton of it. Because that's all you were at first. That's all I think you still are."

And now my own arrow has hit the target, and immediately I feel like shit, but I keep going. May as well dive all the way into this mess. "Insecure about me, insecure about your friends, insecure about your family. Why don't you see how worthy you are? How many times do I have to say it for you to believe it? Because no one is going to believe it until you do."

"Because I'm not!" she screams at me. *Screams.*

She stomps right up to me, and my back is once more against the tree. Her eyes blaze. "I'm not. I never have been. Because if my own family doesn't think I'm worthy, then I must not be." Tears stream down her face and she stares me down, fully convinced of what she's saying. "So you can tell me these things all you want, Price, but I know it's not true. Not really.

Because if I *was* worthy, then you would have told me everything."

She drops her arms and holds herself, still looking at me, all while I try to think of what to say. I came here with a goal, but I've lost the thread, and now I'm confused and can't tell which way is up and which is down. I tuck a rogue curl behind her ear and study her intently. How her hazel eyes are the brightest blue beneath her tears. How soft her skin feels beneath my hand. How her whole body trembles with the effort of holding herself together. So I say the only thing I can. The thing I should have been saying for weeks. "Jodi, I love you."

She coughs out a sob, her apron soaked with tears. "No, you don't."

This time, when she turns to leave, I let her go.

## CHAPTER 37
## JODI

*A*FTER WALKING AWAY from Price, I drive. Eventually I end up at Smith Lake, sitting on one of the weathered docks with my feet in the blue-green water. My whole body hurts and my eyes are practically swollen shut with all the crying I've done.

I'm sure things are over with Price. It doesn't matter he said he loves me. No way will he bother with someone like me, who loses her shit and pushes and pokes him while she does it, even if he told me to. I want to apologize, to tell him I'm sorry, but I can't do anything but sit. My limbs feel heavy, weighed down.

When my phone rings, I don't answer it. But then it rings again, and again, and I worry that someone might actually need me. Which is hilarious, because no one actually needs me.

It's Mom. I blow out a deep breath, because she is dead last on my list of people to talk to today.

Actually, I take that back. Dad is dead last.

The phone rings again.

"Hi, Mom." I don't bother keeping the flatness out of my voice.

"Jodi?" Mom's voice sounds slightly panicked.

"It's me."

"You don't sound well. Are you sick?"

I can't even laugh. "No."

"I was calling because I heard from Jess. She's there? With you?"

"I told you that already."

"You did?" She titters. "Oh, you did."

"I told you, and you didn't believe me. Standard stuff."

The phone rustles on her end. "I'm sure I was just confused, that's all."

I manage to summon enough emotion to be pissed. "No. You weren't confused. In fact, you said that *I* was the one who must be confused. As though I couldn't possibly know that my sister was, in fact, staying with me."

"Oh, don't be dramatic," Mom says.

And I guess today is the day of me being done with everyone and their shit, because I snap, "Stop it. Stop doing that."

"Doing what?"

"Minimizing my feelings. 'Don't be dramatic,'" I mimic.

"Well, it's true."

I straighten, decades of anger coursing through me and finally ready to be unleashed. "You know who you never said that to? Jess."

"Jess was a born entertainer, darling—drama is just part of who she is." Mom says it as if that explains everything.

"Didn't say it to Jason, either."

"Don't you talk about Jason," Mom says, her voice censorious.

"I will talk about my brother if I want to," I say, my voice deadly calm. "Because no one else will."

"He was my *son*," Mom says, her voice cracking.

"And he was my brother!" I shout back, absolutely *through* with holding myself back. If I'm going down, then I'm going down swinging. "And I'll talk about him, and remember him, and love him, because he was a real person who died, not some untouchable saint to be worshipped without discussion."

Her gasp is audible. So is her crying.

I look up at the sun, its position still high in the sky as more tears come. Birds chirp in the trees behind me, and a small boat motors by. In the distance, I hear kids calling to each other and laughing. My eyes hurt, and my skin feels as though it's been stretched taut over my body. I don't know how much more I can take.

Resigned, I ask, "Why did you call, Mom?"

"It doesn't matter," she says.

"Great. Talk to you later."

I hang up before she can say anything more, then flop back onto the dock, my heart wrung past the point of pain, and close my eyes to the early May sun.

*I* DON'T SEE anyone the rest of the day, and I manage to sneak into the B&B and fall asleep before the sun even sets. Jess is nowhere to be found the next morning, and neither is Price, although I can tell he's already been in the kitchen to brew some coffee and lay out the beginnings of breakfast for the other guests. It's just as well, I tell myself. He'll be glad to be rid of me when my apartment is ready again.

I arrive to open the shop and Darius's eyes rake me over, head to toe. He gives me a kind smile. "You look pretty good for a woman who finally detonated."

I wince and ask, "How bad is it?"

"The rumors?"

I nod, bracing for it. I feel raw, as though the tight skin from yesterday has disappeared and left me with an exposed layer to the elements.

He follows me into the shop and heads toward the back, calling as he goes. "Not much, actually. Just that you punched your sister, fired me, told Larry where he could shove it, and yelled obscenities at the regulars."

I can't help but crack a weak smile. "All things considered, that's pretty good."

"I know, right?" Darius responds with a grin. Then he wraps me in a giant hug. "Jodi, my sweet, you have *got* to let a brother know when you need him, okay? You been acting like you're grown and got your shit together for so long that nobody knows otherwise unless you say so." He releases me and holds me by the shoulders, dipping his head to look me in the eye. "Got it?"

I nod.

"So will you please drop the act and tell me what you need, when you need it?" he prods.

I nod again, and my smile is the tiniest bit bigger. "Thank you."

"You're welcome," he says. "Now let's get this place opened up."

We're full into the rush when Jess saunters in and comes behind the counter. "Didn't think you'd bother to show up," I say.

She doesn't respond, just ties an apron around her waist and looks at the next customer. "How can I help you?"

"Um, is this the coffee shop where Price Joseph works?" the customer asks.

I jerk my head up to see who's asking. The woman is that unknowable age between thirty-five and fifty-five, impeccably dressed in athleisure and sporting expensive jewelry, well-coiffed hair and five-hundred dollar shoes. Behind her is a gaggle of women who seem very, *very* interested in Jess's answer.

"Who's asking?" I inquire.

The woman turns to me. "Ooh, are you the owner? This place is so cute! We're all in a book club in Mountain Brook and thought we'd swing down here to see if it's true. If Price Joseph is really around here."

Ah. Mountain Brook. That explains the way the women look, all of them dressed as one version or another of their leader. Mountain Brook is basically in Birmingham and is the richest neighborhood per capita in all of Alabama; these women would give the snobs of New York and Miami a run for their money any day, and are what the Mom Group in the corner can only aspire to be.

"He doesn't work here," I say, hyper aware of how the regulars in the shop are eyeing this new development.

Jess pipes up as she unties her apron. "I'd be happy to give you a tour of his regular haunts if you'd like. For a fee, of course."

I manage to keep my jaw from unhinging even as I clench my hands into fists.

The woman flicks her eyes to Jess appraisingly, perhaps sensing a kindred spirit, and nods. "Of course."

"Jodi," Darius says under his breath. "Are you really gonna let them do this?"

"I'm not sure I could stop it even if I wanted to," I mutter back. "Those women look like they bite."

Darius snickers as Jess walks around the counter. "Let's get you ladies some drinks and we'll get the tour started. Jodi?" She looks at me expectantly, with only a flicker of hesitation in her expression. As though maybe, just maybe, yesterday taught her something.

And I decide to go with it. Because she sure as hell isn't

getting any money from me. "Step right up, ladies." I force a smile.

Once they all have their drinks in hand, the women swarm around Jess as though she's their new chosen leader.

Jess, ever the natural when all eyes are on her, smiles graciously. "You know he used to play football, right? Let's get started with a look at where Price went to school."

# CHAPTER 38
# PRICE

$\mathcal{M}$Y PHONE BUZZES repeatedly, but like my brother several days ago, I'm loaded with laundry and am walking into the basement. Once I've finally started a load, I pull the phone out.

CHIEF

Price, get the hell over here.

WILL

We've got a situation.

CHIEF

Now, Price.

WILL

Chief's about to blow a gasket.

AARON

Dude.

CHIEF

I don't care if you've got guests at the house or not, get your ass over here.

Now.

I palm my wallet and grab the keys off the keyring in the entryway, then head to my truck. Throwing my phone on speaker, I dial Will.

"Are you on your way?" he asks.

"What's going on?" I take a turn too fast and the tires chirp.

"Hard to explain. Just get here."

Adrenaline is pumping. "Is Jodi okay?"

He laughs. Actually *laughs*. "Excellent question."

I speed through a red light and crane my neck to see inside the coffee shop, but all looks well. When I turn my head to see what's in front of me, however, I slam on my brakes.

"What the fu…?" I breathe.

Will laughs again. "You must have just pulled up." He disconnects and I park, unbuckling my belt and sliding more than a little apprehensively out of the cab of my truck.

Chief is standing off to one side with his hands tucked into his belt buckle, looking super pissed. Beside him is Buck, appearing even more pissed than Chief. But then there's Will and Aaron, both of whom were clearly working out based on what they're wearing, and both of whom are watching me with shit-eating grins on their faces.

And that's when I know I'm fucked. Because the only time Will smiles like that is when one of his little brothers is about to get into trouble.

"There he is, ladies!" Jess gestures from the sidewalk in front of the fire station toward me, smiling brightly at the group of women standing off to the side. All of their heads swivel as one to look at me, and a few of them squeal.

What the actual hell is going on? But even as I think it, I realize exactly what's happening. Because half of them are reaching into their bags and pulling out the book.

I freeze, not knowing what to do. What does a guy do in this situation? What would a boy band dude do? Immediately, I think of all the shows I watched when I was younger, and in every instance, the guys ran. So I consider it, strongly, before realizing I have no chance at this and I need to suck it up and deal.

With a glance at the coffee shop to ensure that Jodi is not watching, I cross the street. "Ladies," I say, smiling. "To what do I owe this pleasure?"

I hear snickers and growls at the same time.

Jess steps forward. "Price, these lovely women came here all the way from Mountain Brook to meet you. Said they were big fans." She raises her eyebrows at me, and I get it. *Play the part*, she's telling me. And while I'm not a fan of Jess, I'm also no fool.

So I turn a big smile at them. "What an honor! And you brought the books."

One of them speaks up. "We did. Will you sign them? Maybe take some pictures with us?"

Jess clears her throat. "Beth here was just telling me about all her followers, and how *she* saw you on one of her friend's livestreams. Seems you're very popular right now."

Beth holds her hand out, and when I grip it, she gives me a firm handshake. I raise my eyebrows. "Nice to meet you, Price. And Roll Tide." She winks at me and dips her chin to the University of Alabama shirt I'm wearing.

I grin, immediately at ease. "Roll Tide."

She steps forward and pretends to whisper. "There's a few of us who are Auburn fans, but I try not to hold that against them."

"I heard that, Beth!" says one of them. "War damn eagle, bitch!"

They all cackle, and it's clear they know how to have a good time. That, plus the fact that all but two are carrying White Claws and have clearly been in the sun for a while.

"Jess here took us on a walking tour of famous Price haunts," Beth says, whipping out her phone and swiping a manicured nail through professional-looking shots of my high school, the bed-and-breakfast, the coffee shop, and the fire station. "If you'll give me permission, I'd like to share them with my followers."

I blink. It feels like an invasion of privacy, but anyone can find these places if they try hard enough. What would Jodi want?

Beth waves the moment away. "Think about it. Let's sign some books!" Beth says, smiling and waving the rest of her crew forward.

I do as requested, then Jess sidles up to me. "Can I borrow him for just a second? Thanks." She grabs my arm and leads me off to the side. "These women just paid me five hundred bucks to do this."

I raise an eyebrow. "So, in addition to taking advantage of your sister, you scam people out of their money, too?"

She scowls at me. "I know how to read the room, Price. Look at them. They're dripping with money, and they're happy to spend it like they want. There's nothing wrong with that."

"I didn't say there was."

"Then let's figure out a way to monetize this. There's money in muscles," she says with a smirk.

The wheels start turning as I look over at the group. While they've ignored Chief and Buck for the most part, my brothers are definitely of interest to them. I re-join Beth and her friends, and point to Aaron and Will. "You know, those are my brothers."

Beth's eyes light up. "You don't say."

I smile back at her. "I do say. And now I have a question for you."

"I'm listening."

"You think your followers would be interested in an old-fashioned firemen's calendar to help us fundraise?"

"As in, the three of you all sweaty and covered in soot,

wearing only the bottom thingies? That sort of thing?" She clasps her hands beneath her chin.

I chuckle. "They're called turnouts. And yes, that's what I mean. Would they?"

She smiles broadly. "Ab-so-freaking-lutely, Price. I'd be happy to get the word out. What's the fundraiser for?"

"The station. Turns out we owe a lot of back payments thanks to some state mismanagement of funds."

"Alabama government not working? *Shocking*," she says, rolling her eyes in solidarity. "Come on. Introduce us to your brothers. Ladies! Have I got a treat for you!"

I saunter over to Will and Aaron and wrap my arms around their shoulders. "This is Will. He's the oldest and a fireman. And this," I grip and shake Aaron against me, "is Aaron. He's a paramedic. He's engaged, but he'll still take pictures."

Both of them stiffen against me and I laugh. Under my breath I say, "Go with it, guys. This is gonna get the station out of debt."

Half an hour later, the women have left and Chief is glaring at me. "What in the hell was that?"

I shrug and point to Jess, who's still hanging around. "She got this party started, Chief. I just finished it."

Jess wiggles her fingers. "They came into the shop asking if Price worked there. I saw an opportunity." Then she turns to me. "I want in on whatever you're doing next."

"Hard pass," I say. "But thanks for giving me an idea."

"Listen," she says, her tone changing as she again guides me away and speaks softly. "I need out of here. Jodi won't loan me money—"

"You asked your sister for money?" I interrupt, my voice harsh.

She at least has the courtesy to flinch. "I thought she had it, okay?"

I stare at her, my blood boiling. "You thought she had it," I repeat. "After her apartment burned, and you've been staying with her in a room I'm giving her *for free* and she's been paying you to do a shitty job at the shop with money she doesn't have. Probably even let you have her tips, didn't she? But you thought she 'had it.' What is wrong with you?"

Jess's eyes well up and she wrings her hands. "I'm sorry! I didn't know."

"No," I say, leaning into her and lowering my voice. "You didn't *think*. You didn't consider her. Not even slightly. Not for your entire life, and sure as hell not now. It literally did not occur to you to think about anyone other than yourself, even though everything was right there in your face. Am I right?"

Tears spill freely down her face and she hiccups and nods. "I said I was sorry, okay?"

Will's hand wraps around my arm and tugs me back as he says, "I think she's trying to apologize, Price."

I grit my teeth. "I don't believe her."

"Not your place, man," Aaron says, getting in my line of sight. "You know family has to deal with family."

I consider my brothers as Jess sniffles, hidden behind them. "Fine. You're right. I'm not happy about it, but you're right."

Aaron grins. "Atta boy."

I step around him and aim my next words at Jess. "You need to talk to your sister. Stop apologizing to me, and say it to her."

She sniffs and wipes beneath her eyes. "I will."

Exhaling, I look at Will and grin. "Ready to hear how we're gonna save the station?"

# CHAPTER 39
# JODI

*I* CLOSE THIRTY minutes later than usual, thanks to everyone gathering at the shop to talk about what they saw when the group of women were here to find Price. Between Mrs. Withers, Miss Betty, and a rotating cast of characters at their table, I'd heard more stories than a book of fairy tales.

I brace myself for the drive home, knowing I'll have to see Price and not having any idea how to avoid him. But I guess I'll cross that bridge when it gets here.

Before I get to my car, I hear my name. Turning, I see Jess crossing the square from the bookstore. I stiffen, my stomach still a disaster from yesterday's confrontations and not doing any better after watching her parade those women out of here to take them on a hunt for Price.

"Can we talk?" she asks.

Resigned, I nod, already drained at the prospect of having to stand firm and tell her once again that I'm not going to give her money. But I'll do it—tell her no—because I know it's what she needs.

"Can we go back inside? Or, at least, not talk here, in front of everyone?"

I look around. It's the regular kind of busy that a day like this has: mothers taking their kids on walks, Chief and a rotating set of firemen spilling onto the sidewalk a block away, and cars driving slowly along the square. Plenty of people to take notice of us.

We go inside and I lock the door behind us, then turn to look at her.

Jess stands in front of me and fidgets, picking at her nails, but I wait. Until yesterday, I would have started talking, unable to bear the awkward quiet we found ourselves in. And maybe part of my newfound silence is exhaustion, but I embrace it, leaning into the simple power of keeping my mouth shut.

Finally, Jess looks at me, and for what feels like the first time, I see how small she is. She's my height but thinner, no longer the larger-than-life person who'd commanded the attention of every room she walked into. And for the life of me, in this exact moment, I'm not sure who's changed: her or me.

"I owe you an apology," she starts.

My heart squeezes tenderly and I inhale, still holding her eyes. I manage to quell the instinct to give her a hug and tell her it's fine, and force my expression to remain neutral.

She continues. "I've been a shit sister lately. Turns out that Nashville is full of girls just like me, all of them wanting to be the next big star, all of them talented. And for all that Mom, and even Dad, made me think that I maybe had a chance at making it, I don't think I do. Not really."

I bite my lip and stay quiet.

She laughs humorlessly and gestures at nothing, looking up at the ceiling. "I mean, who knows. Maybe I do have a chance. But it's not your job to make me feel better about it, and I think that maybe, somehow, I thought it was? Even though I've not talked to you about it at all. Maybe I figured you just sort of *knew* what was wrong and could fix it somehow." She slides her gaze back to me, and I notice how hollow her eyes have grown.

I swallow and thread my fingers together, nodding. "Talking would have been good," I say.

"Yeah," she agrees. "And I think—I think I've been a shit sister for a lot longer than 'lately,' haven't I?"

I start to shake my head, but stop. "You've...not been the greatest," I hedge.

"I've been shit," she repeats more forcefully. "And I'm sorry. I think I've spent most of my life being self-centered and bratty, and I got a lot worse when I went to Nashville. After Jason..." she trails off.

"No—say it. We don't talk about him enough. After Jason, what?" I offer a small smile.

She sighs. "After Jason, you were the only one who managed to keep her shit together, you know? Mom and Dad lost it. It's like they forgot they still had two kids who deserved their love. But you—it was almost like you weren't affected."

I gape at her. "Seriously? I wanted to curl up in my bed and never come out. He was the only one who ever saw me."

A shadow crosses her face, as though she's going back through her memories and looking at them in a new light.

I continue. "Someone in the family had to function, Jess. It shouldn't have been me, but it was."

She nods and twists her lips. "You're right. We were all a mess, and Devon—shit, she was a ghost. I'm not sure what we would've done without Ceci."

"I'd almost forgotten that," I say. "The way she just came to Devon's and took charge. And she barely knew Rick at that point, too."

Jess chuckles. "The point of all of this is: I'm sorry. I'll do better. I'll probably screw it up at first, but give me time."

I smile. "Apology accepted. But can you tell me one thing?"

"What's that?"

"What brought this on?"

"Oh." She grins sheepishly. "Price."

I furrow my brow.

She fiddles with her thumbnails. "He, um, basically told me I was a selfish brat who didn't know how good of a sister I had." She raises her chin. "He's right."

Warmth floods my chest at the statement and I open my arms wide. "Get over here."

She steps into my embrace and we hug tightly, her petite frame slight against my own. After a moment, with her head still on my shoulder, she says, "Jodi?"

"Mmm?"

"I miss Jason."

I squeeze tighter. "Me, too, Jess."

*W*HEN I GET home, Jess having made her way over to Kerry's house, Price is whistling in the kitchen. I'm attempting to tiptoe past him, certain he can't possibly realize I'm there, when he appears in the doorway between the foyer and dining room.

He smiles, leaning casually with his broad hands gripping the frame on either side of him. "Hey, kitten. I was wondering when you'd get home."

I don't know if it's his dazzling smile, or the deep green of the t-shirt he's wearing, or the kitchen towel slung over his shoulder, but I feel myself go physically weak in the knees. Which isn't fair. Because he's done with me. He must be; I know I would be.

Except...he's smiling and calling me *kitten*.

"Um, hi," I say, and I'm certain I look as confused as I sound, because he grins even broader and steps toward me.

"I'll get that for you," he says as he relieves me of my tote. "Have I told you about that first day here? It was *killing* me that you wouldn't let me carry your duffel up the stairs. And then, idiot that I was, I hoofed it up there and stood there like a jerk while you huffed and puffed up three flights." He shakes his head and looks at me fondly.

"What's happening right now?" I ask, craning my neck to take him in. He smells so good, that perfect soap-and-laundry scent mixed in with eau de Price, and it's not helping me think clearly.

"What do you mean?"

"What do *you* mean, what do I mean?" I counter.

He juts his chin and sticks his lower lip out. "What do *you* mean, what do I mean what do you mean?"

"Price!" I say, exasperated. "We broke up! Why are you being so nice to me?"

He laughs. Full-on guffaws for a solid fifteen seconds. Then, "You think we broke up?"

I feel like that old white Persian cat meme, where he's sitting up and holding his hands out as if to say *Would you look at this shit?* "We fought. Behind the coffee shop." I say the words slowly, to make sure they sink in.

"So what?" He genuinely looks confused, as if suddenly I am the one making no sense.

"So, we said mean things to each other. That's that." Right? That's that. We fought, we're done. That's what happens when I lose my shit. People leave. But just in case, I spell it out. "I went nuclear, Price. I pushed you and screamed at you. The last time I did anything even remotely close to that, literally all three of my family members left town. Not all at once, of course, but still. It was easy enough to see what made them leave, and it was me."

His face clears. "Oh, baby. No. No, no, no. Sweetheart, we are Velcro. There is no getting rid of me. Ever. Wow—you really don't know how to fight, do you?" He steps closer. "You walked away when I said it, but I meant it: I love you. The way I feel for you, Jodi—it's real. It's so fucking real that it's scary, but I don't care. So yeah, scream and kick, poke, punch, go ham, but you're stuck with this here hunk of meat. Like, forever. Even when my meat isn't so hunky." He stops and tilts his head. "Forget that last sentence."

"But—"

"There are no buts," he says gently. "Do you remember what I said during that argument? I scaled the wall. I'm on your side. There's no getting rid of me, as long as you'll have me."

I stare at him, trying to process what he's saying. It feels impossible. Haltingly, I say, "So, we're not broken up?"

"Not even close."

"We're still together?"

"We are if I have anything to say about it." He cups my chin, and I lean into his touch. As his thumb strokes my cheek, he says, "I love you, Jodi. I'm sorry it took me so long to see you. But I promise you, I will spend the rest of my life making up for it if you'll let me."

His silver-blue eyes search mine, and I blink hard to keep the tears back. Because I hadn't realized it. "You—you love me?" My voice is soft, still a little disbelieving.

A smile blooms. "Always. Yesterday, today, and tomorrow. I absolutely love you."

Before I can respond and tell him I love him, too, his smile turns wicked. "And now I'm going to demonstrate." He picks me up, tossing me over his shoulder as though I'm weightless, and walks us to the bedroom.

# CHAPTER 40
# JODI

*H*E KICKS THE door shut, his hand on my butt as I keep hanging like a sack of potatoes. I angle up.

"Um, Price?"

"Yes?"

"Can you put me down now?"

He toes his shoes off, then sets me down, sliding my body over his as slowly as possible. I feel every hard plane of his chest, every ridge of his stomach, and the very impressive package he's sporting beneath his pants.

When I look up to meet his eyes, they're smoldering. I catch my breath, still trying to grasp that this sexy, beautiful, compassionate man is mine. That he wants me. That he loves me.

He takes my hand and places it on his chest, and I feel his heartbeat. "I'm all yours, kitten. You're in charge."

A surge of affection roars through me. Because it's what he gives me every time: the safety and knowledge that I control whatever we do, even if it doesn't seem as though I'm the one in control.

"Wait," I say.

He stills.

"The modeling. You said something about wanting me to be

proud of you, that you thought you needed to do more at the station first?"

Grimacing, he nods. "I'm so sorry for not telling you—" he starts.

"It's not that," I say, cutting him off. I press my palm against his chest in emphasis. "I know you're sorry. But you need to know that I have always been proud of you. Of *you*, not your body, but you. Your heart. Your mind. You see the good in everything. And *I* see *you*. I always have, Price."

His eyes soften. "You did?"

I smile as a low laugh escapes me. "I did. Even when you were utterly oblivious of me."

He shakes his head and grins as he regards me. "You are amazing, Jodi Bristol. The absolute best thing to happen to me ever, you know that?"

I tip up on my toes to press my lips against his neck. His pulse races beneath his warm skin, and I close my eyes and inhale his scent. "I love you, Price."

With a shudder, he pulls my braid from behind my back and pulls the elastic off, then threads his hands from my temple to the base of my head, loosening the hair and massaging my skull as he goes. I moan, my eyes rolling into the back of my head as he slowly unplaits my hair, brushing his fingers through it. He hums, lifting my face to his for a tender kiss. "Thank god. Because I love you, too, Jodi," he says as he releases me. "So much."

I look at him and smile, then lift his shirt. He takes it the rest of the way off, and I run my hands over his warm, tan skin, moving my thumbs across his nipples and grinning as his hands tighten on my hips. I look up through my lashes. "Show me. Show me how you love me."

He gives me a slow, almost feline smile. "It would be my absolute pleasure."

He begins by removing my shirt, then smooths his calloused

fingers over my shoulders and around my back. "Yellow," he murmurs, taking in the color of my polka dot bra. Leaving it on, he undoes my jeans and starts to push them down. "Are you matching for me?"

I quirk an eyebrow. "Guess you'll find out."

He chuckles softly, running his lips over my hair and down to the shell of my ear. Taking the lobe between his teeth, he whispers, "I plan on it. And I'm going to make you soak them."

Warmth pools between my legs at his words, my body instantly obeying his command. I kick my shoes off as he shoves the jeans down and off and drops to his knees in front of me.

He looks up. "You always match, kitten. So help me, you have ruined me for polka dots. I will never look at them without imagining what you would look like in them." He runs his hands over my butt, the curves of my hips and stomach, then presses his lips against my belly. As his fingers stroke over my calves, my thighs, down to my ankles and back again, he licks the sensitive skin right above my panty line.

I push my hand through his silken strands as his mouth moves lower, scraping his teeth along the fabric gently. "Don't," I gasp.

"Don't what?" he murmurs, his voice vibrating against me and making me whimper.

"Don't be gentle." I grab the back of his hair and grip hard to reinforce the message, and he chuckles.

"There's my kitten," he says, "turning into a demanding little creature on a dime." He strokes a thumb down my seam and licks his lips at the wetness he finds there. "Good girl," he purrs, pulling my panties down and smirking up at me. Then his eyes darken and he goes deadly still. "As for being gentle, I won't be if you won't."

And with that, he sinks his tongue into me, gripping my ass so tight that I'm torn between pleasure and pain, my hiss opening into a groan. I tilt my head back and let myself dissolve into the twin sensations.

After a moment, he moves a hand between my legs and shoves a thick finger into me. I cry out and yank his hair, angling his face up to mine. His lips shine with my arousal, and as we look at each other, he snakes his tongue out to flick my clit, then pushes in a second finger.

"Fuck," I whisper, trying hard to remain standing.

"Give in," he says.

I jerk his mouth back to position as my answer, moaning as he works me. We're nowhere near the bed, having stopped right inside the door, so he's the only thing I have for balance.

He sucks me so hard my knees buckle, and I let loose a curse. "Price!" I yell, my core tightening as he pushes his fingers even farther inside of me, angling them and pressing exactly where I need them.

"*Now*, kitten," he says, and his voice brooks no dissent.

I see stars, one arm hanging limp while the other barely holds onto his silky hair, pulsing around his fingers again and again. "Holy," I say, unable to form a coherent thought.

He surges upright, lifting me with him, and has me on the bed in two swift steps. I hear his pants unzip, and angle myself up on my elbows. He stands before me, and my mouth goes dry. Wide shoulders tapering to trim hips, golden skin that begs to be kissed, muscled thighs from running, and of course, the whitest butt on the planet.

I grin, unable to stop myself, and he narrows his eyes at me.

"Are you ever going to stop laughing when you see me naked?" he asks. "You're gonna give me a complex."

I shake my head, my smile growing wider. "No. But the Speedo tan situation makes a lot more sense now that I know I'm dating a hot as shit model."

He raises a playful eyebrow. "I told you I'm not modeling

anymore." He crawls onto the bed and begins kissing his way up my body.

"What if I'm okay with it?"

He huffs a laugh. "Is that the orgasm talking?"

I reach down and wrap my fingers around his cock, delighting in the way his whole body jumps at the suddenness of my touch. "No," I smile. "I mean, if you're done, you're done. But I'm good with it." I am, too. After the initial shock wore off, I thought it was pretty hot.

I also want to see more of his covers. Especially if he's the only person on them.

"I'm pretty sure I'm finished," he says. As I guide him onto his back, he continues, "I've got an idea for one more thing, but—"

I straddle him and take off my bra, and his eyes snap to my breasts.

"We're not talking about that right now, *fuck*, kitten, you're killing me," he moans as I grab my tits, squeezing them, kneading them and pinching my nipples while I circle my hips on top of him.

"Good," I say, thoroughly enjoying the easy torture he's allowing me to put him through.

He reaches up to replace my hands with his own, but I lean back, not letting him touch. Instead, I rise up on my knees and run a hand down my stomach and to my clit, circling it and playing with myself while Price watches.

"Fuck, that's hot," he says.

After a minute, I shift and move between his legs, then gather my hair into one hand. "Hold this," I say, then lower my lips to his cock.

This is only the second time I've gone down on him, but he assured me the first go-around that it was pretty hard to screw up a blow job. Still, I promised not to be gentle, so I decide to see how far I can take him.

Honestly, it's kind of like a lollipop and banana all rolled up in one velvety steel package. After licking the head and hearing him mutter a string of obscenities, I take him all the way to the back of my throat while pulling on his balls.

"Jesus fucking Christ," he gasps, yanking my hair so hard it pops me off. "You can't—"

I smile wickedly up at him. "I can. And I will."

He unleashes another round of curses as I lean down to lick him, balls to tip, and slide my hand up to squeeze his nipple as I take him into my mouth again. He jerks and hisses in pleasure, lifting his hips to meet my mouth over and over. I find my rhythm, feeling powerful as he murmurs praise and moans my name.

Eventually, he pulls me off. "Any more and I'm a goner," he growls, flipping us so that he's on top of me. "And I plan on coming while I'm buried inside you."

He grabs a condom and has it on quickly, his mouth crashing onto mine, his beard losing all softness as his tongue plunders me, claiming me as his. And I welcome it, threading my legs through his and relishing the anticipation, the way his cock presses against my hip and belly, our breaths coming faster, more urgent, until finally the emptiness within me is too much to bear, and I break.

"I need you inside of me," I say. "Please, Price."

He cups my chin in his hand, his dark silver eyes holding mine. "Guide me home, Jodi. And don't ever let me go."

I reach between us and position him, and he slides into me. Home.

# CHAPTER 41
# PRICE

"C'MON, BOYS, LIVEN up!" I call from the middle of the group. I'm surrounded by the station's firefighters, and Lisa, my favorite photographer, has her camera trained on us. "Act like you're enjoying this."

Will grumbles behind me. "There is nothing enjoyable about what's happening right now."

"Suck it up, buttercup," I shoot back. "Maybe if you'd done your job as Assistant Fire Chief, I wouldn't have had to do this."

*This* was the absolutely brilliant idea that I'd been working to make happen for the past month, ever since my chat with Beth from that ridiculous "tour" that Jess had taken the Mountain Brook women on. *This* was a full-out photo shoot to create a calendar of the Firefighters of Talladega. We were starting with group shots to get everyone comfortable, and then we were going for individual shots. Plus some shots of the Joseph Brothers, since according to Jodi, Devon, and even Ceci, the three of us on the cover would skyrocket sales.

They aren't wrong. We *are* a fine-looking bunch of assholes.

"Fuck off," Will growls, then slaps the back of my head. "Finances weren't in the job description."

"They most certainly are," I say, smoothing my hair back into place. And I would know, because now I'm the Assistant Chief.

I'm still not sure how Chief managed to promote me without pissing off the rest of the station, but everyone was supportive when he talked to them. I'm guessing no one wanted the gig, but I'm not complaining. People around town look at me differently now, and while I can't be sure that at least part of it is because they're imagining me half-naked, I'm telling myself that it's because they finally realize that the Assistant Chief position means I've got a brain along with a body.

"Okay, guys, give me a smile!" Lisa says, the camera shutter clicking continuously.

After a few minutes, she declares the group session finished, and the crew immediately sighs in relief, breaking apart and moving to either side of the bay and onto the sidewalk.

"You ready to show them how it's done, Price?" Lisa asks with a wink.

In answer, I slide the suspenders off my turnouts and whip off my t-shirt, then spread my arms wide for Lisa's assistant to spray some baby oil on me.

"The fuck?" Buck asks incredulously. "Are you kidding me right now?"

Aaron laughs. "Just wait till it's your turn, Buck."

"Like hell I will," he says, crossing his arms and giving a scowl almost as good as Will's. He looks at Chief. "Are we really doing this?"

"We are absolutely doing this. Price says we're silver foxes," Chief says, preening.

Will blanches and Aaron howls along with the rest of the crew.

"All right boys, watch and learn," I say, swaggering over to my place in front of the apparatus.

The laughter keeps going, but to my surprise, it actually gets kind of quiet as I drop into the headspace I need to be in. Find the light, constantly move, use my environment, be aware of every part of my body from my boots to my fingertips to my nose, bend in ways that feel unnatural but look good as hell on camera, and pretend I'm the sexiest motherfucker to ever grace the camera lens.

I hear cat calls and slide my eyes away from the camera. Then I grin, because Jodi has appeared in the middle of the square, front and center, between far more people than I'd care to count. Miss Betty is aiming her phone at me, as are several of the Mom crew. Mrs. Withers is literally in a lawn chair, fanning herself, and I'm pretty sure she's got eyes for Buck.

"I love you for more than your body, Price, but hot damn!" Jodi calls.

Ceci issues an ear-splitting whistle. "Get it, Price!"

I can't help but laugh. Because of course, the entire town lost its mind as word got out. The police department had to block off half the square, and even now a couple of them—all women, I'd noticed—were "patrolling" the area. Even though we all know the only people who might get out of hand are Jodi, Ceci, and Devon.

"I think we're good," Lisa calls, immediately checking the images.

I join her, wanting to see how they are. "Damn, Lisa, you're good," I say.

She stops on one of me laughing at the camera, relaxed and leaning against the gleaming chrome. "That's the one," she says.

As she flips through the rest, I concede she's right. "But you know I need a few of those for Jodi."

She snickers. "Of course."

We move through the guys at a clip, mainly because most of them won't do it for longer than five minutes, but I coach them from my position beside Lisa. And since Lisa is a pro like none other, she manages to get some really great shots.

When it's Chief's turn, the whole crew comes back to watch,

and I issue a silent thank you to the town for not needing our services for the couple of hours this is taking.

"Take it off!" Ceci calls, not at all seeming to care that her husband and children are with her.

The scene has grown, and some enterprising grade schoolers are now selling lemonade for five bucks a cup, which people seem to be handing over without hesitation. Jess weaves between the crowd as well, selling pastries and iced coffee from the shop.

Chief refuses to "take it off," as Ceci requests, but he gamely poses for a few photos. When he's done, he motions for Buck, who declares he's giving Lisa five shots and that's it.

"Make 'em good, Lisa," I mutter.

"I've been snapping shots of him and Chief the whole time," she says back. "I've got some great ones. Don't worry."

"You brilliant, brilliant woman."

Then me and my brothers are up. I throw them a broad smile. "Let's go, bros."

Because I've been shirtless this whole time—may as well give the town what they came for—Aaron immediately goes to pull his shirt off.

"Atta boy," I chuckle, then start laughing as Devon yells from the square.

"That's my man! Woo!"

Aaron blushes, turning away from her and giving me a look. "If this doesn't work, you owe me, asshole."

"Look at you! Did you increase your workouts ahead of this?" I ask instead, poking at his abs. "Trying to give me and Will a run for our money?"

"I hate both of you," Aaron says.

We turn to Will. "Shirt off, broseph," I instruct. "Give the ladies what they want."

His jaw tightens. "I'm not comfortable with this. I feel like a piece of meat."

"Right now, you are," I admit. "Just roll with it. Give me ten minutes."

He stares at me, probably thinking that it's intimidating, but he's been giving me that death glare for years. So I throw him a shit-eating grin in response.

"Fine." He turns and stalks into position, then pulls his shirt off.

"Holy *shit*, I'm engaged to the wrong brother!" Devon calls from across the square.

Aaron laughs and it's Will's turn to blush.

I join my brothers and turn them to Lisa's assistant for a quick oil spray.

"I can't fucking believe I'm doing this," Will grumbles, flinching as the spray hits his torso.

"You gonna rub it in, big boy, or shall I?" the assistant asks, his eyebrows waggling.

I snicker as Will slaps a hand to his chest and starts rubbing, eliciting even more cat calls from the crowd.

Finally, we get into position and Lisa starts shooting. I guide us through different positions and poses, and Lisa offers encouragement as we go along.

"That's a wrap!" Lisa says.

Will moves faster than I've ever seen him, lunging for his discarded shirt.

And because I'm a prick, I don't remind him to wipe the baby oil off before he puts it on.

Sue me.

Lisa and her assistant start breaking down the lights, and that cues the crowd to disperse. Jodi picks her way through the people and comes over, and I try to pull her into a hug.

"Not until you wipe that oil off," she says, her eyes bright. "But damn, babe. That was hot."

Heat runs through me at her words. "We're not done," I whisper in her ear.

She looks up at me in confusion.

"Give me, Lisa, and her assistant fifteen minutes, then come up to your apartment."

"What are you up to?" she asks.

I smile. "Do you trust me?"

She nods.

"Then I'll see you in fifteen minutes."

# CHAPTER 42
# JODI

ITH THE PHOTO shoot finished, I stroll back to my shop to check on things. Darius has it all under control, especially since Jess had been selling drinks and pastries to the crowd earlier.

I finally got back into my apartment two weeks ago, and Jess moved in with me. She's working at the shop a couple days a week and also at a doggie day care in town, with a goal of saving up to move back to Nashville and try once more. Things are definitely better between us, but we're not exactly besties just yet.

"What's going on up there?" Darius asks, nodding toward the apartment.

I shrug. "Price said to give him fifteen minutes and come up."

Darius grins. "Have fun."

I check my watch, see that it's time, and head up. As I open my door, I see the photographer and her assistant have set up lights and rearranged a few things, including the set of framed book covers of Price as a shirtless firefighter, a shirtless soldier, and a basically shirtless doctor. They were easy enough to find once I knew it was him, and it helps that there are entire social media pages dedicated to him at this point.

The bed is definitely the focus of the room now, and they've draped some kind of gauzy white fabric against the red brick wall behind the frame. The windows are open, and a soft breeze blows in. Price waits on me, grinning like a school kid.

"Is this…" I start.

"A photoshoot for just the two of us?" he finishes. "Yes." He beckons me closer and holds out a bag. "I got you a few things."

I peek into the bag and find a rainbow of lacy colors. Lingerie. My cheeks burn as I look up.

He gazes at me tenderly. "I want you to see what I see, kitten. Will you let me do this for you? I'll be with you."

I nod, a blend of excitement and nervousness pulsing through me.

The assistant excuses himself, leaving the apartment, and Lisa turns to me. "It's just us, Jodi, and we'll only do what's comfortable."

I grip the bag tightly. "Um, okay."

In the bathroom, I inspect what Price gave me. The choices range from a white silk shorts-and-button-down pajama set with black piping around the edges, to a variety of lacy confections. And there, beneath all of them, is a royal blue and white polka dot bra and panty set. I smile and put them on under the white silk pajamas, then step back into the main room.

And immediately my jaw drops. Because there's Price, kneeling on the bed only in black silk shorts that match mine, his golden skin gleaming in the light as he works with Lisa to make sure everything is set up. "I want it to be perfect," he's saying.

He glances up and sees me, and his eyes darken with desire.

Lisa turns as well, then gestures me toward the bed as she smiles. "You look beautiful, Jodi."

I barely hear her as I make my way to Price, who holds his hand out. I swallow hard, taking it and letting him guide me onto my knees with him.

"Gorgeous," he murmurs, his hands stroking my face and neck.

"Yes, you are," I say quietly.

He chuckles and reaches for my braid, pulling out the elastic. Unleashing my hair is one of his favorite things to do, so I close my eyes and submit to him. I hear the shutter of the camera begin to click, and my eyes pop open.

"Pretend it's just us," he coaches. "Don't look at the camera. It's me and you." He kisses my forehead, then temple, then jaw, and finally presses his lips to mine.

I sigh into the kiss, the gentleness and adoration of it, and give myself over. He cups my chin in one hand and runs his other down my neck and into the vee of the silk top, drawing goose bumps in his wake.

Seeing what's beneath the top, he makes a noise of contentment. "You know how hard it was to find polka dot lingerie?" he murmurs.

"I have an idea," I say softly, taking the kisses he gives me.

He positions himself behind me, still kneeling, and moves my hair over my shoulder to kiss my neck. He starts to undo the top, and I arch against him, lost to the sensuousness of his touch, the whisper of his breath against my skin. With the top undone, he tips my chin to kiss me again, one of his palms flat against my stomach. Distantly, I'm aware that Lisa is still shooting, but I ignore her as I twist and pull him to lie on the bed. Propped up on his elbow, Price threads his fingers through my hair, then lifts one of my knees, bending it against his chest.

We continue like that, Price gently shifting me into one position after another, slowly removing the pajamas until I'm only in the bra and panties, and the shoot morphs from something sweet and gentle to decidedly hot and naughty, with me pressed against Price as he palms my ass and breasts. I breathe heavily, unable to control the way my hands rove over his body, my fingers dipping into the waistband of those sexy silk shorts.

Eventually, Lisa disappears downstairs, clicking the door shut behind her, and Price lies on the bed and hauls me to him, his eyes wicked and bright. "Did you enjoy that?"

"What do you think?" I ask, my blood on fire from his touch.

He slides his hand down my stomach to the apex of my thighs, then pushes a finger inside of me. "I think you knew exactly what you were doing when you put these on," he murmurs.

They're crotchless. "You knew what you were doing when you bought them," I counter, my breath hitching as a second finger joins the first.

"Maybe," he rumbles. He bends his head to my breast and takes a nipple into his mouth, sucking it into a peak and drenching the lace.

I moan. "Fuck, Price, I'm already so close."

He pushes his fingers in farther, and heat swirls and gathers into a tight coil. When his thumb finds my clit, I soar across the edge, gripping his shoulders and shuddering as the orgasm washes over me.

It's barely finished before I'm pushing his shorts down and fisting his cock, desperate for him to fill me.

He reaches for the condoms in my bedside table and puts one on, and I roll us, straddling him, still clad in the bra and panties. I sink onto him, inch by glorious inch, and watch as he squeezes his eyes shut.

"You are…perfect," he gasps, snapping his eyes open to spear me with his gaze. "I will never, *fuck,* get over this. Over you. How you feel, so tight. Mine. You're mine, Jodi. Say it."

I ride him slow, arching and swirling over him, taking him

how I want. "I'm yours," I whisper. I lean over him, my hair curtaining down. "And you're mine, Price Joseph."

He thrusts into me, his hands gripping my hips. His silver eyes are bottomless, and in them I see the promise of years to come. "I'm yours. Always, kitten."

## EPILOGUE: SIX MONTHS LATER

### PRICE

*I*S THERE ANYTHING better than a Christmas parade?

That's a rhetorical question. Because obviously, there is not. Not when Chief is dressed as Santa and standing atop Glenda, the ladder apparatus, waving and ho-ho-hoing as Buck drives it down the street, the rest of us walking beside it and tossing candy out of our boots at the kids as they line the square.

The high school marching band leads the parade, followed by the Boy Scouts, the Girl Scouts, the local Shriners chapter, a slew of other groups, and of course, the Dancing Grannies, complete with their own boombox blaring seventies hits. We're nearly at the station, meaning we've hit the end, but all that signals is it's almost time to light the tree in the middle of the square.

Rick and Devon helped Jodi and Darius set up a booth outside the shop to give away hot chocolate, so after I empty my boot of the last of the candy, I make my way there. All around me, people are bundled against the chill of the early December air, and kids zoom between parents like the balls in a pinball machine, hopped up on sugar and excitement. Twinkling lights line the shops in the square, and wreaths hang from light posts.

The whole thing is downright wholesome, which is in direct contrast to the thoughts I have as I watch Jodi bend over to pick something off the ground, the leggings she's in doing a spectacular job of showing off her assets. The things I could do to her in that position…

Aaron appears and shoulder-checks me, pulling my mind out of the gutter. "Is that who I think it is?"

I follow where he's nodding toward a corner of the square, and there, standing off to the side and looking around like she's searching for someone, is Tori Welch. I laugh gleefully. "Oh, shit. Merry Christmas to us. Has Will seen her?"

Aaron's eyes light up with mirth. "What do you think?"

I shake my head. "No way."

"Fifty bucks says he talks to her if he sees her."

I smirk at him. "I'll take that bet. He won't. He's still pissed at her."

He lifts a shoulder. "We'll see."

I make my way to the hot chocolate stand and step behind Jodi. "Hey, gorgeous," I murmur as I pull her against me and kiss her neck. I'm hoping it's just ticklish enough to make her wiggle against me in those leggings.

She giggles, pressing her ass against me as her pom-topped hat falls off her head. "Price!" she admonishes, leaning down to grab the hat.

Obviously, I take the moment to pull her hips against me, then raise my eyebrows when she fakes a scowl in my direction. "Wanna ditch this place?" I ask.

"You're incorrigible," she says, swatting playfully at me and letting me snuggle her against my chest.

"And you should be illegal in those leggings," I say in her ear.

She lifts her head for a kiss, and I happily oblige.

"I got us an early present," I say, reaching into my pocket. "Well. It's mine, but I'm hoping you'll join me."

She furrows her brow at the key I hold out.

"I bought it."

Her mouth pops open, and her hazel eyes are wide and green in the holiday lights. "You didn't."

I smile broadly. "I did." I'd been on a mission to buy the house across the street from the inn as soon as I heard the owners were considering selling. They had grandkids in Tennessee and wanted to move closer, so when they were ready, I was first in line. Being Assistant Chief had a lot of perks, it turned out. And thanks to a few final high-profile romance cover gigs, I had enough for the deposit. "Move in with me?"

Jodi's eyes get even wider and start to water.

"Oh, sweetheart," I say, reaching up to wipe a stray tear as it tracks down her cheek.

"You really think we're ready?" she sniffs. "I mean, we've not even been together that long—"

"Jodi," I interrupt her. "I was ready six months ago, when I realized how much I missed having you under the same roof as me when I was off-shift. We're Velcro, remember?"

She laughs and sniffs again, wiping at the tears that keep coming. I don't bother trying to stop them at this point, because I have learned that my girl is a crier. Once she got past keeping her emotions in, it turned out she had a lot of them. And crying happens at least three times a week. Minimum. Happy tears, sad tears, frustrated tears, all the tears.

I love every last one of them.

"Say yes," I urge. "Please?"

And as the lights of the Christmas tree blink on behind me and the crowd erupts in cheers, Jodi leaps into my arms and whispers, "Yes."

*Thanks for reading The Barista's Guide to the Perfect Steam! I hope you loved it. I'd be grateful if you'd take the time to review it on Amazon and Goodreads!*

*Be sure to head to my website and join my mailing list for news about the next book in the series! www.authorvaleriepepper.com*

*Speaking of the next book, turn the page for a sneak peek at The Grump's Guide to Chaos!*

# THE GRUMP'S GUIDE
# TO CHAOS

TORI

I HAVE MADE a terrible mistake.

Huge.

And while I could, perhaps, be talking about the past twenty years of my life, I am in fact talking about the past twenty minutes.

Note to self: do not ever—*ever*—walk unannounced into Mom's house again.

I want to bleach my eyes after what I just saw. No child, no matter her age, should be subjected to seeing her mother getting it on with some guy on the couch.

We're not talking some casual making-out, either. I wish. Quite the opposite. I stumbled into a very much *not* casual, very much clothing optional situation when I opened the front door.

At the ripe age of thirty-seven, I know that people of all ages are sexual beings, and I heartily approve of each person getting theirs. Pleasure knows no bounds and all that. But I could have gone to my grave without seeing what I saw.

I barely manage not to retch at the memory, and instead turn my focus to the cheery scene in front of me. The Talladega holiday parade has just finished, and the square is filled with people. Chief Suarez is dressed as Santa, like always, though he's a little grayer and a little thicker than the last time I saw him. And like always, he beams with pride as he lights the tree in the center of the square. I'm on the edge of the crowd, but I swear I can see the man's eyes twinkle in delight. It's almost enough to keep the image of my mom and whoever that was at bay.

My stomach growls, clearly over the scene at my mom's and finally seeming to realize it's been well over twenty-four hours since it's been fed, so I go in search of sustenance. I find it in the form of a cute coffee shop, but when I tug on the door, it's locked.

"Coffee and hot chocolate are over there," a voice warbles near me.

I barely manage to keep my expression in check as I take in the woman to the right of of me. She's wearing a knitted purple beanie with a hot pink pompom waving jauntily on top, her scarf is striped like a candy cane, and she's nearly engulfed in a pink puffer coat. She's a technicolor elf of sorts, and I grin. "Good to know, thank you."

She peers closer, her eyes narrowing behind thick lenses. "Tori?"

I blink and try to remember how I would know her. "Y-yes. I'm sorry, I don't—"

She waves me off. "Pfft. I'm Mrs. Withers. I was your neighbor a long time ago—you were a little thing, maybe ten, when you all moved."

The statement is an unintentional wallop of pain against my chest, and I struggle against the emotion in my throat. "Ah. Well, nice to meet you again, Mrs. Withers."

She pats my arm and toddles off, waving her hand at people I vaguely recognize but can't place just yet.

I make my way to the coffee and hot chocolate booth, my head down as I root around my tote for my wallet. Keys, sunglasses, lipstick, lip moisturizer, tinted lip moisturizer, phone, book, silk hair tie…where the hell is my wallet?

I trip over my own two feet—a common occurrence—and jerk my head up and arms out to keep my balance.

"Ow!" someone yelps beside me.

"Oh no, I'm so sorry!" The words are out of my mouth before I even lay eyes on who I've hit.

"It's okay," the blonde mumbles, holding her cheek and raking her eyes over me. "Just, watch where you're going? There are kids and dogs all over the place, and let me be the first to assure you that they're all deadly in one way or another." She's smiling by the end and holding a gloved hand out. "I'm Ceci. You new here?"

I shake her hand, pleasantly surprised by the grip. "Tori. Not new, just…returning. For an unknown length of time."

"Well, welcome back," Ceci says, then gestures ahead of her. "Were you heading to the Daily Dose booth?"

"Um, yes. Just need to find my wallet," I say, looking back into my tote and wishing, like always, that I could be a little less scattered. But that ship sailed a long time ago. Then I see it. "Found—"

"The drink's on me," Ceci says, ignoring my unfinished sentence and looping an arm through mine, hauling me forward without another word.

I stumble again but manage to keep my feet under me, wondering exactly what kind of super-human power this woman has, because I am not the person who lets herself get *handled* by someone. And Ceci is most definitely handling me.

"Darius!" Ceci yells as we approach. "A drink for our new friend here."

I grimace at him, but relax when I see the understanding smile on his face.

"Ceci, maybe ask your friend if she wants to be attached to you like that," Darius says and laughs. Then he looks at me, amusement in his dark brown eyes. "Don't mind her. She's aggressive, but she's also a mother to four-year-old twins, so we let her get away with it."

I nod and try to rub feeling back into my arm now that Ceci has let go of it. "Got it. Aggressive mother of twins."

Ceci levels a glare at Darius that I'm not sure is entirely playful, but he doesn't seem fazed. He blows a kiss at her and looks back at me. "What'll it be? We're rolling straightforward tonight: drip coffee or hot chocolate, with or without marshmallows. Both are good, but the hot chocolate is legit."

"In that case, hot chocolate, please. With marshmallows." I look around the booth. "Do you have anything to eat?"

"You mean other than the marshmallows?" he laughs. "No, but the restaurant over there is open," he says, pointing diagonally across the square.

I take a sip of the hot chocolate. "Oh. Wow," I say. "That's…"

"Told you," he says and winks. "Ceci, that's five bucks."

"Highway robbery," she sniffs, but hands over a ten and waves him to put the rest in the tip jar.

Immediately I like her even more. "Thank you, Darius, and Ceci, thanks for the hot chocolate."

She swings her gaze back from where she'd been searching the crowd. "Not a problem. And if you happen to see a smoking-hot man with two little gremlins with him, will you tell him his wife is ready to go?"

I grin and tip the cup at her. "Absolutely."

I head towards the restaurant Darius mentioned, weaving through a still-thick crowd and holding tight to my cup.

*Coming Spring 2024!*

# ALSO BY VALERIE PEPPER

GUIDED TO LOVE SERIES

*The Mechanic's Guide to Getting the Boss's Daughter* (series starter novella; free to newsletter subscribers)

*The Widow's Guide to Second Chances (Book 1)*

*The Grump's Guide to Chaos (Book 3) - Coming Spring 2024!*

NOVELLA

"To Have and To Scold" in the *Holidays & Hook-Ups* anthology by The New Romance Cafe (June 2023)

# ABOUT THE AUTHOR

 Valerie Pepper is an incurable optimist and a firm believer in the girl getting the guy, or the guy getting the girl, or the girl getting the girl, or the guy getting the guy, or basically any way it needs to happen to make a real-life happily ever after, even if it takes more than one try.

When she's not writing, you can find her reading, hiking, listening to whatever music suits her mood, and hanging out with her family. She's fascinated with the idea of a capsule wardrobe, but loves clothes and shoes and boots far too much to make a real go of it.

She's currently living out her own happily ever after with her husband, kids, and dogs, and maaaaaybe too many shoes. She lives in Birmingham, Alabama, and is the recipient of the Contemporary Romance Writer's 2021 Stiletto Award. Learn more at www.authorvaleriepepper.com.

# ACKNOWLEDGMENTS

Thank you, as always, to my husband and kids. You don't read my smut, but you support and encourage me every day. Thank you for celebrating every milestone with me, and for being just as excited for each new development on this path as I am.

The Cheeto Dust Crew: my amazing critique partners Ivy Fairbanks, Alicia Wilder, and Kat Saturday. Thank you for calling my characters out on their shit, and making me a better writer because of it.

SRE: The best damn group of indie writers on the internet. Thank you to Jamie for pulling us all together, and thank you to each and every one of you for making me snort-laugh, cringe, cry, and feel all the emotions in between. Thanks especially for the Wet Henrys, and all the publishing advice shared (and sometimes shouted). In alpha order because I can't remember otherwise:  Bella, Dani, Effie, Eliza, Elliot, Florence, Irene, J.L., Karen, Kelsey, Kitty, Lexi, Luna, Maia, Stacy, Tirza. SRE for life!

Thanks to my editor, Jennifer Sommersby. Thank you to Sarah Hansen of Okay Creations for another beautiful cover.

ARC readers, Bookstagrammers, and BookTokkers: Thank you, thank you, thank you. Thank you for the love you've given me and my books. Thank you for giving me your time, your enthusiasm, your memes, your exclamation points, grabby hands, and hearts. It means so much to me.

And to you, the reader. Thank you for giving me your precious time. We all need a little escape every now and then, and that's what books have always been for me. As a writer, my goal has always been to be worthy of your time, and I hope that I have.

xo,

*Valerie Pepper*